FOLLOW ME THROUGH DARKNESS

Seek the light

DANIELLE ELLISON

SPENCER
HILL
PRESS

Spencer Hill Press

Please visit our website at www.spencerhillpress.com

First Edition: October 2014
Danielle Ellison
Follow Me Through Darkness/ by Danielle Ellison –
1st ed.
p. cm.
Summary: A girl escapes a controlled community and races through a forgotten world in hopes of saving everyone she loves before time runs out and their existence is wiped away.

Cover design by Hafsah Laziaf/ Icey Designs
Interior layout by Jenny Perinovic
Author Photo by Jennifer Rush

ISBN 9781939392145 (paperback)
ISBN 9781939392688 (e-book)

Printed in the United States of America

To Margaret Polk, Donald Snider & Cheryl Olcott

Three teachers who came into my life at various times and impacted it differently, but in equal measure. You believed in my dreams way before I ever knew I was allowed to dream them. Thank you for never letting me give up on myself.

And to everyone fighting for your dream: may you never give up.

THE HUMAN SOUL STANDS BETWEEN
A HEMISPHERE OF LIGHT AND ANOTHER OF
DARKNESS ON THE CONFINES OF TWO
EVERLASTING HOSTILE EMPIRES
— NECESSITY AND FREE WILL.

-THOMAS CARLYLE,
ESSAYS, "THE OPERA"

ALL I'VE EVER WANTED IS FREEDOM, but I never imagined it would be like this. There are no rules that I'm forced to follow, no bylaws or Troopers or barriers to keep me inside. But there is also no ocean, no sky, no sun; there's nothing but torches and endless underground tunnels. For five days and fourteen hours, all I've had is darkness.

The smell of sweat and rotten food permeates the hot, sticky air. Sometimes a baby cries; the sound of its squalling sticks to me, jams into my pores like the humidity. I'm trapped, and it's worse than the safehouse because I can almost feel the walls and the tunnels caving in on me, burying me. I wish I were home with Sara, with the ocean and the school children and Thorne. Oh, I miss Thorne.

"You're lagging, little girl," Bayard barks at me.

"I have a name," I snap. "Neely, remember?"

He grunts in response, and I follow him closer. Bayard is the third person I have followed through the Burrows, and so far he hasn't been very friendly. Most of the people here are nice, but they're cautious. They're unlike anyone I've met before in the Compound. There, we were connected to each other, and here I can go hours without seeing anyone except Bayard.

1

I miss Rover. Rover told me jokes, and he always had that line of dirt over his nose that seemed to match his freckles. Even Josef had a way about him—a happy, amiable smile. Bayard makes me feel like I've been bothering him for the last ten hours.

His bushy beard, dark skin, and tattered clothes almost meld his image into the walls. If not for the torch he holds, I'm sure I would lose him completely.

"I hear you met a Cleaner," Bayard says.

For a second I think there's something mocking in his voice, but his eyes are intense on me. That's not a look of mocking. I nod, glancing down at my hands.

Some of my fingernails are cracked, one is missing, and all of them are red and puffy from the force of my hands across the pavement. The Cleaners are louder than anything in the Compound, piercing and whirring and relentlessly searching for any form of life. Anything they can suck up and destroy. Rover called them vacuums. One of those machines wrenched a tree from the ground and sucked it up through a chute that was connected to a large, metal sphere. I'd covered my ears as I ran, and the whirring sound hovered over me. The wind caught me, and my feet flew up, fingernails gripping anything they could while Rover drug me into the Burrows.

"You were lucky," Bayard says.

Whatever "lucky" counts for. None of this is lucky. I've been a target since I set foot outside the Compound, since before I even left it really. I'll be "lucky" if I even make it through the Old World in time. Forty days isn't very many.

"Which way?" I ask when we reach a crossroads. Bayard huffs at me and then points his torch left. My shoulders ache from my pack, so I readjust it and move left just ahead of him. My pack is still heavy, still full, but how long will it be until I run out of my own food?

The Remnants—that's what the people of the Old World call themselves—are generous, offering up whatever food they're eating. When I first arrived, I was shocked by the strange, dirty people and the language. I'd almost questioned my decision to venture out here, but then one of them handed me a bowl of food and encouraged me to eat. Soon I realized they were more than I believed, giving and friendly and full of life. The taste of stringy meat and gristle still lingers on my tongue. I never ask what I'm about to eat when I accept food and I try not to think about it, but the smells around me are too pungent to push the negative thoughts away.

We pass under a measly sliver of sunlight. A dot really. A dot forcing itself through the same kind of metal hole the Rover pulled me through. I wish I could feel the sun seeping through, but the warmth of the spot is lost before it touches my skin. I want it to touch my skin. Five days without it is too much. How much longer will it be? Time is pushing me to the ground, and the weight of it is enough to make me give up and stop trying. I glance at the watch Xenith gave me out of habit.

With each minute that passes, I feel my life slipping away. The numbers are large and blocked, and they tell me the days, the hours, the minutes I have left until my deadline. Xenith said it was powered by the sun, and there is no sun underground, yet it still counts down the time until my life changes forever. Unless I stop it.

When we stop to sleep, when my feet ache more than I expected them to at five days in, I always mark the days I've lost on the map Xenith gave me. Not because I need to but because I want to see them in as many ways as possible.

The marks are piling up, and I know that soon the days will all be gone.

"Where are you going?" Bayard asks.

The question makes me pause. I haven't told any of the others. Xenith instructed me to only tell the people he approved, but I have a long way to travel with Bayard. And not talking is lonely. I've been not talking about what I know for months now.

"San Francisco," I say. But my next stop is to see a woman named Cecily Lopez. The Mavericks helped Cecily and her twin sister escape from the North before I was born. Their escape changed everything.

Bayard whistles. It gets caught in his throat, and he coughs through it. "That's the other side of the world. You'll never make it there, little girl like you."

"You don't think I can just because I'm a girl?"

Bayard stops walking, shines his light in my direction. The brightness of it makes my eyes water. "I don't think you can because it's a death mission. The world's a dangerous place. Always has been. No one has ever made it to the other coast on their own above ground."

"Then I guess I'll be the first," I say.

Bayard stares at me for a moment, then grunts. His light shifts away from me, and we walk on.

I NEED TO SEE THE SUN BEFORE I GO INSANE. Bayard tells me there are two more days, and then I will go up to the Old World. I will step on the ground above and walk among the dead. Or what they always told us was dead. And haunted—a place where people are hunted and disease destroys and nothing is safe. But I'm not sure what to expect anymore. This place, these tunnels burrowed under the land, isn't even supposed to exist. Nothing was supposed to be here, and yet it is. I know now that the Elders started keeping secrets long before I was born.

What else have they lied about?

I can't help now but reconsider all the things Xenith ever said to me. I was so quick to dismiss him back then, but he knew. He knows so many things about the Old World. And I'm here now. I'm *underground*.

"How did your people come to live here?" I ask, glancing down at the metal tracks on the ground. It's a question I've asked both guides, but they refuse to answer. They didn't trust me, not with the mark I bear and the place I come from. I'm a stranger to them. A threat from the Compound, despite Xenith's seal of approval. I hope this guide will answer my questions. I need to know these answers from someone else's

5

perspective, someone without a motive—and because after all the impossible being possible, I want to know the truth.

Bayard snorts. "My people? We're your people as well."

I don't respond. They don't feel the same as me, yet I can't deny that I finally understand what I didn't know before: that they are more than Remnants and I am more than the director's daughter.

We walk a few more steps before he clears his throat to answer me. "Before the Preservation, before the Elders got involved, these tunnels connected the sides of the country. Trains travelled underneath the ground delivering food, supplies and people to other places."

I didn't realize trains were this big, not really. I saw a picture once in a book, and even next to the people who waited on the platforms, the train wasn't that much taller. If the trains fit in here, they are much larger than that picture. Most things never are as small as they seem to be in pictures.

"Do you know the story of the disease, Neely?"

"I know what they taught us in the Compound."

"The US was mostly gone. Entire cities wiped out, no economy anymore," Bayard says as we walk through the tunnels. There's a noise above as one of the Remnants move on the platforms around us. Josef said that was where people used to wait and catch the trains. Now it's where the Remnants sleep in the warm months.

"It started with the ravens. They say the ground was covered in so much black that it was as if the night sky had broken into pieces and landed on the ground. Feathers. Feathers everywhere." Bayard's voice falls silent. We walk on along the path next to metal strips. "The scientists used to experiment on mice, and there was an incident during the downfall of the United States where all the mice were released. A form of protest. They think the birds ate the mice, and all the birds got sick."

"I know that part," I say quickly. "The scientists learned the ravens' flesh was blackened and that the blackness was eating their flesh off. It spread to humans until everyone was covered. But what happened at the end? Before the Preservation? Before the disease was destroyed?"

"To understand the end, you gotta understand the beginning," Bayard says, his voice short.

We walk on in silence, vaguely hearing the echo of the other Remnants somewhere above us. I look up and try to see someone, but there's nothing. There's not enough light. I can barely make out the rounded top of the tunnel above us, high and cloudy from the smoke of the Remnants' fire pits. The smoke swirls above my head, seeping out into the other world through those little holes of sunlight.

"The people got fevers that made them act out, be irresponsible, irrational. Within hours, the skin changed and the symptoms spread rapidly from one person to the other. One by one, until the disease was widespread across the United States," Bayard says. "After much death, a cure was discovered. The blackness disappeared. Humans were saved."

But they weren't. Bayard grunts again, and the silence consumes the space around me, the torch he carries lighting the path. There's no noise except the echo of our feet, of his boots that clomp as we walk across the dirt- and rock-filled tunnel. I listen, counting each step. There are many things in the tunnels: trash, large bugs, smelly old rags that were once clothing, broken glass boxes with buttons, round rubber things.

His deep voice startles me against the silence, and I miss something he said. "But then the cured started going crazy, and instead of their flesh being eaten by the blackness, they started feasting on the flesh of others. They had no control, no humanity. The cure had failed, and in a few months, the whole world became a skeleton of what it was. Everything stopped, they say."

The way he says that has too much sadness to it. I can't imagine all the death. There isn't much death where I come from—not in the same way. We have no real sickness and absolutely no disease. We are too perfect for diseases, too pure. People only die in the Compound when it is their time. When they are elderly and their body fails. Sometimes there are accidents or unexpected deaths when bodies are tired or too complicated or worn too early. Like with my mother.

"Then the Elders came," Bayard adds stiffly. "They'd risen up in the midst of tragedy, of a falling nation, and they had money, power, and hope. They'd discovered a new cure to this failure, had a plan, and everyone believed them. They needed someone to believe in. That's when the Preservation started."

There's another sound from above, but again, I see nothing. Maybe they're all ghosts and nothing is real. I could probably believe anything at this point. Maybe they are ghosts and this is a dream—some kind of nightmare—and I'll wake up back at home and it will be as if the last two months never happened.

"During the Preservation—" Bayard's voice brings me back to reality. This is the reality, even if I dream it isn't. "—those who'd never been infected, called the Clean, were tested. If they were found not to be a carrier or have a gene vulnerable to Raven's Flesh, they were marked with the branding. But they only chose only the best of the uninfected, the people at the top of the broken world, those with the best genetic makeup. The strongest. The rest were forgotten, left to rot."

A sick feeling rattles around in my stomach. "They never told us that they only took the best or that the others were left behind," I say.

Others. The Remnants and those who probably didn't even have time to call themselves anything. The lives down here have meaning, even if they didn't before. The Elders were wrong. All people matter, all lives count.

"I'm not surprised," Bayard says. "The Clean forced themselves underground to survive and start a new life. The infected ended themselves eventually, I guess."

I don't miss the disdain in his voice. That was centuries ago. The Raven's Flesh is gone, but we still get the branding. The brandings are uniform, all given at birth throughout our history and painted into our skin. Everyone I know has one on the back of his or her neck. Three circles that get smaller, one inside the other. The circles exist to remind them of the cycle of the Preservation: disease, death, salvation. And then the circles crossed in an X because they are saved. Clean. Perfect.

Has it always been a sign of the Elders' deceit?

"That's the end. Now we all survive the best we can," Bayard says, falling silent. That's it. But it's only the beginning. "Have you ever seen the Elders?"

"No," I say. They are a mystery, a force we can't see. They never visit us in the Compound unless they come to see my father. They've been in our Compound once, but I was too small to remember. It was when my grandfather died and I was still believed to belong to Sara. Before the Elders knew to look twice at me.

My mind drifts to back Thorne. The boy I love, the boy who was branded as my twin, even though he isn't. I press my fingers into the half-circle on the back of my neck. My branding is not the same; I'm one of the exceptions. Twins have a different branding, one that marks them as one half instead of one whole. It's the mark I have. The mark Thorne has. We got it before Cecily Lopez and her sister left the Northern Compound, before the Elders stopped giving it anymore, and the branding has changed Thorne and me into something more than normal. What would it be like if he was here? What would he say to this story? This mission?

"No more questions, then?" I whisper no, and Bayard scoffs in the silence. "Is something bothering you? You seem to always have a question in need of answer."

I smirk. "Touché, old man."

Bayard goes silent, waiting. I wouldn't usually share details, but I'm with the man a few more days. Just long enough to escape. It shouldn't matter if he knows something about me; it's not like we're going to be friends after this. "I'm just thinking about Thorne."

"Who's that?"

"He's my..." But I can't finish the thought. He's a lot of things. "He's someone I love that I left behind."

Bayard sighs. "You can go back home someday, and he'll be there, ready to see you again. I'm sure he's thinking about you as well."

I force a smile. "I hope you're right."

But will he be there? Will I go back home? I've hurt Thorne. Even with hundreds of miles of distance between us, I know that. There are some things that aren't easy to forgive.

"I am. My daughter, my family will be home once I return. The people you love don't leave so easily if they truly love you."

I inhale as we walk and press my finger into the branding on my neck. It's a lot to hope that Thorne will understand this, that his love for me is stronger than this, because Bayard's right. The people who love you don't leave, and that's exactly what I did. I faked my death to leave him, and he'll never know why. A spark rushes through me from my branding, a warm heat coursing through my body that jolts me forward. The shock of it makes my feet fumble under me, and I run into Bayard, knocking the torch from his grip. My breath hitches at the sudden darkness that stretches before me.

MY BREATH HITCHES AS I SEE the outline of my father waiting for me at the end of a dark hallway in one of the lower levels of Headquarters. The branding on my neck tingles. Father is grinning, happy but devious. His blue eyes shimmer, and it chills me to the bone. Each step toward him feels as if it's taking me further away from where I want to be. Each step makes my branding burn a little more.

There's a sudden jolt in my stomach, and I feel nauseous. It catches me so off-guard that I can't catch my breath again. Thorne. His fear attacks me, this constant pressure washing over me. Where is he? What's causing this? Thorne is never scared. Not like this. I look around the hallway, but there's only my father at the other end.

A scream echoes, barrels toward me. Pain spreads through my whole body, and I fall to my knees. I should get up, but nothing wants to move, muscles on strike and stiff. Fear and shock trample me. Thorne's fear. Thorne's agony. It's like he's dying, or I'm dying. The screams engulf me while I add my own to them, like a chorus. The sounds refrain down the hallway—whether his or mine, I don't know anymore. Then the pain subsides, but the fear and confusion are still very present. Thorne knows it's coming again, and he's terrified.

"Look what I discovered, Cornelia," my father says, pulling me to my feet.

My fingers grip a large windowsill and my father's arm as he holds me up to see. Beyond the window, Thorne lies, his arms and legs shackled to a table in a stark white room. There are poles and tubes running from his arms to a large machine in the ceiling.

I yell Thorne's name at the sight of him. Caramel eyes look in my direction, dark and glassy. His voice cries in low, steady groans, and then I read my name on his lips.

There's a noise, a simple buzzing, and a flicker of the lights in the hallway as the room he's in fills with light. His body convulses. His wails are louder than before, and each one I mirror. The pain and fear is more intense than anything I've ever felt. The branding burns on my neck, but it's so minor it barely compares to everything else. We connect more in times of intense emotion, and this is the strongest I have ever felt race through me. The emotions he's feeling are so twisted and connected that my body is trying to process. It can't. I can't even think straight; everything is too jumbled. I want to run, but my body doesn't seem to work. Burning waves vibrate through me—spreading and running through my veins. A constant piercing pressure, pulsing and throbbing. Fire burning through everything.

"Please!" I beg my father. "Let him go." It almost feels like it's happening to me. I don't know what he's feeling or which emotion is the strongest, and that makes all this harder. I can't take it from him. I can't carry it for him. I can't do anything except feel his terror and do nothing.

Father's stance doesn't change, his arms crossed over his chest, his eyes forward, his smile barely there but intentional. He's so far from who he used to be that I don't know if anyone can save him.

"That's interesting, isn't it? How you can feel what he's feeling?" my father says. He leans down to me, wiping a spot of blood off my lip. I must've bitten it. His eyes find the branding on my neck, and he pushes a finger against it. "Do not forget that I can take away everything you hold dear in your life if you disobey me."

Father signals to someone through the glass. He steps away from me. "See you at dinner, Cornelia." The door closes and resounds back to me in the silence.

Thorne's pain is gone, just like that, but the memory of it lingers. It must be that memory that continues to ring through his body. Exhaustion, fear, pain, confusion, love—they all make me sick as they merge in my stomach. Thorne catches my gaze through the window. His eyes are heavy, darker, exhausted, and I can't handle the look on his face: the pain my father put there, the love he carries for me, the confusion about all of this. I can't handle it, so I look away.

BAYARD LOOKS AT ME, his eyes studying mine. "You need to stop?"

He picks up the torch from the ground, and the soft glow of it lights an area between us. I lean against the wall, gasping. After a second, I push away and apologize. Bayard grunts at me, his eyes narrowed and face scowling.

I inhale a breath as we walk, but it's hard to do. My head feels heavy, and I want to sleep, to curl up against a fluffy pillow and rest. I can't shake the feeling of Thorne. About how I left him. How I let him think I died. How I betrayed him. Where is he right now? Would he recognize me if he saw me here, covered in dirt and shaded in lies?

"You sure you're okay?" Bayard asks.

I nod, inhale the stale, sour air again. It burns in my chest until I have enough to form words. I need to steady my emotions, to change the subject. "How long have you been in the Burrows?"

"I was born here. Most of us who live here are from original families," Bayard talks without hesitation, continuing the story of the past. I like the distraction of his voice echoing around me. "The Elders never thought to check below, and they didn't care about the rest of us. Our families were the ones who were left to die, either by the infected or by the elements. The infected killed each other, and we survived as ghosts."

The Elders don't care about anyone but themselves. Even now. "How have you survived?"

"The Mavericks provide for us. People from the camps bring us some supplies every few months: torches, food, water. After 300 years, we've figured it out. There are some Remnants who go above occasionally. I am not one of them, but my youngest daughter, Faye, likes to explore." Bayard's voice is rough as he talks about his daughter, and when I look at him, his eyes are narrowed, brows furrowed.

"You don't approve?"

"I don't want her to get hurt. There's a difference. To love means to worry and want to protect, and that's all I want for her. Safety," he says softly. Perhaps I have been too hard on Bayard. His demeanor isn't about our journey or me; it's about the people he loves. Love, worry, protect. I understand that concept completely.

"Why don't you go live above? Why stay in the darkness for centuries?"

Bayard holds the torch betwcen us so the glow of the pyre reflects off his face. His dark eyes and dirt-covered face explore my own, and then he gives me a curt nod. "This is all I know. Why should I trade this place for something that could be worse when I am safe and warm and have all I could need?"

I gulp back everything I'm feeling. The inadequacy. The urge to turn around and run all the way back to the Compound. There are reasons to go above. I miss the feel of the sun, seeing the ocean and the sky. To experience the endlessness of the three as they meld into one. I say none of this though because it's not my place to question him. His life isn't mine. I don't know what it's like out here, and my time isn't enough for me to pretend as if I do.

"Why did you leave the Compound, Neely?" he asks

I start to walk past him, and he claps my arm. The harsh line of his lips demands an answer, but gentleness is present in his eyes. It's that gentleness that reminds me of my father before all of this. Before he was made into something else.

"Because I had no choice," I say.

"We always have choices." He releases me and walks on, the light of his torch leading the way.

I had a choice; he's right. My choice was to say nothing, to do nothing, and lose everything—or I could leave. I could fight. That's what I'm doing, and it may end up costing me everything anyway.

"What's in San Francisco?" Bayard presses in my silence.

"I'm looking for someone," I reply. I don't want to tell him about the Mavericks yet; even though the Remnants respect the Mavericks, not all of them agree and not all of them can be trusted. I'm told the Elders have ears and eyes everywhere.

Bayard mumbles something under his breath. "This whole thing was rushed—you coming here, us helping you out. There a reason for that?"

I shrug. "It's urgent. I only have thirty-two days left to make it there."

"What happens if you don't?"

"I will lose."

"Lose what?" he asks.

I avoid the question. I look around the Burrows while we move, studying the metal bars along the ground the best I can. I count the pieces of trash we pass and hum inside my head. I listen for the sound of his boots clomping. But even all the distractions can't stop the word from coming out.

"Everyone."

He doesn't hear me. The word is barely whispered, inaudible and lost in the echo of darkness.

THERE'S AN ECHO AS I *move down the stairs and into the dark depths of Xenith's quarters. Mint lingers around me as if he's painted the walls with his familiar scent. In all my life, I've never stepped into his quarters. I know that being here means something more than I ever expected to give in this fight. There's no turning back after this. But I can still hear Thorne's screams in my ears, feel his pain again and again. I'm doing this for him, for my father, and for all the people the Elders have ever hurt. I have to stop them.*

Xenith is hunched over a table, his blond hair falling in his face. His hand moves fiercely on the paper spread across the table. I can't help but stare at him. He isn't Thorne, whose beauty is simple and holistic, olive and dark, but Xenith is undeniably attractive. He has a strong chin, a sharp jawline, and blue eyes, dark and vast like the ocean. I've always liked his eyes, ever since we were kids, because he could never lie. The truth was always swirling in them. I wonder if it still does.

"Neely," he says without looking up from whatever he's working on. "Are you lost?"

"No."

Xenith moves the paper over to a different stack and continues writing. The pencil in his hand moves quickly and I try to see what the words are, but they aren't in English.

"I'm here because—"

He holds up a hand to me, and I bite my lip, waiting. His hand moves across the paper on his table, never pausing and never faltering. He doesn't look up, so I wander around the room. To my left is a shelf full of trinkets. One is a small, round glass object with faint white lines etched into it. I reach out a hand, but Xenith says my name as a warning without even looking up. I step away from it like I've been scolded and feel childish. Alone and lost in a big world. I move toward another shelf filled with books. My fingers graze one of the spines as I wait for him to stop me. He doesn't.

I watch him as he brushes his hair out of his eyes, leaning over the counter and writing like a madman on sheets of paper. Maybe he is a madman. A crazy, dangerous, genius of a madman. For someone who's only eighteen, sometimes I feel like he's so much more than I can ever be. As if he knows more than I can begin to understand.

I shouldn't be here with him. If Thorne or my father found out, then I'll be in more trouble. I can find another way. I step back toward the stairs and hear him slam his hand on the table. When I turn around, he has a smile on his face.

"Sorry. I was in the middle. Some things you have to finish before you can start others," he says. He moves toward me and raises an eyebrow. "Leaving so soon?"

I shake my head. "I need to talk to you."

He laughs. "I figured since you've never set foot in my quarters before."

"It's important."

Xenith nods his head at me and points at the far side of the room toward a beat-up leather couch. I lead the way, and we sit, me on the couch and him in a chair next to it. My heart dances in my chest, trying to escape or make too much noise and tell on me. I shouldn't be here. Thorne wouldn't like me trusting Xenith. He never has.

"Do you want a drink?"

I shake my head. "I'd rather get this over with." My mouth is cotton, but I'm more scared of accepting anything more from him than I am about to.

"What can I do for you, Neely?"

His voice is smooth, confident. I know he's been expecting me. Xenith has a way of knowing things that others don't—especially with me. I inhale so a deep breath fills my lungs and calms me down, clears my head. I'm here because I have to be.

"I need to leave the Compound," I say. "As soon as possible."

If he's surprised, he doesn't show it. His gaze is steady, focused on my face, and he shrugs. "Why are you coming to me?"

"You're the only one who can help me. I know that you can, that you know the way things work." I lean forward on the edge of the chair. "I know that you know the way out."

Xenith meets my stare. "What is it you're asking?"

He wants to me say the words, to paint the picture I see, even if he already sees it. If I can't say it, then how could I everactually change it?

I sit up straighter. "The Elders have something planned for me, something more than me being a director. I've read things about what they've done, what they plan to do. And my father is different. More out of control. I don't know why, but I think they've done things to him. I found files in his office, notes on cases where the Elders had been experimenting on twins, and there was something about me in there."

"What was it?"

My mind races back to the pages I read. "It said that I failed the experiment. It didn't say what the experiment was, but on other twins, they used the branding and it changed them." I pause. "I think it's changed all of us. Whatever they are doing, whatever they're up to, it's not good. My father told me they had a plan for me, Xenith, and I don't want to be part of any plan they have. I definitely don't want to be the director. I want the truth."

"About what?"

"Whatever they are doing. To me, to Thorne, to all of us." The globe on the shelf catches the corner of my eye, and I turn to look at it. The lines that outline the Old World are barely noticeable up close, but even from here, I can see them. America used to have life, and maybe it still does. Maybe the Old World isn't as old as we are told. "I don't believe anymore that we're the only ones alive from the Preservation. I know there is someone in the Old World who can help us." I look away for a heartbeat before looking back. "I feel it."

Xenith's eyes grow dark, unmoving and still. He shrugs again and leans back in the chair. "But why are you coming to me?"

"Because you hate the Elders." Because they're responsible for your family dying. I don't say that, but it's shared in a glance. He leans toward me, his hands crossed in front of him and resting on his knee. "And because I read things about your ancestor, Nicholas Taylor, who claimed there was still life outside. I believe him, and I think you know it's true."

"My help has a price. Even for you—especially for you."

"I know," I say. I don't look away, which I know he expected. I know coming to him requires something of me. Xenith doesn't give away information or time for free. There are whispers of people turning to his family over the years and the cost of information or time or a much-loved item. I'm ready for whatever he's going to ask of me.

Xenith moves from his seat. I see him smile before he turns his back on me. He moves toward another shelf in the far corner of the room, takes down a book from the back—the same one I was looking at before—and sets it to rest on the table.

"I can help."

"Just like that?"

He smiles with a nod, and his shoulders drop. "There's a group in the Old World, a secret organization if you will, called the Mavericks. They've been around a long time and have a lot of power. They can help you. You can help them, too. You just have to get to them."

I nod in agreement, unable to process it all. He's helping me. I'm going to leave the Compound and go into the Old World. It's an adventure, a quest like the ones I've read about. Suddenly, it's all very overwhelming. I don't know if I can do it. Xenith's eyes study me. I can't let him see that I'm not sure, so I stand and move from the couch toward him. He turns to shield the book from me, and our bodies are only inches apart.

"What do I need to do?" I ask. I fight down the part of me that wants to move closer. That part has always wondered what it would be like to be closer to Xenith. The other part, the stronger one, has kept me away.

"Nothing. Wait for my word. I'll get things together for you." His gaze sends an unnerving chill down my spine, but I don't move. "Is there something else?"

I step back.. There's one piece of the puzzle that has to be fixed. The most important piece. The real reason I need to get a life away from here. The words hesitate in my mouth, frozen. It won't be something easy for Xenith. In fact, this will probably be the worst thing I could ever ask him, and yet I have to ask him. "Can you protect Thorne while I'm gone?"

Xenith clenches his jaw. His blue eyes peer into mine, harsh and sharp like ice.

"Please. It's that or let him come with me," I say. Xenith knows what happened. He knows my father tortured Thorne. Everyone does.

"That is not an option for so many reasons."

"Why?" Xenith doesn't answer me, and I can't leave until I know Thorne is safe. "Then promise you'll protect him. I love him."

He laughs. It's short and crisp and purposeful. He's mocking me. "You're branded to him. That's not love, Neely. There's a difference, I promise."

I shake my head. I don't know what he means, and I don't care. I can't leave Thorne here. Not alone. "I need to be certain he will be safe from my father while I'm gone. You're the only one who can do that."

Xenith is quiet. He and Thorne are far from friends, but will he risk Thorne's life? If I'm not here, then no one will be able to stop my father. No one except Xenith. He moves with the book to the side of the table where he stood when I first entered, and he's silent until he sets it on the table with a sigh.

"The cost for that, Neely, is too great."

"What is it?" I ask, moving toward him. I'll do anything to protect Thorne. Anything.

He looks up at me, his light hair falling in his face. It's like he has control over those strands and the way they fall perfectly to half-cover his eyes. He moves to meet me in the dead space. He's inches from my face, his warmth mingling with mine.

"You."

I huff and take a step back. He wants me? That is a joke. There's no way he can be serious. Why would he want me?

But Xenith isn't joking. "Me?"

"You," he smiles, taking a step forward so he's close. The heat of his body fuses with mine, and I can almost hear his heart beating. His breath brushes my skin, and I shudder. "Thorne is protected, and you're trading yourself to me. Your life for his."

I freeze, looking at him. Xenith doesn't look phased by the response, but my mind is racing. "You want to kill me?"

"No."

I shake my head. This is insane. My life for Thorne's— but he's not going to kill me. What does he mean then? I shouldn't have come here. I shouldn't have given in. I can find another way. I turn away, and Xenith calls my name.

"I'm not speaking of your death—your life is worth a great deal more than you know. I promise you that. And when I ask you, you have to hand your life over to me. Of course, even if you say no, it all still falls on your shoulders."

I still don't understand what he wants with me, and his half-answers are annoying. "What does?"

"There's a change coming," he says with a pause. "The Elders aren't so happy with the way things are going. It's been in talks for a while, but I know they're going to act sooner rather than later."

"Act how? What are you talking about?"

Xenith shakes his head. "I can't lay all my cards out on the table. Not until you've decided what you're willing to risk or stand up against."

This is the chance. I can be free from the Compound, from my father, from all the things I'm supposed to be, but I'd have to give up Thorne. I'd have to leave him. To let him go. A pain forms in my chest at the thought, but leaving him is the only way I can keep him safe and stop the Elders.

My life for Thorne's. If I stay, he's taken from me or worse. If I leave, I'm not with him, but at least he could live. That's what matters. Him living. With or without me. That's all that matters.

"I'll do it," I say. Even as I say the words, I push down my feelings of uncertainty. I'm losing Thorne by saying yes. Can I live without him?

His gaze freezes on me. "You really should take some time to consider—"

"I'll do it," I say again.

Xenith smiles and touches my cheek. His hand is warm, calloused, and rough as it rubs against the smooth skin of my cheek. The contrast sends another shiver down my spine, and I have to resist the urge to turn into it. I can't want his hand on my face. I can't want his fingers to caress me.

He leans into my ear, his warm breath tickling me. A rush of breath escapes my parted lips. "It's done then. I'll be in touch."

I TOUCH THE WALL WITH MY FINGERS, and it crumbles in bits to the ground. Things I can't see crackle under my feet as I walk. I don't even want to imagine what I'm stepping on, yet it's all I can do. Dried-up food. Bits of broken glass. Rocks. Rusty nails. Insects. Bones, most definitely bones, probably from whatever it was that I ate before, tossed into the dark corners and left to rot.

What do they do with their dead? People die. My mother died. Thorne's father died. Xenith's parents died. The Healers burn the bodies, and we scatter them into the ocean. Am I walking on dead people right now? Children, babies, adults? 300 years' worth of people?

A weight scatters over my foot. I squeal, and Bayard turns to me.

"Some-something was on my leg!"

"Probably just a rat."

I raise my eyebrow, even though he can't see it. "Rat." I shake my leg because it still feels like something is on me. I shiver, and Bayard starts to walk again.

"Next time that happens, try to catch the little bugger. Those are a delicacy in these parts." I can hear the amusement in his voice.

I can't wait to get out of here. Away from the iron and dirt walls. From the smell and the darkness and the rats. This was is not why I came here, to be trapped underground, and I know it's part of my journey but I'm ready for the next part. I'm ready for the end.

I run into something hard and bounce back like a rubber ball. Bayard looks down at me, his brow furrowed and his face taut with annoyance. Twice I've run into him.

"We'll be sleeping here tonight. This is a safe area."

I look around him at the minor stretch of tunnel with makeshift steps leading up to a higher platform. Up here, torches line the walls, and the golden glow is bright enough that I can see my feet for the first time today. My gray-laced shoes are cloaked in black, but I can't tell if it is dirt or darkness.

All around me are oddities. Everything from glass bottles to keys hanging off strings to tattered books litter the ground and are crammed into the shelves that have been built into the walls. The whole space is overflowing in Old World treasures.

"Third tent down from here," Bayard says.

His steps are wobbly and wide as he moves in front of me. I adjust my pack on my shoulders and follow behind him. As we pass the row of books, I try to make out any of the titles, but it's too dark. Some of the covers are destroyed, while the others are just out of reach for me to see. I desperately want to explore them. I've only touched twelve books from the Old World. A small group of us used to meet on the beach next to the barrier that separates the Compound from the Old World and dream about this world.

Rowan was the first one to bring us a book. The forbidden stories were wrapped in the shell of "approved" reading, books that the Elders and the director deemed good for us to know. Those approved stories all fit the same kind of mold and were nothing like the books Rowan brought us. Books about a king and his knights and the great battles and injustices they fought. Or the one about creation in a garden of perfection with Adam and Eve and the misery they set forth by pursuing the forbidden. We shared the stories, passed them around in secret for the entire year before Rowan was transferred. I never had the chance to ask him how he got the books. Now I know I never will.

Bayard puts his hand on my shoulder, and the sudden movement makes me jump. "You'll be out of here soon. I know it's hard if you're not used to it."

I look up and meet his dark eyes. There's a hint of a smile at the corner of his mouth, probably forced and more out of pity than anything else, but it warms me. The look's gone as quickly as I see it.

The flap of the tent in front of us pops out in our path, and with it comes a lady shorter than me. Her hair is back in a bun, pulled close to her head except the poof that rests on top.

"Bayard Toffy! Look at you! It's been ages since I've seen you!" The woman's practically yelling it, she's so excited. I'm sure there's no one around who doesn't know we're here now.

She and Bayard hug, chattering quickly in a language I don't understand. I never knew the people in the Old World spoke differently until I got here. To be fair, I never knew there were people. English was the standard before the Preservation, but Rover said the Remnants spoke in Spanish once they were established. That way, if any were found, they could pretend they didn't understand. We don't get to learn Spanish in the Compound; we learn only enough about the Old World to teach us a lesson about gratitude.

They stop talking and look at me. "This here is Neely. I'm guiding her above," Bayard says in English. He looks me with something almost like pride. The look sticks with me and rattles something in my heart. It's been so long since my father wore that expression. So long since he's been anything like a father.

The woman's eyes grow three sizes wider. "Why does she want to go up there?"

Bayard looks between us. "She's only passing through."

"Where's she from? There's nothing up there, girl. Nothing but death and danger."

I open my mouth to speak and close it again when I realize I have nothing to say.

Bayard crosses his arms. "She's on a mission, Francine. No need knowing any more than that. I was hoping we could sleep here tonight. We've a good two more days of walking ahead of us."

They say a few more words in their adapted Spanish language, Francine stealing glances at me while they talk. They pause, and then Francine smiles and hugs me. She takes the pack off my back and hangs Bayard's torch on the wall.

"You're just in time for supper," she says in her high-pitched voice. "My Jordan did some hunting today. We had a lucky day, we did."

They use that word a lot. *Lucky.*

Francine winds my arm through hers. She's so welcoming that I can't keep up with her whirlwind movements. She whistles through her teeth, something that Kai tried to teach me to do more times than I can count, and people from the first two tents poke their heads out.

The next thing I know, we're all sitting on the ground around a cauldron of stew. There's a thin boy who keeps smiling at me with his missing teeth and dirty face, and an old man made up of bones who keeps staring at me—well, my branding on the back of my neck—mouth ajar. I let my hair down around it to block his view, and my hair is matted together. I'm more like a Remnant each day. The thought isn't as horrible as I imagine. It feels nice to belong with them, even temporarily.

Bayard sits across from me, talking to the others like they are long-lost friends. The sight of it makes me miss my own friends. The ache forming in my chest disappears when some little girl hands me a chipped, black bowl. A boy comes behind her and slops something tan into it. Even as the others wait for food, they giggle and talk excitedly over each other. I smile as I watch them. They look like the kids I taught in the Compound, yet they live nothing like them. How does someone live in darkness forever and carry so much contagious light?

Francine stands up. "Let's say a blessing and give thanks."

And they do. Each one of them lifts up a voice and chants the same thing while I sit and listen. I don't need to know what they are saying to feel the joy. The Compound is about control, but this world is family and freedom. They deserve more than this life, and I want to help them all find it. Stopping the Elders, finding the Mavericks—I can do that for them. Fight for the innocent at the Compound and the ones forced into hiding. Save us all.

"Thank you, Jordan, for the delicacy of tonight's dinner!" Francine beams. The young boy who put food in my bowl blushes and buries his head into his bowl. I lift the spoon up from the thick, pasty stew and catch Bayard's eye from across the circle. He's smiling while he chews, his face completely bright with something hilarious. I look toward Jordan and the food and back at Bayard.

A delicacy. Rat stew.

I am not strong enough for this.

"Something wrong, honey?" one of the women next to me asks. Her belly is wide and round with pregnancy, and I can imagine her having that baby at any time. I stare at her stomach as she rubs it. "You can touch it," she says. I shake my head.

"How far along?"

"A few more weeks," she says, face lit up with happiness.

I smile, but the thought of having a baby in this world is baffling. There's nothing to look forward to, nowhere to go, and yet the Remnants are alive. I lift my spoon and can hear Bayard chuckle in the crowd, but I avoid looking at him. I close my eyes, stick the spoon in my mouth, and try to not think while I chew. Just chew. And when I do, it's familiar. Tangy and spicy. Stringy and gristly.

I've had rat before.

That should be comforting, but it's not. It makes me want out of this place that much more. It makes me long for Thorne, for home, for times like before. All things I'm not allowed to wish.

WE ARE NOT ALLOWED TO make wishes in the Compound. There's no need to desire anything more, but that's one of many rules Sara loves to break.

"Did you get candles?" Dad asks her. His jacket hangs on the chair behind me, and his shirtsleeves are rolled up, tie undone. He looks very at rest, unlike the times when he's working in his office with his "director" face on.

Sara places a chocolate cake on the table in front of us. She always does this for birthdays. It's a tradition from the Old World, one where all the people feed cake to each other. It's silly, but Sara loves it.

She shakes her head. "I didn't want to cause a commotion trying to find them."

Kai bumps shoulders with me while our parents search through cabinets. His face is round and smiling. "Birthday girl," he says.

"Don't forget birthday boy!" Thorne adds as he sits beside me on a stool. The two of us smile at each other. "We don't need candles."

Kai stands next to Thorne, and I study them together with their dark hair and dark eyes and skin like they never leave the sun, just like Sara. I am all auburn hair and light skin, equal parts my mother and my father, and I wonder how, for those first two years of life, anyone thought I was related to the Bishop family.

Dad moves next to me, and Sara stands across from the four of us. Though we aren't all blood, we're some kind of makeshift family. Two halves that were shoved together, imperfect and lopsided but somehow whole. Dad and me are better with the Bishops.

"Thirteen," Sara says. Her eyes glaze a little, like she's reliving a memory.

"Make a wish, even without the candles," Kai says.

Thorne and I hold hands as we close our eyes. I wish that this would never change. When I open them, Father hugs me and presses me against his shoulder, while Sara hands Thorne the first piece, me the second, and Kai the third. Kai stuffs a bite in his mouth and then rams some of it into Thorne's face. They always do this, too. The Old World had weird traditions. Thorne yells and tackles Kai to the floor.

I stay out of it and enjoy my cake. Sara wanders around the room, trying to make Kai and Thorne stop getting icing all over the living room furniture.

Father sits next to me, and even though I'm thirteen now, I like having him here. He takes a bite of his big piece of chocolate cake and smiles at me. "You look more and more like your mother every day," he says.

"You told me that in your note this morning," I say. Father smiles. He leaves me a note every morning. He has for as long as I can remember, and earlier this year, since I was old enough to take care of myself, he's been leaving for work before I wake up. Even after he's gone, he leaves me breakfast on the stove and a note on the counter.

"It's true, though," he says. Father doesn't talk about Mother much. Most of what I know of her comes from Sara. But when he does, his eyes light up and his face changes from sadness to happiness to a deeper sadness. "You're a lot like her. Too much sometimes."

"How?" I ask softly.

He tilts his head to look at me. "You have her eyes and her nose and those freckles right there." He points to my cheek. "She was smart, beautiful, always made everyone laugh, and she was fiercely devoted."

I smile widely.

"And she had that smile," Father adds. I hug him, and he pats my head. In his arms, I feel safe.

"Hey, Neely!" Kai says. I turn around in my chair, just time for him to smash me in the face with cake. I lick my lips and then jump into the boys. No one makes us stop, even though the floor, the walls, and the furniture gets covered in icing.

When we are done, my father announces that he has to go back to work, and he lets me hug him before he goes, leaving a trail of brown icing on his white shirt.

MY SHIRT USED TO BE A DIFFERENT COLOR. Cleaner, brighter, not as smudged.

Maybe the darkness of the Burrows is rubbing off on me. Tainting me.

THEY'RE TRYING TO SUFFOCATE ME. These Burrows seem to go on and on, never getting smaller or shorter, only thinner and closer together.

WHAT WOULD MY MOTHER SAY if she knew I was here? Everything would've been different. My father would be normal. She would've sang songs to me instead of Sara. I wouldn't be branded to Thorne. And I wouldn't be here.

I'd be home, and it'd be all I needed. She'd be there, instead of dead.

THERE'S A FIGURE UP AHEAD that I recognize. My heart beats faster, and I imagine that it's Thorne. That he's waiting for me. He's right there, holding out his hand, talking to me. I just have to reach him.

"We're getting closer," Bayard says.

Closer.

I look forward again, and there's nothing there.

"WHAT'S THE REASON YOU'RE DOING THIS?" Bayard asks me. We've finally stopped to rest and eat, and my body is thankful for it.

"What do you mean?" I ask, studying his face while he chews.

"I'm not supposed to ask you questions, and I reckon it's none of my business. But you're pretty near the same age as my daughter, and if she was traipsing through the Burrows and in the Old World, well..." He looks down at the ground and then back at me. "I'd want to know everything I could as to why she was being so foolish."

"You think it's foolish?"

His eyes don't leave mine. "Depends on the reason."

I look away from his gaze, the warmth in the darkness of his eyes and the flickering torch too much for me to handle. I want nothing more than to tell him everything. No one except Xenith knows what I'm doing. No one except the two of us—and Kai—even know I'm alive. I should tell my story, right? I should share and let the people who matter know what I'm doing, so if I die...

"You don't have to tell me," Bayard says with a heavy sigh. "I get that it's important."

I shake my head. Of all the people I've met, I'm surprised myself, but I think I can tell Bayard. He'd understand it.

"You don't know what it was like in the Compound," I say. "It was perfect. I mean, perfect. And then one day, I looked around and I saw the deception. I didn't want to see it, and I tried to ignore it but−"

"But you can't unsee something."

Neither of us speaks for a moment, and Bayard's eyes darken. What has he seen in his life? "The Elders are evil. Everyone's being lied to, and I want to help them."

Bayard is quiet. "So you left to get help?"

I shrug. The only thing I can say is that I'm leaving for everyone there. It makes me feel less selfish. Because when I think about why I left, I know the reason is more than that. I'll never be able to wipe away what the director−what my own father−did to Thorne. I'll never stop feeling the pain, never undo his screams, and never stop wondering why. Why me. Why us.

"I shouldn't talk about it. I don't want to put anyone else at risk," I say.

There's the fact that they wanted to use me. The fact that they experiment on their own people, want to control and change their own people, that everything I know about my whole life isn't real. Maybe even Thorne and me.

That's the part that feels the most desperate. I have to know if we're real or manufactured. If our feelings, our love, is theirs or ours.

Bayard looks at me, his eyebrows furrowed together. "The people you love are a burden to you?"

I shake my head. "I'm the burden on them. I've caused some problems in their lives, and this is part of how I fix it."

"I'm sure it's not as bad as it seems. I doubt they'd want to lose you. I know I couldn't lose my Faye. I'd have no life without my family."

I look away from him toward the ground. I feel the same way, and that's why I'm here. I need to save them, and selfishly, I need to know about Thorne. I have to know. "I just need to keep going."

"Then let's go." Bayard groans as he stands and wipes some breadcrumbs from his beard. I get up too, reach for my pack, and we start off again, led by the unsteady light of the torch.

THE STARS ABOVE US *provide the only light, and it's unsteady, a deep contrast to the calm waves. Waves so calm that it makes me nervous, as if in the silence Xenith can hear my heart racing and the crashing of my thoughts. I dig my toes into the sand, but I can't be reading this. It's really real, the Old World, and everything else is false. They lied. Everyone's been lying.*

I crumple the pieces of paper in my hand before Xenith takes them away from me and straightens them out across his chest.

"This is really happening?"

Xenith nods, his expression grim. "I wouldn't make it up. I told you there was a change coming."

I stare at the paper. Ultimate Compliance. The Elders want to use the branding to make everyone in the Compound into some sort of machine. Some kind of human that follows directions, doesn't think, doesn't question anything, and is emotionless. I knew they were up to something with twins, but with everyone? They'll strip them of their own thoughts and feelings and move them all to a new Compound. The blueprints are enormous and fortified, bigger and better than even this one. They'll start making transfers in two months. They already have a list of people and families they want to move.

"They've mastered the way to make it so that no one questions. There's already no free will, but this move will wipe away everyone completely. All traces of humanity and individuality —gone."

I think on that, and the pieces click together. "They've already started using on it," I say quickly. Xenith looks at me. "My father. That explains the change in him. They've changed him into something for their own use. He was never so heartless before."

I run my eyes over the list Xenith found of all the families set to move to the new Compound. People I grew up with, children I've taught during my placement, friends. The Bishop family is one of them: Sara, Kai, and Thorne. The only people I really love. My father has succeeded in taking Thorne away, just like he'd promised. I can't let this happen. I can't let them all be turned into whatever it this is that the Elders are creating.

Xenith clears his throat. "There's one more thing that you should know, Neely." He pauses, and I look up at him. He hands me a new sheet of paper. My eyes scan it, reading the slanted handwriting.

Sara has mentioned that she's noticed some potential effects from the twin branding. I shall examine that tomorrow and see what I discover.

"What is this?" I ask.

"My mom's," Xenith says. "She was the one who switched you at your birth. She monitored you for years, and then Thorne as well, until she died."

I knew that Liv Taylor had switched us, me for Thorne's twin sister, but I didn't know she'd been watching us. Why would she keep tabs on us? "What was she looking for?"

"Not her. The Elders. She was trying to protect you."

Protect us from the Elders. None of this makes any sense. I look back down at the paper.

Sara has reported back to me, and we believe them to be connected. They are small, but when one cried, the other cried. When one laughed, the other laughed. The full effects are entirely undeveloped unless I can get closer, but I suspect them to have some emotional alteration because of the branding. The effects will only increase as they age unless it can be undone sooner. If my guess is true, then it's not safe for either of them. Especially her. Amelia knew the plans they had for Neely from the beginning, and if they discovered this truth now, they would take her. I will proceed in keeping all Amelia's secrets for Neely.

Liv Taylor knew that we were connected. "What secrets did my mother have?"

Xenith sighs heavily. "I don't know. I swear. We never talked about Amelia."

My eyes drift back to the page.

If Neely and Thorne are emotionally drawn to each other because of the branding, there is no indication yet of how deep that emotional connection goes or how it should impact their lives together and separately. I believe it to be part of the reason they are always together, as whatever they feel draws them to each other. Should my predictions be correct, then they may never be their own person. The branding caused that, and I caused the branding by lying about her birth and testing. I hope I do not regret my decisions.

I inhale. My head is spinning. Liv Taylor, even when we were kids, thought Thorne and I were so close because of the branding. She died when we were eight, but even back then, she knew we were something. If what she's saying is real, then it means that Thorne may not actually love me. That our feelings may not be genuine and may instead be some sort of experiment. I close my eyes. That can't be true. He's the one sure thing I have. If he's not real, then what is?

"You okay?" Xenith asks.

My eyes narrow in on him. "This is what you meant the other day when you said there was a difference between me loving him and the branding."

"Yes," he says. "I'm sorry, Neely, but you had to know. You said that you thought the branding changed you, and it did. You said you thought the Elders had a plan for you, for everyone, and they do."

Somehow I'm the center of all of this. "What does it mean?"

"It means you have to leave. If you want help, then you have to find it. Save yourself; save everyone. There's a group who can help you—the Mavericks. I'll plan it all out for you."

A group in the Old World. He's mentioned them before, but how does he know? How am I supposed to trust what he's saying? If there was someone with the power to stop the Elders, then why haven't they?

"I'm just supposed to believe all of this and go? I don't know anything about these people."

"The Mavericks have been fighting the Elders since the Preservation, since the walls of the first Compound were built. They're the only ones."

"Why should I trust them?"

"You trust me, don't you?" he asks. I nod, afraid to say aloud that I do. "Then you trust them. I'm one of them. My whole family has been. They originated with my family nearly three hundred years ago."

I cross my arms around my chest. "Then why can't you go?"

"Come on, Neely," Xenith says. He reaches out to me but changes his mind and steps closer instead. "You came to me. You wanted out of this place. You wanted to stop your father, to keep Thorne safe, to 'not be their pawn.' That's all you. It's not me. They aren't the people I care about. Besides, you know their plan, and if you're here, you can't run from it." He pauses, tosses his hands up in the air. "I'm giving you what you wanted. If you want to be freed of them and if you want to know the truth, then you have to go."

From here, I can see the indentation of his jawline and his strong chin. His eyes are wide, dark blue like the ocean after a storm. I take a breath.

"It's only you who can go, Neely. For more reasons than you know." The way he says it seems almost as if he's pleading with me. He wants me to go.

"You said there's a plan," I say.

"There's a spot where the barrier is open," he says. His eyes dance excitedly. "I have maps, records that my family has tracked for years. All we have to do is make sure you're there at the right time and smuggle you out."

That's all. He makes it sound so simple.

He looks out over the ocean, and I take the opportunity to study his face in the darkness. The arch of his nose, the shape of his lips as he speaks. It's hard not to look at him when he has such authority over things. "I have a route planned for you. The people of the Old World have set up camps. They have ways of communicating, systems for trade, networks of people. It's the only way you have a chance," he says, and his eyes meet mine. "You just have to follow the route to the Mavericks."

He's completely serious. His gaze doesn't falter, doesn't mock. He's waiting for my response. What can I say? He's got everything figured out. He's got maps and lists and names. He's got me. He'll smuggle me out, send me on my way, and...wait.

"There's one problem," I say.

"What's that?"

"How will I get out? I mean, I'm the director's daughter. I can't just disappear."

Xenith crosses his arms over his chest, and his blue eyes search me, find something in my soul. I can feel them latch on there. I know that's an image that will never leave me, a feeling that will stay, somehow.

"You won't disappear. You'll die."

I suck in air. "What?" My voice is an octave higher than normal.

"Everyone in this Compound will think Cornelia Ambrose is dead."

"How?"

He doesn't blink. "We'll fake your death."

I don't respond. My brain is trying to absorb everything and failing. He keeps talking.

"You'll stay hidden until the time is right for you to leave. No one will know anything except you and me. And, well, I'll probably need some help from someone to help us pull this off. Not Thorne. Maybe Kai, since he's a Healer. That can be of service to us." His voice hardens. "Every person in this hell will believe you died—and then you'll save them all. And yourself."

My hands shake in about the same way as my stomach. Thorne would mourn me. I would be dead. My remains would be thrown into the ocean, and a small, empty vase would sit in someone's house to remind them. I can't possibly do that to them. I can't let them suffer; I can't keep this from them. But it won't matter if they all get transferred. I'd never see Thorne again anyway. At least this way there's hope.

"Do you really think it will work?" I ask. The voice that comes out doesn't sound completely like mine.

"Yes."

I inhale. A deep, cool breathe of air. Die. I can die and leave. It's the only way.

His hand reaches out to cover mine. "I've been planning it, Neely. I wouldn't risk you unless I was sure," he says. "You don't have to do it. Any of it. You can stay here.. You can change your mind right now."

I close my eyes.

I could change my mind. Right now.

I have an out, this one last chance to stay. To go home to Thorne and pretend like this never happened. To have a life here with Sara and Kai and Thorne. To walk by the ocean and not think about what could be beyond it. To live. To love. To be content. But I can't do that. How can I do that when it's only temporary? Only days until I lose them all?

I nod. Xenith smiles, really smiles. I've never seen him really smile. It lights up the night sky, and it almost–almost–makes my heart flutter. I shake away the feeling. This is a not a time to have a fluttering heart. Not where he's concerned.

He claps his hands together. "Then let's plan your death."

SOMETIMES THE BURROWS smell like death. Or how I imagine death would smell. It's only a moment, fleeting but powerful, and it comes along when I don't expect the pungent scent of something rotten.

Bayard whistles while we walk. It's a pretty tune, soft and melodic, repetitive. It echoes off the Burrow walls and reminds me of the ocean. The way the waves sound when they wash in and out of the shore on summer nights when the air is crisp. Will I ever see the ocean again? Will I ever feel the breeze or walk through the tide or see the sun rise over the endless blues?

Bayard whistles a high note that gets stuck somewhere in his throat and cracks. He coughs and stumbles. I reach out to steady him.

"You okay?"

"It's a little warm," he says quickly. "Chokes me up."

"It's not a race," I say.

He looks at me, sweat building on his brow. "Isn't it?"

THREE MORE HOURS and I will feel the sun again. I will be free from this darkness. Leaving is scary, having to face what is beyond and above, but never getting out of the shadows is inconceivable. Like I was better off dead.

The air is different on this side of the Burrows, almost thinner so it's harder to breath. The tunnel seems narrower and darker. It definitely feels hotter. I'm uncertain if it's real or if it's all in my head. Much like the rest of my life. But the scent is different, too. Not as rancid and musty. There's something odd that burns my nose and makes my throat itch.

"What's that smell?" I ask. My head is pounding, my stomach is churning, and my nose is on fire. The air is thick. Surely, Bayard feels it, too.

"We're almost there," he says.

"Do you smell it?" I ask as the scent gets stronger. It's almost as if we're walking into a pit of rotten eggs. I hold my breath, air filling up my lungs, and try not to breathe in until I have to again.

Bayard never answers.

I can see the end. This round flow of light burns into the darkness and imprints on the ground. I want to race toward it, but a churning grips my stomach.

"Bayard..." I start. I stop walking and bend over. The tunnel is spinning. I crouch against a wall and use a hand to support me.

"Neely," Bayard says. He gasps in sharp breaths next to my ear. The rancid smell around us fills my nostrils, and my fingers hurt from the pressure of leaning into the wall. Then, the air gets thicker, like smoke.

I start to ask Bayard a question when my stomach churns and vomit rushes out instead of words. It splashes off the ground, and I groan. The piece of cement under my fingernails chips off a large chunk and falls onto the floor just as a scream echoes down the tunnel. Someone else's scream, dripping with pain. It rushes toward us with the sound of feet and more screams. It all happens in seconds, but it feels like my deadline has passed three times over.

"What is it?" I ask.

Bayard coughs again, and I see the worry in his eyes. "They're all dead."

A heavy weight sits in my chest. "How are they dead? What's happening?"

He considers me, like he wants to say something else. His eyes get glassy with tears, and he blinks them away. "I have to get you out. Run, Neely."

The smoke chokes me, drenching me like Thorne's clothes after the fishermen burn off the unused bits from the day's catches. But even those smells couldn't prepare me for this one. The scent is nauseating and sweet, yet rancid, and I can almost taste it on my tongue. Cries of pain and panic, screams of names blend together around me, and Bayard yanks my hand and pulls me along, abandoning the torch. We run. I glance over my shoulder as we go, and that's when I see a faint glowing light coming from the other side of the tunnel.

It's all on fire behind us.

The crackling of flames engulf the air. A pop or a spark off the metal. Screams grow fainter, and the people we left behind flash in my head. The children, the pregnant woman, the old man. Are all those I swore to save dead?

We're not far from the entrance to the Old World. Bayard runs next to me with strength I didn't imagine him to possess. I don't look back again, but sweat pours from my skin, soaking my shirt. I focus on the running and fight down the urge to vomit that plays at my throat, at my nose, at my stomach. My pack rubs over my sticky shoulders, but we go. We move forward in the thick smoke until I can't see Bayard anymore. Aside from smog, there's complete darkness and the ever-increasing absence of screams. I wish for them to come back. The silence means death.

"Neely, here!" Bayard yells.

Bayard stands ahead of me under a small shaft of sunlight, face bright red from the heat of the fire that seems to be behind us. The exit to the Old World is above him, looking just as it did when I first arrived. Except this time smoke dances in the beams.

Heat and flames barrel toward us as Bayard and I move toward it. On the wall across from us there's a ladder with missing rungs that goes up, up, up toward the sunlight. Toward freedom.

"You go first!" he says.

I put a hand and a foot on the rungs and start to climb. The metal burns my hands, but I keep going. The smell of burnt flesh traces the air, but none of it is mine and I know that people in the Burrows are dying around us. What I don't understand is how this happened.

The hole is sealed shut when I get to the top of the ladder. I push on it, but it doesn't budge. I can only use one hand or I'll fall. It doesn't work. I look down toward Bayard, and the fire is spread all below us.

"Bayard! It won't open!" I yell. I can barely see him, but I hope he can hear me. I pound and push at the round metal opening. It's not working. I can't get it open.

Bayard tugs at my leg. He squeezes past me on the ladder, half-on and half-off of it, and pounds something metal against it. The noise is almost lost in the hiss of the fire that fills the space below. The only escape is through the hole, and it's stuck.

This is how I die.

Tears sting my eyes. The acid scent of burnt hair sticks in my nose. It can't be the end already. I won't let it.

I move up next to Bayard, and together we pound at the metal covering. The small holes of light bounce off my skin, but in the heat of the fire below, I don't enjoy it as much as I thought I would. I let the tears fall and mix with my sweat.

There's a loud pop and a clatter as the metal rung Bayard held falls to the ground. I look up and there's light. So much light. Blue skies even. Bayard laughs, overjoyed and relieved.

"Go first, Neely!" he yells and helps me maneuver around him on the hot ladder.

I can smell the fresh, crisp air outside, and I pull myself up as Bayard pushes me. I'm short, so it's harder than I thought. I land on a black ground, and my body is shaking, burning with sweat and thirst as I reach back for Bayard.

"Take my hand," I yell. He's farther down than he should be, and I reach out for him. "Take another step up!" But he doesn't. His eyes meet mine, and I expect to see fear in them, but I don't. They're peaceful. "Take my hand! Bayard, come on!"

"No," he says, and my brain is scrambling, trying to process what this "no" means. This is life; that is death. This, unlike all other choices, is an easy one.

"You can't!" His name is on my lips, and then he lets go of the ladder. I only see a flash of him before he's lost in the orange tint of the fire.

"Bayard!" I yell his name. Over and over I yell, with no response from him. Only the hiss of flames answers back.

Bayard sacrificed himself for me. I gasp in a breath, even though I'm sobbing. He saved me. He made me go first, and then he—what? Gave up? How could he give up?

All of those people, the ones I swore to save, died while I live. I cry because I failed them all. Their faces, the ones I've met, flash in front of my eyes. Rover and Josef. Nadine. The old man at dinner who kept staring at my branding. The boy who caught the rat for the stew. The ones who helped Rover pull me in from the Cleaners.

They are all dead. I've killed them all. If I failed them, then I can never save the others. I can never save anyone.

I know I need to calm down. Xenith warned me that he didn't know how far I could push myself before the connection started working again. If an emotion is too strong, then Thorne could feel it, and he can't know I'm alive. I take a breath.

I think of the children at home. Of Sara. Of Kai and Thorne. I think of Bayard's determination to get me out of the Burrows. He succeeded in that. I take breath after breath until the emotion levels out and I can breathe.

Too many have been sacrificed now, and I can't stop. I can do this. I can make it and save the others. I can do it.

"WE CAN DO THIS. There has to be a way to do this," I say.

Thorne shrugs and gives me that "I don't really feel like doing this" look. I brush it off. I want my own space; surely he does, too. He can't feel everything I feel because that's going to get really awkward. Doesn't he ever plan to kiss a girl? Because I don't want to know what he feels like with her when that happens.

I snap my fingers and motion for him to stand. He sighs overdramatically and pulls himself up off the floor. I swing my hair over my shoulder.

"We should focus. I can send you emotions when I want, so maybe if we mean to block them, it will work, too." That's what I've been saying for a month, and we still haven't had any luck.

Thorne clenches his jaw, but he nods slowly and takes my hand. There's a little spark now that we're touching. His emotions are steady: a little doubtful, a little motivated, and a little irritated. That's reassuring; at least I'm not the only one.

"Ready," I say. I let him push his emotions through first because he can put on joy and happiness quicker than I can.

The joy washes over me, and I try to block it. I picture it in my head, a literal wall that keeps him out, but it doesn't work. I fight hard to keep him out of my emotions. Just trying to keep him at bay makes my head start to pound. I feel him breathing harder next to me, struggling. I gasp and pull away from him. It didn't work.

"You okay?" he asks, lowering himself to the ground. I nod. "You?"

"Maybe we're doing this wrong. Maybe it needs to be more natural," Thorne says, patting the space beside him. "Think about your favorite memory, about how you felt."

I bite my lip. Favorite memory. Once when we were six, Sara, Kai, Thorne and I slept on the beach. We weren't really allowed to do that—no one is—but Sara let us do it anyway. We had this little fire going, even though it was warm, and the waves were calm and Sara told us stories about when she was little. She had lots of stories about my mother, about Kai and Thorne's dad, and about Asher, the brother that neither of the boys remembered much. My father came by and it was late, but he sat up with us instead of taking me home and shared his own memories. I was calm, safe, comfortable.

"You're cheerful and peaceful," Thorne says. I nod back. "Now keep me out of it."

"How do I do that?"

He shrugs. "What do you do to keep people out? Build a fence, lock the door, lie."

"Lie? That seems weird. You can't lie about your feelings."

"Sure you can," he says. "Try."

I feel Thorne's emotion, and whatever he's thinking of is sad. I'm curious because that's so unlike him, but I'm even more curious if I can keep him out. I focus on the feeling of that night, the cheerful, contentedness of it, and I slam a door on it. Lock it. It makes my head hurt, but it's a dull pain. I inhale, keep my focus, and keep the door closed, even though it feels like something is pulling on it. I'm not sure how long it lasts before I have to gasp for breath and lose it all.

Thorne's hand rubs circles on my back. "I didn't feel it," he says.

I look at him. "What?"

"I didn't feel anything from you. Did you feel me?"

I shake my head. "Just for a second before I closed you off. Your head doesn't hurt?"

"Barely," he says. He smiles this huge smile. "Let's try it again. This time, see if you can break into me."

We try again. I don't feel anything he's feeling when he blocks me out. It feels a little like I've lost something, but I know this is how it's supposed to be. Each time I try, my head hurts, but it works.

"Maybe it will get easier," Thorne says.

"Maybe," I say.

The next time I try, I do the lie-about-what-I'm-feeling method. Instead of frustration, I show him that I'm happy and smile so big that my lips hurt.

MY LIPS ARE PARCHED FROM THIRST, and when I finally pull myself up my body cries out. Under my pack, my back is sweaty, and everything on my body seems to ache. Even my ears. I feel the grime on my cheeks, streaked clean where tears washed it away. How are all those people dead? They were innocent. They were alive. They were happy, even though they were struggling. They were free. They had their minds. That is how I will carry them with me and why I can fight for this. For them.

I wipe my hand across my cheek. How did that fire happen? It was out of control–a tunnel of flames that came barreling toward us and destroyed everything in its path. Everyone. I was almost out safely. Somehow it feels like that was intentional, and if it was, then I need to get out of here.

I pull my pack off my shoulder and dig through it for some water. My hand grazes the brown map Xenith made for me as I yank the bottle out and sip at the rest of the cool liquid. I'm almost out. I tilt my head up toward the sky so the sun beats down on my face. I count in my head and refocus.

When I open my eyes again, I move a few steps away from the hole. Around me, the Old World is more beautiful than I'd imagined. I was outside only briefly before—the distance between the truck and the entrance to Burrows—but this place is very much alive. The sky is endless blue, pearly and bright, and scattered with white clouds. The sun shines through thin trees, its rays dancing off the few leaves. A light patch of browning grass stretches across the landscape, tall and bushy and tinged with broken pieces of blackened concrete and rocks. Just beyond I make out the shapes of buildings. Most of them aren't complete anymore, but even from my distance, I can imagine what they used to be. I want to go see them closer, but they seem farther away than I have time for now.

Once all of this is over, I will come back.

I will go anywhere I can and learn about the Old World. Before the fall, before the Preservation, before this.

If I survive, then I will go everywhere.

I place the now-empty bottle in my pack, and the brown paper map crinkles when I take it out. I smooth it out so I can read over it one more time. I have it all memorized, but I want to see it there again. To be reassured that this trip is what I need to do. More Remnants died than I can count, and now I have to fight for them along with myself and Thorne and everyone else.

Odessa, Texas.

Little arrows trail off the name and point to the directions. Cecily Lopez is supposed to be here in a little casino, and she's expecting me. I stuff the map into my pack and walk west as Xenith wrote out on the page. I leave everything behind to burn, but I know as I go away from it that this place will haunt me. Maybe forever. Definitely until this is done.

WHEN MY DAY IS DONE, I go straight to the barrier near the ocean. Something about this place calls to me. It has left some kind of mark on my soul, a mark I'm not sure I can make go away. Thorne has warned me not be here. Kai has warned me. Sara has told me in her own way. But I can't stay away.

"You should set up a tent so you can sleep out here," Xenith says.

I look at him with a smile. "If I did, you'd always know where to find me."

"I already do," he says. His hair is getting longer, hanging in his face like Thorne's does. "You really shouldn't be out here all the time."

"I've heard." We are both silent, but his gaze on me is too intense. "I should go."

"Are you my friend, Neely?" Xenith asks. I don't move, but he does and I am frozen to this spot.

"Yes," I say. "I think so."

"I don't have many friends," he says. He's a heartbeat away from me, and my breath stops in my chest. I'm not sure what's happening, but the look in his eyes is unfamiliar. His hand is on my arm, on my cheek, in my hair. My eyes lock with his, and I know he's planning to kiss me. Do I want him to kiss me? Xenith says my name softly, and then he's on the ground.

Thorne is standing in the spot he was just in, cursing. Xenith crawls across the sand, cradling his face. Thorne looks at me, and I feel his emotions through our connection. The anger, the fear, the jealousy. Thorne moves toward Xenith again, his foot inches from Xenith's body before I stop him.

"Don't!" I yell to Thorne. I pull him away. "Don't."

"He was—"

"It's nothing," I say.

"You don't own her," Xenith hisses.

I slide my hand into Thorne's. "It's nothing. Let's go." I need to get one of them away, so I pull at Thorne, say his name. He looks at me. "Don't."

He nods slowly and tosses another look at Xenith before he pulls me away, our hands still attached. I steal a glance back at Xenith, but he's already gone.

Thorne doesn't let go of my hand as he pulls me up the beach. I say his name, try to get him to stop, but he ignores me. We're almost to the house before I manage to pull my hand loose from his grip.

"What's wrong with you?" I yell at him. His back is to me, and he's breathing hard. I can see his chest expand and retract. "What was that?"

"He was going to kiss you!" Thorne turns to face me.

"I know that," I say. My voice is low at his expression. Thorne's emotions run through me like heat and weight and pain. The idea of me and Xenith is hurting him and it shouldn't. Xenith doesn't mean anything to me. The wind picks up around us, tossing the waves across the shore, as we walk toward the housing units.

"You were going to let him kiss you?" He crosses his arms, indignant in his stare.

I cross my arms back at him. I don't owe him an explanation. "Not that it matters, but no."

"No what? You weren't moving. He was."

"You don't know what happened back there. You just come in and punch him!" I don't know why I'm yelling or why I'm defending Xenith. I'm embarrassed. I'm frustrated and angry with Thorne. "You don't have a say."

"I don't have a say?"

"No," I snap.

"Fine. You can kiss whomever you want to kiss, Neely. I don't care. I'm sure he'll open the door right up for you if you go to him." Thorne takes a few steps away from me, his hands clenched at his side.

"I've never wanted to kiss Xenith! You're such an idiot!" I yell after him. I turn around, too, and walk in the opposite direction. I don't care though. I don't want to be anywhere Thorne is.

A hand is on my shoulder, whipping me around. I see a mass of brown hair and then feel the smooth sensation of lips on mine. It takes a second for me to catch my breath and register what's happening. Thorne is kissing me. His hands are on me, and my lips are glued to his, not wanting to be anywhere else. Then his lips are gone. He takes a step back, and we look at each other.

Thorne just kissed me.

"What was that?" I asked.

He smiles, any traces of anger before gone. At least temporarily. "That was something I've wanted to do since I was thirteen."

Thirteen. He's had feelings for me as long as I have for him.

"What stopped you?"

"My mom and our situation. She didn't want it to be odd for anyone else," he says. "But I don't care about them anymore."

He reaches his hand out to me and pulls me forward. His lips find mine again, and this time, I'm ready. I let them take me over, and my hand slides over his back. A shock rushes through my body, a fire, a spark that works *from the inside out. I pull him closer. My heart pounds, on the brink of explosion. I'm on fire. For the first time, I'm whole. I'm alive. The other things don't matter, and his touch fills that missing piece.*

"I can't believe it took me so long to do that," Thorne says in my ear. "We need to do that more often."

I nod, smiling. "Do you feel different?"

He looks at me. His fingers trail up my arm and leave a warm sensation in their path. To anyone else, the question would've seemed odd, out of place. A kiss can't change you. But Thorne only nods. "I feel you more than I did before."

"Me too," I say. He kisses my forehead. I feel it in my toes. His hand squeezes mine, and I feel it in my heart. His lips touch mine, gentle and quick. It lingers on my soul, the imprint of a shadow in the light.

THERE IS SO MUCH LIGHT AROUND ME, and it's a refreshing change. I feel more awake, more connected. The city I walk through is lined with old houses, not much unlike the ones in the Compound. There they are also uniform, though not as big as some of these appeared to be from far away. Aside from the houses, I pass large stores, not tall like the faraway buildings, but long. Imprints of words align on the sides, though mostly I can only make out a few letters. A "W" and a sign that's shaped like a jagged square and a circle. Whatever they were, I don't know now. I pass a large building with many broken doors that all connect. There's no top anymore, and most of the left side has been destroyed.

I'm surprised that they have held up this long. The Preservation was hundreds of years ago. Even in its brokenness, this world is beautiful. Deep browns and grays of sand and mountains spread out across the horizon. Decrepit buildings stand with overgrown greens. What was it like when it was thriving and alive with people? When the buildings were whole? It's not nearly as bad as the Elders painted it, but then again, if they had told us of its beauty, maybe more of us would have been discontented by the Compound. At least, those who were able.

I walk down a street of endless nothing. There are no remains of other buildings, no houses, just trees and dirt and hot concrete. Everything is hot in Texas. My street turns left and onto a bridge. Xenith said Cecily would be on the other side.

Pieces of the bridge are missing when I walk across. The holes are small enough that I can go around them, but there are more as I continue on. What if the piece I'm standing on decides to crumble and take me with it down into the water? I would die here before I even made it anywhere. I'd be dead just like all the people in the Burrows. Like Bayard.

An ache forms in my chest. He would never have fought to get out. Even if he was harsh at the beginning of our journey, I understand him now, and I miss him. Bayard made it clear that the Burrows were his home, that there was nothing that could separate him from them and nowhere else he wanted to be. He wouldn't have been able to live, to press on and move forward, while carrying so much grief. He would never have liked it above or been able to carry the loss. Those were the people he loved. He would die for them, and he did.

Selfishly, I hope that's not my fate.

A breeze blows around me, whipping my hair through the air, and Thorne would love it. He would love the way this bridge stands here, even though it's falling apart. He'd stick his hands through the holes and touch everything—the sides with the jagged edges and the beams that run every way. I can almost feel his excitement coursing through me, even though he's not here. He'd call it "marvelous" and "unique," and he'd joke about jumping into the water, even though he'd never, ever let either of us do it.

I miss him.

Across the bridge, the landscape changes to brown. There's not much green here, trees or leaves or otherwise, and a large, red building fills my view. That's the one. Xenith said I would know it.

The doors open when I push them, and my eyes are flooded by darkness inside but they adjust quickly. The doors stay open a crack behind me as I step forward slowly. It's so eerily quiet that everything inside me wants to run out.

"Anyone here?" I call into the darkness. I rub my hands together nervously. A tingle jolts through my body, the same way it does when Thorne and I feel each other through the connection. I miss him so much I'm imagining things now. "Hello? I'm looking for Cecily Lopez. I come from SMC128." There's no response. No indication that anyone is even here. I have one more card to play. I inhale the stale air. "Xenith Taylor sent me here."

There's only silence. I feel the tears building up inside, but I push them down. I haven't come this far to cry. They'll let me in. They have to.

I lean back against a large machine, and a pole hanging off of it rams into my arm. At closer inspection, the pole is more like a handle. I pull down on it but nothing happens. There are four little squares above the lever, and all of them contain pictures. One looks like a cherry.

A loud voice echoes in the darkness. "Nay-hm?"

I jump at the sound and brace myself against the machine. Someone is speaking to me—a man's voice—but I'm not sure what he's asking for or where he is.

"Excuse me?" I ask, searching the darkness for movement.

"Don't move," the voice calls, and I freeze, ignoring the prickles running up my arms. "State your name."

"Neely Ambrose," I say quickly.

There's only more silence on the other end. Then a loud buzzing sound fills the room.

"The door is to your left," the voice says to me. "Go down the hallway. Turn left. Knock twice on the third door."

I do what he says, and it's easy to find. The hallway is simple enough and the ceiling is tall, wide open, and vast. I try to imagine what it was like to see this place in its prime. Large chandeliers bright and beautiful when they were lit. Tall ceilings and long hallways. There are no pictures on the walls, only marks where they used to hang. Like everything in this forgotten world.

The third door is white, and my fingers run across the grain as I knock on it. There's a scuffle behind the door, a thud, and then a click as it opens to me. A man hovers over me, big and tall, muscle and fat interweaving to make him monstrous. He grunts in my direction.

"I've journeyed here to meet the survivor," I say.

He holds a hand up to me. "Neely Ambrose?"

I nod. The big guy looks me over, top to bottom, before he grunts and pushes the door open. I exhale and take half a step forward.

"We've been expecting you," he says. I catch a glimpse of something that shimmers tucked into his belt—a gun?—as I enter. Something heavy settles in my stomach, the familiar feeling of anxiety.

Candles and a large fireplace dimly light the room. It's warm in here. My body is tingling. Directly in front of me sits an older woman. She only has one eye—the other is covered with some kind of patch, and my stomach leaps into my chest as her eye follows us across the room.

She doesn't greet me, only watches me through sallow skin and sharp lines that decorate her face. Her hair is streaked brown and gray, wrapped in a tight bun atop her head. "Have a seat." Her voice is rough and hoarse, as if she grew up eating glass.

There's a chair opposite her. I'm halfway to it when I see him and gasp, sudden emotions flooding my body all at once.

Thorne is standing right in front of me.

THORNE IS IN FRONT OF ME on the other side of the opened door. His back is to me, but I know him anywhere. When I see him, I wedge myself behind the wall and door and try not hit it. If it moves, then he'll see me, too. Why is he here? I press my ear to the wood, careful not to close it the half an inch, though I'm sure he can hear my heart pounding against it. If the door closes, he'll know someone else is here, and he can't know that. Why is he here? I can't see his face, and I want to. The thought makes my heart pound faster.

I try to calm myself, but his voice trails through the space. Xenith yells something I can't make out, and then there's a crash and the sound of glass breaking.

This is because of me.

I shouldn't, but my hand is on the doorknob. Thorne is here, and everything inside of me wants to go to him. His voice is clearer, and I catch my name.

"She's dead, Thorne. I'm sorry, but Neely is gone," Xenith says. I've never heard him apologize to anyone, especially not to Thorne. And his voice sounds so convincing. I'd believe it if I didn't know the truth.

I peek around the corner and see Thorne shaking his head, holding Xenith against the wall, a bookcase shoved over on the floor. Xenith is so tall, but Thorne is stronger, and the sight of them both there like that is almost too much. I'm causing all this pain to the people I love.

Thorne releases Xenith. "Why do I feel her?"

Xenith straightens out his shirt. "Why does someone who loses a leg still think he can walk?"

I take a step into the living room where they are as every cell in my body urges me forward.

Thorne's back tenses, and I wish I could feel what he was feeling, but the blockade is keeping that away. "It's not like that. I wake up in the middle of the night, terrified and alone. That's not me—that's her. Sometimes I'm overly confused, conflicted, unsure, scared. That's not me either. How do I feel her if she's dead? It's the worst kind of torture. Losing her is bad enough, but some days it's like she never left. Like one day I'll wake up and see her."

Xenith catches me in the doorway, and his eyes grow fierce. I take a breath and realize I've opened the door wider. What am I doing? I'm going to ruin everything. I inch backward, back toward the room so I lose sight of them. I shouldn't, but I try to feel Thorne's confusion, his sadness. There's nothing because of the blockade.

"I miss her." His voice trails back to me. I have to hold my breath so I don't call out to him. "Don't you miss her?"

I can't see Xenith's face anymore, but I imagine it. Etched with pain, deep lines that appear in an instant. "Every second."

He's really good at lying.

I lay on the floor of Xenith's bedroom, sneaking peeks through the crack of the doorframe, waiting for the shadow that tells me Thorne is gone. It doesn't come. Not for a while. So long that I fall asleep like that, my name the last thing I hear.

Over and over.

My name.

I'M NOT SURE HOW MANY TIMES Thorne has said my name now. I can't stop staring at him. This has to be a joke. A trick. Maybe I'm dead, and this is the afterlife. He touches my hand, my arm, my cheek, and in an instant, my chest hitches. He whispers my name, and his relief crushes me so deeply I have to exhale in order to stand correctly. I can't believe he's here. How is he here?

Tears fill my eyes as my brain, my body, my entire being shifts with elation. That I'm alive. That he's touching me. And all of his emotions add to mine. The relief, the longing and joy as he touches my cheek. It feels like floating. Heat runs through my branding and down to my toes.

I meet Thorne's dark gaze, and he pulls his hand away swiftly. His emotions change, and I intake a breath as I get hotter. He's disappointed and angry. I don't need to feel that; it's evident on his face, the way his eyebrows dip together and he slides his hands into his pockets.

I've imagined our reunion every night since I died, since before I left the Compound. There would be kissing and tears, and he'd look at me in that way that only he can because I'd just found a way to save him from a fate he didn't know was coming. It'd be the most blissful kind of dream, and I'd never want to wake up. It wouldn't be like this—in the presence of strangers and shrouded in confusion.

This is not as blissful.

"How are you here?" I ask.

I search Thorne's eyes and see the spark that lives there. The one he tries to hide when he's with everyone else. The one that's only for me. I missed him so much. Looking at his face, seeing how tired he is and his heavy eyes—all I did was miss him. I reach out through our connection, trying to search his emotions for something, but he's blocking me out. I hate when he does that. It so rarely used to happen that he didn't want to let me in, but now? This is what I've done, what I've caused.

"How are *you* here?" he asks back. I almost see the word on his lips. *Dead.*

Next to us, Cecily clears her throat. I turn to her, nearly shaking. How is he here?

"Something to eat?" she asks. As soon as she mentions it, my stomach churns. I nod slowly. Maybe food will wash away the aching and fill the pit in my soul.

"Boris!" Cecily yells. His name makes me want to laugh, though I'm not sure why. The feeling fades as soon as he appears again. "Get our guests some sandwiches."

He nods and leaves the room without a word or a sound. My eyes keep drifting to Thorne as he sits, and I can't help it. I never thought I'd see him here.

"He's a lump, not good for much other than protection, but he makes a great grilled cheese, so I keep him around," Cecily says, and then her focus is straight on me. "Have a seat, Miss Ambrose."

I do as she asks and sit next to Thorne.

"Mr. Bishop here tells me you're on a secret mission, though he didn't seem to know the details."

I look at him curiously. He doesn't know anything. Knowing Thorne, he wouldn't need to. He'd go anywhere for me, do anything, and this is no exception.

"Why are you here?" Cecily asks, pulling my eyes from Thorne to her.

"Xenith Taylor sent me. I need sanctuary with your people," I say. The Remnants. Because they know him and his family and I need them to help me get safely to the Mavericks.

Silence closes in around us, and lets the doubt in Xenith sink in. Maybe he's not as powerful as he thought he was, but then Cecily nods her head slowly.

"Young Mr. Taylor has a tendency to overstep his bounds. What makes you think I will help you? You are the director's daughter, after all. How do I trust you?"

"I'm here in front of you. I've made it all this way, and Xenith trusts me. He trusts you. That's enough."

I feel Thorne's emotions then. A sudden impulse of red-hot anger and irritation. I try not to look at him, not to be thrown by it, but it's hard.

"Even in my circles, some cannot be trusted," Cecily says. That's the same warning Xenith gave me. Not all Remnants are innocents. "Why do you seek the Mavericks?"

"The Elders are enacting a plan on my Compound, on my own life, and we need help to prevent it." I feel another ripple that sends my head spinning, and I steal a sideways look at Thorne. He's confused, and I can't tell him all the reasons I had to leave right now. It's not the time or the place.

She nods from her chair, and her eye widens. This woman has survived so much, and sitting here with her eye narrowed on me, I can't help but wonder what evils she has faced.

Seconds slip away from us. I push up the hair on my neck and angle myself toward her. Cecily stares at my branding and adjusts her position in the chair. Her face remains blank, keeping her secrets locked tight, but I know she bears the same mark because she and her twin were born in the Northern Compound. All twins back then got the branding.

Cecily doesn't look convinced of anything. If she's surprised or caring, she doesn't show it on her face. Her lips remain in a thin line. Thorne takes my hand, lacing our fingers together, and every place our bodies touch sparks through to my soul. It's been months since I felt our physical connection, and I have to fight away the urge to kiss him so I can feel this more intensely.

We only connect through the branding when one of is feeling a stronger-than-normal emotion or when we want to feel what the other person is feeling. Usually, it's just a steady hum, like a heartbeat, and I carry my own feelings. But when Thorne is around, when he's feeling something intense, when I'm tuned into him or touching him, then it's a different thing entirely. It's like a drug sometimes, our connection, and I can't get enough. Other times it's a burden I don't want to carry. The two change too often to keep track.

He pulls us to our feet and shows her his branding. Together, we are complete. If our branding was put together, it would be beautiful. Where mine is dark, his is light. Our curves of color fit into the emptiness of the other person's—two halves that make one whole and fill in the void. We each have the opposite half of a circle, with a line in the middle where our halves would join. That line is crossed with another, so if I look at it sideways, it resembles an X. The same X that exists across the regular branding.

"Sit," Cecily says, and as we do, she turns to show us her marking. Her half is the same as mine.

Thorne releases my hand, and the change inside me goes from burning to nothing. Stillness. The usual pulse of my heartbeat. But the loss of the fire always leaves me wanting more.

Cecily stands up and walks around the room, her shape silhouetted on the ceiling.

"You are not twins," she says as a statement instead of a question.

"It was to save my life."

"How?" she asks. Her voice is weak.

I glance at Thorne, but he doesn't move and avoids my gaze. "For the first two years I was alive, it was said I was his twin."

"Seems like a big mistake to make."

I nod, gulp down a lump in my throat at the thought of my mother. "My mother died giving birth to me, and Thorne's twin died at birth. I was switched with his biological sister as an act of protection. No one except Thorne's mom, Sara, knew until I was two—not even my father."

"Why would one lie about that?"

The room is quiet but anxious, and I feel it in the air and in Thorne's emotions. I need to tell Cecily all I know so she'll help. Maybe we can use the branding to connect, to remind her where she came from and how she fought her way out.

"My grandfather had malicious plans, and from what I know, and they switched me to hide me. I honestly don't know all the answers. No one ever really talks about it."

"How old are you both?"

"Seventeen," Thorne answers.

"You were born two years before my sister and I got out," Cecily says with a pause. "They spent years separating twins after Deanna and I escaped, just in case any others were exceptions as well. Why would they let you remain together?"

"Your escape made the Elders test and separate twins. It was revealed, at the time of our test, that we weren't related," I say. "Since we weren't blood relatives, they didn't believe it would affect us. They tested us, but there was no proof of anything abnormal."

Because Xenith's mom lied, but I don't say that.

Thorne is quiet, his eyes not leaving me. I have a lot to tell him about the things I've learned. I hope I get the chance to explain all of this.

Cecily's head bobs around in a way that makes me worry it could fall off her neck. "When we escaped, the Elders began to fear twins instead of treasure them. Before then, twins were special and desired—preferred, even. After that, they were no longer allowed to be born." Cecily's voice is heavy. "There were no twins born in the decade after us, and all before us were separated. If the Elders really feared them, they'd go to any means to prevent their birth."

Preventing their birth? That's not something I knew. "I know they were experimenting on twins before their birth."

Thorne's brow creases, but he says nothing.

"Yes," Cecily says. "Treatments from conception to birth given in utero. The Elders believed twins held some great knowledge that they wanted for themselves. For decades they sought the answers, but the answers caused other effects they would not realize for many years."

"What were they looking for?" Thorne asks.

"The Old World had many beliefs about twins, from the dawn of time until the Preservation," Cecily says. "In their mythologies, twins represented creation and sacrifice, a partnership. Twins were cast as two halves of the same whole, sharing deep bonds. Some said twins had psychic or emotional connections and secret communication. Centuries of humans believed that twins had a connection, a strength that transcended normal understanding."

That's how Thorne and I are. Stronger together, a balance, a weighted scale. I've known what Thorne felt all my life.

"Because of the stories the Elders connected twins?" I ask.

Cecily nods. "There's power in belief. It shapes who you become. The Elders believed twins were half a person, and the branding would allow them to remain one. Early on, the Elders tested twins to determine how deep that connection ran, and well, they always got the answers they were searching for."

If the connection is that deep, then what would it feel like to not have someone else on the other end of my branding? To be alone after being with someone for so long?

"How?" Thorne interjects.

"Because the branding alters genetic code," I say aloud. It's starting to make some sort of sense. If the branding alters everyone in some way, then it alters twins. The purpose was supposed be similar—control and lack of free will—but it wasn't. Not with the treatments given to twins. That was how the Elders did it.

Cecily clears her throat, and when I look up, she and Thorne are staring at me. "The twin branding and testing caused more trouble than the Elders believed it could. You can't play with genetics and not have consequences. The branding was the glue of whatever concoction the Elders were cooking in the womb."

Then how did it work on Thorne and me? What did it mean for us? Was it truly the reason we are the way we are? I was never given a treatment, but I was glued to him, part of him.

"It served also a marker that these two people were different, important to them," Cecily says. "The

Elders kept them together, studied them as they grew, and used the research to perfect future births." She stares at us for a long time, sorrow evident in her eyes. "They believed you were unaffected. I assume they were wrong in that belief?"

I nod, not letting my gaze waiver. "What happened back then?"

Cecily doesn't get to answer. Boris steps into the room with food and water. Cecily looks away as Boris hands me a sandwich, and the hot cheese burns the roof of my mouth.

I'm halfway through the sandwich when she asks me about the Burrows. "There was some kind of casualty there today. We weren't sure you would make it."

"My guide helped me escape before the fire."

"It was a fire?" she asks. I nod. She says something to Boris in the Remnant language. "Eat up, then get some rest. Boris will return to show you to your room. We can talk more tomorrow."

They're gone before I get the chance to ask if they know how a fire could've started in the Burrows and what they know about it. Thorne stares at me, and when I reach out for him, because my hand has a mind of its own, he pulls away.

XENITH PULLS ME OFF THE FLOOR. My head is groggy with images of Thorne, with the sound of him crying for me in the other room with the boy he hated more than anyone.

"Is he okay?" I ask as Xenith lays me on the bed. I scoot over and sit up.

"As okay as he ever will be."

"I want to tell him," I say. I need to. "You need to."

Xenith shakes his head. "That's not happening, Neely."

"Why? He can help. You know that we're stronger together!"

"I told you that I couldn't get you both out at the same time. You know that. The Elders were already suspicious of your connection—you said so yourself," he says. I did say that and it's true, but that doesn't make this easier. Branding connection or not, I still want him with me. "And you leave in three days. Thorne Bishop can't help you now. You can't tell him anything. You're dead, Neely."

I start to protest, and Xenith holds a finger to my lips. "You made a promise. You can't tell Thorne anything. Nothing. You gave me your word, and I will know if you break it."

"Xenith."

"Neely, you gave your word. No telling Thorne. If you can't handle a task as simple as that, then you shouldn't be going."

"Fine. I won't see him again once I leave here anyway."

"Fine." The word is sharp, and I know he means it. I would never have the opportunity to tell Thorne anyway, but Xenith stares at me until the awkward minutes feel too long.

IT'S BEEN TOO LONG SINCE I've had enough to eat, and my stomach is full after one greasy sandwich. It feels as if Boris has been gone for hours, but it's probably only been minutes. Thorne keeps staring at me, his emotions and mine jumping between a heavy weight, a ripple, and a warmth spinning in my head. Underneath all that, under the worry and confusion and anger and fear, there's a lightness. He still loves me. The reassurance of that is more than I expected.

"I don't understand any of this," Thorne says, breaking the silence. "I knew I was coming here to see you, to help somehow, but I guess part of me thought you were really dead and Xenith was attempting to end me."

I inhale a sharp breath as the weight of his sadness rushes over me. It's only a fraction of what he must have felt. I'd experienced him after I died, by chance and without him knowing, and I'll never forget the way he said my name, pleaded to Xenith as I listened in the next room. That was like getting my heart ripped out of my chest. Holding my body when he'd thought I'd died? I don't want to imagine what that was like. That loneliness.

I can almost see it, even though I don't remember more than the retelling from Xenith. He told Xenith that he'd felt something was wrong when I'd died and he had to come back for me. The story of Thorne vomiting over the fisherboat. Him wading into the water and pulling me to shore, trying to bring me back even though he knew it wouldn't work. The anger he must've felt and the fear and the sadness all at once.

"I saw them send your ashes into the water," he says. "I lost you, and it was like losing myself. I kept waiting for you to be there, and every day you weren't."

I close my eyes and feel Thorne pulling away whatever weight he'd sent through our connection. Even when he's mad at me, he's carrying more than his share of our emotions. I never want to be on the other side of that. I couldn't handle losing Thorne; I'm not as strong as him.

I bite my lip. There are too many words that taste bitter on my tongue. I'm not sure which ones are the best ones to say, so I don't use any of them. We sit in the silence while my brain tries compartmentalize all of the pain that I caused him. The emotions fall through me until I feel the normal, steady pulse of my heart and breathing. This is the feeling I had while I was separated from Thorne. The new normal of it just being me.

"How did you get here?" I ask. I don't know which emotion to give in to first, so my brain says that I need to understand instead. There's got to be a reason, a way he came.

Thorne looks at me, his warm, caramel eyes still familiar. "The same way you did. Xenith."

At the sound of his name, I look up to meet Thorne's eyes. Xenith went back on his word to me to protect Thorne no matter what. I shake my head and move across the room. Xenith wouldn't lie. Not to me.

Thorne rises and takes a step toward me. "You look surprised that Xenith would help me. You shouldn't be. He'll do anything if the price is right."

"He wouldn't do that," I say. But part of me knows I'm lying to myself, even if I don't want to accept that.

"What do you want to hear instead? Want me to prove it?" Thorne holds onto my arm, and I feel the sensation of something lodged in my throat, then of it sitting in my stomach, solid and steady as he feels it on this own. His worry. "Xenith didn't get me out," he says slowly.

The words fall from his lips, and I feel an erratic jolt in our connection, a shock bolting through my system. I jerk my hand away so I don't feel it again. That jolt means Thorne is not lying. That jolt is an undeniable truth. Xenith betrayed me; he risked Thorne.

I run my hands over my face. This can't be happening.

"I'm here to help you. I thought—I felt you. I thought I was crazy because you were dead. I thought I was crazy," he says, shaking his head slightly. His fingers graze my arm again, as if he can't not touch me. I can't handle him touching me, not right now. It's too real.

I take a step back and pretend that I don't feel his frustration. "How did you make it here before me?"

"I travelled aboveground."

Above. Xenith told me that wasn't safe. He told me I had to travel through the Burrows. I guess that wasn't really safe either. Why wouldn't he let me travel above? Why would he send Thorne up here when it could mean his death?

"Why did you leave?" Thorne asks.

Tense silence fills the spaces between us. In seventeen years, I've never questioned what to say to him. I don't even know where to start or what answers to give him or which ones matter the most.

"You know why I left the Compound," I say. I turn on my heel to avoid any more conversation. He lunges for me and pulls my body toward his, and it responds on contact with heat and fire. His face is inches from mine, so close I can feel his warm breath. I can smell the salt of the ocean in his pores. I can see the pain in his eyes that was never there before.

"I meant *me*. Why did you leave me?"

I swallow but can't look away from his face. What can he read in my eyes when he looks at me? Does he know all the times I wished for something more than him? For something completely my own? Does he even know why he's really standing here?

"I—"

My voice cracks as if tears are going to come through. I force them back. The door opens behind us, and Thorne releases my arm. Boris stiffens in the doorway, his eyes going back and forth between us.

"I'm to give you a place to sleep," he says. A small smile creeps across his face. "One room or two?"

Thorne says two.

THORNE EXTENDS TWO YELLOW DAISIES out to me, smiling like a schoolboy.

"What are you doing here?" I ask.

"I came to help," Thorne says. "And I brought you some flowers. Only two though. You know how the old man is about picking his daisies."

I take the flowers from Thorne and set them on the table next to me. He's already wandering around the schoolhouse, floors creaking after him as he opens windows. "How did you know I was here?"

He doesn't answer until he's opened all four windows, and the breeze is nice. Thorne crosses his arms and leans against the doorframe. "Aren't I allowed to be a man of mystery?"

A smile breaks across my face. "Sara told you, didn't she?"

He sighs dramatically. "The women in my life conspire against me." He jumps and moves around me quickly to pick up the paint. He crouches down and dips a brush in the paint, and it drips to the floor. "Where do we start?"

"You don't. You don't have to do anything."

He looks up at me and slowly rises to his feet. "I know I don't. I want to. Painting the schoolhouse is my favorite thing to do, you know."

I laugh because he's trying so hard to be serious. He smiles, and his eyes light up when he looks at me. I feel a wave of love and joy coming off him and into me. "I thought you were going out with the boats today?"

"Changed with Carl so I could be here. You know how much he likes me." He winks. He moves his paintbrush down along the wall and stops mid-stroke. "Although if you want me to leave, I can go. I know how hard I am to look at for so many hours."

He tosses the brush back into the container of paint and starts to walk away. I know he's teasing me, but I don't want him to go so I take hold of his hand. A fire rushes through us when our hands touch. I can feel every cell in my body moving, and every hair stands on end. It's a sensation I'll never fully be prepared to feel, but I'd be lost without it.

"Stay," I say.

Thorne doesn't let go of my hand. He licks his lips, and his desire to kiss me rushes through and mixes with my own for him. "Can't. I'm busy." As soon as he says it, our connection jumps, sending a shock through me.

"Liar," I joke. "Please stay."

"Now you want me to stay? Only seconds ago you wanted to be rid of me."

"Never. I don't want you to waste your day on something you don't have to do."

"I want to do it. Anywhere you are, I want to be," he says. His fingers trace my cheek and send tingles through my body. "Even if it does give me nightmarish flashbacks to second year when someone spilled her juice all over me and everyone said I had an accident." He shudders dramatically. "Why did I ever stay friends with her?"

"Because she has this remarkable smile?" I suggest and smile at him.

"No, I think it's because she's so messy," he says. In a movement that happens quicker than I even know possible, Thorne reaches for the paintbrush and wipes it down my arm, cold and yellow. I yell out his name.

"Neely! What a mess! Hank Callahan will be upset that you're wasting his paint!"

I aim another brush toward him. "You're going to pay for that."

"Please don't promise things you won't deliver on," he says.

He runs out the door, and I chase after him around the schoolhouse in two circles. His brush finds my face, and then he pulls me toward his chest and turns me around so my back is up against the wall.

"I hate you," I say. Our connection jumps, flickers like a flame that's struggling to stay lit.

Thorne smiles. "Liar," he says as presses his lips against mine. No one is around to see us, but we part quickly. The rules are still the rules: we can't be seen kissing in public. I smile at him as we separate. We spend the next three hours stealing kisses while we paint inside the schoolhouse.

FOR THREE HOURS, Cecily has been telling us about the Old World. She's only lived here for fifteen years, but she knows the entire history. She helped establish a whole network of Remnants to the Mavericks, and it's impressive.

"There were seven Compounds back then," Cecily says. She sits in this rocking chair, and every time she moves it creaks. The sound of it keeps me on edge and unsettled.

"There still are seven," I say.

She looks at me with a gleam in her eye. "There are only two left. The Mavericks have taken down the rest."

"Wouldn't we know that?" I ask.

"Have you been to any of them? Heard of anyone coming from somewhere that wasn't the North? The rest are gone. They've been disappearing for over a century now."

The other Compounds are gone. I'm not sure why that feels so unreal. The Elders have lied about everything. This isn't any different, but...

Thorne asks her a question that I don't hear. He's been very attentive to her, though he acts like he doesn't know me at all. I can't figure out what he's feeling. He's completely blocked his feelings, and it's probably exhausting for him. Blocking each other out takes a toll eventually. We both know that from the years we spent testing it.

Cecily inhales and rocks in her chair. I can't help but wonder what else she's experienced. "My sister and I always knew we were different. We had dreams from childhood, the same dreams at first. Then, as we got older, they were dreams of the past, of the future, sometimes of the world that we didn't know existed right outside the barrier. Deanna and I weren't the only twins with the branding, but we were the first to escape."

"How did you do it?" I ask. We've never been told anything about their escape.

"We planned it telepathically. The things the Elders do to twins, the tests, caused mental abilities. The Elders had been planning for that, unknowingly, and for this one. For centuries now, it's been building."

"The abilities?" Thorne asks. He sits on the edge of the chair, anxious for more details. He gets that way sometimes.

"When the testing started after the Preservation, twins were born with different-colored eyes or hair or traits. Small things that made them different," Cecily says. She pulls a small, thin knife from her pocket and starts cleaning out her fingernails. "By the time we were born, every set of twins had a connection. Things kept secret until we escaped. They created us, and then they punished us."

The Elders put us in this situation.

They created us.

I wonder how true that is for Thorne and me. How true is that for everyone else with the branding? Nothing in my life, or in anyone in the Compound, has ever been real. It's all been created. We deserve something real. Everyone. I'm just the one who knows that I need to search for it.

Cecily looks toward the back of the room where Boris nods and places some items on the ground. "We've got some supplies for your journey. Food, mostly. The others have been contacted and will be waiting for you. But there's nothing except more trouble waiting."

"I've experienced the Cleaners and—"

"We have more enemies than the Cleaners. The life of a Remnant is not a simple one."

"What kind of enemies?" I ask.

Cecily's eye is pea-sized and bleak. There is no emotion, as if it's only a lifeless dark marble. Empty and desolate, but not without power. For in that bleak, dark eye, I see my own fear.

"The kind that will kill you without question," she says.

She says the words without blinking, but there's a flash across her face similar to the one someone gets when they are remembering, reliving the past like it's the present. I know, in this instance, Cecily knows more than she's willing to tell us.

"Xenith didn't prepare you at all?" she asks.

"Prepare me?"

She exchanges a look with Boris, who comes to stand next to her.

"Do you have a weapon?" she asks. I dig in my pack and show her the small knife I carry there. She laughs a short, harsh laugh that sounds as hollow as I feel right now. "He sent you to the Old World without every piece of knowledge or a weapon? He must have a death wish for you—or you have one for yourself."

Cecily snaps her fingers, and Boris moves. There is no noise except the shuffling of Boris's feet. Thorne doesn't look away when I seek his familiar gaze. Whatever tension was there between us before has temporarily been replaced by something worse. Boris returns, and Cecily clicks her tongue.

"I probably shouldn't give you this. It won't be much of a help if you don't know how to use it, but it's better than nothing." Boris sits the gun in front of me with a clink. It's oddly shaped and shiny. I don't want to touch it. I've heard what they can do, how they can shoot fire into people's hearts and stop their blood flowing. I don't reach out for the gun, but Thorne does.

Cecily touches his outstretched arm. "Can you throw a punch?"

He smiles slightly. "I'm sure I can figure it out."

Boris, who has been quiet through this whole conversation, finally speaks. His voice is no less alarming than the first time I heard it.

"Do you run?" Boris asks me.

"Yes," I say.

"I hope you're fast."

Thorne and I share a look. A loud ringing buzzes through the air three times. Cecily shuffles to her feet. "I must go. The Remnants will help you the best they can—not all, but most. Not all the camps are safe." Her words are quick. Cecily kisses my forehead, and then Thorne's.

"Now is the best chance you will have to go. I will leave you to find your way out."

And she's gone, Boris trailing behind her. Thorne and I look at each other. The uncertainty is evident in his eyes. He's just as confused as I am pretending not to be.

Thorne sits next to me so our legs are grazing. A tingle runs through me at the slight touch. Then, his fingers entwine with mine, and with them come the familiar tingles and chills and spark, the ones that I'm so used to feeling with us. The ones I desperately don't want to get used to living without and yet the same ones I'm uncertain about.

"I'm going with you in case you missed that," he says.

"You don't even know what I'm doing."

"Then tell me."

I pull my hand away from his and stand, stuffing the food Cecily gave us in my pack next the map and the book. "It's dangerous." I don't look up at his face.

"I know." I hear him shuffling beside me, and I ignore the urges to search his face.

"We could die," I say, pulling my pack over my shoulders. I can't steady my emotions enough to block them from him, and I can't tell which ones are getting through. My hand reaches for the door when I feel his hot breath on my neck.

"I know," he says just above my ear.

I turn to look at him. Our bodies are so close, and his heart is beating as rapidly as mine is. The scruff on his chin is only subtle, but in the short distance between us, I can see it.

"I can't tell you anything," I say finally. My hand is too sweaty, too nervous, and it slides from the doorknob.

He leans in closer to me, his arm reaching around my waist. "Okay," he says. I inhale a breath just as he opens the door and smiles at me. "But you will."

I start down the hallway. My heart is racing so rapidly that it could explode and all that will be left is the shell of my once-living body.

We exit the same way I entered, past the lever cherry machines and the tables. I don't see Thorne, but I know he's following me. He's always following me. I can feel his questions and doubts, and I try to ignore them, though his are louder and harder to ignore than my own.

THERE ARE VOICES ARGUING *loudly from the beach. It's 2 AM, and it's supposed to be quiet here. There's never anyone out this late. Except me.*

And, I guess, sometimes Xenith.

The only times I see him are the nights he happens to be here when I'm walking along the shore. I can't explain it, but for whatever reason, his presence in those sleepless nights is calming. Sometimes we talk, but most nights I just sit on the beach, him close enough that his scent is carried to me on the wind but far enough away that it doesn't look like anything it isn't.

At first, it doesn't seem like anyone I know, but when I get closer, I can tell it's Xenith. His blond hair is unmistakable, even in the darkness. The other person pushes him, and he stumbles across the beach. He laughs—it's short and crisp and mocking—and then, in the next instance, I see Thorne run across the beach and tackle Xenith.

I race toward them and push my way between Thorne and Xenith.

"Stop it!" I yell. I pull at Thorne's arm, sending positivity through the connection to get him to calm down. I switch my focus. "Xenith, stop!"

It doesn't work at first, then Xenith is the one who steps away, hands up.

"What's going on?" I yell, my breath raspy.

Both boys are silent, heaving in breaths of air. Xenith is the first one to talk but only after a smug smile forms on his lips.

"Thorne and I were just having a little conversation, but then he couldn't handle that mine was bigger."

I shake my head and look at Thorne.

"He knows about us," Thorne says. "About the branding."

I stare at Xenith. "How?"

Xenith crosses his arms over his chest, the smile still on his lips. "Give me a challenge. Other people here may not have a clue, but I'm not like them. Plus, you two aren't very good at hiding it. You're like bunnies at mating season."

"He's not going to say anything, Thorne. He wouldn't."

Xenith and I stare at each other, a battle of wills. He's amused, and it's written all over his smile and the way his eyes light up.

"You're so sure of me, aren't you?" he says.

"You would've already," I say. I don't look away from Xenith. His eyes are intense on me. I know he's not really going to say anything. I don't know how I'm so certain, but I believe it.

"Maybe I'm waiting for the right moment," he says.

Thorne steps toward Xenith. I hold my hand up against his chest to stop him, but he speaks anyway. "Don't act like this doesn't affect you. You know exactly what it would mean for us if the Elders found out."

"I don't care about you," Xenith says, stepping into Thorne's face.

Thorne is silent as they stare each other down. All I hear around me is the sound of the waves, but even they are too loud for comfort.

"It's not about me. If you say anything, they'll punish her, too. And then, you'll be next. Do you think they'll just let you keep breaking all the rules?" I look at Thorne, but his eyes are on Xenith. "Where do you go all the time? I know you're places that you shouldn't be. You miss town meetings, skip classes, ignore the Troopers. I think even you have limits on how much damage you can do."

Xenith is quiet, and he shuffles nervously in the sand. "They can't hurt me."

"But you'd let them hurt me?" I say. Both boys look at me. It's not Thorne I'm looking at though; it's Xenith. I hope there's something else to him, something more than this boy who would threaten to expose me. That's not the boy I know. Not the one I am friends with. Maybe he's just saying it to push Thorne. Maybe he doesn't mean a word of it. But knowing that he could say something—that if he wanted to, he could separate Thorne and me forever? I have no words for that.

"Let's go," Thorne says, taking my hand.

"Neely, I wouldn't do it. You know I wouldn't do it—" Xenith starts.

"Don't even talk to her," Thorne snaps, pulling me away.

"Neely..." Xenith pleads again.

I yank my arm from Thorne and move back toward Xenith. I study his face, and his smile is long gone, replaced by that depth that always surprises me.

"I don't like games," I say to him.

"I'm not playing one."

"You're always playing one," I say.

Xenith doesn't respond, and in the silence, I walk away with Thorne.

THORNE AND I HAVE only been walking a few hours—most of them filled with silence so heavy I could almost forget he's beside me if his emotions weren't so loud and confused, rushing into my consciousness.

I don't think he wants me to know what he's feeling through the connection, but there's so much of it all at once that it's uncontrollable. The confusion of what I'm not saying and the anger that I've been alive this whole time. The worry, the wonder, the reasons *why* I lied about all of it and what I'm doing here. It's like my whole body is convulsing between nausea and weight and heat. I can't sort it out. And then there's the joy. The floating and elation and soaring because I'm really, really alive. He hasn't lost me.

The emotions all fight for his soul, for my soul, and I fear the wrong one will win it.

I try to examine other things while we walk and quiet the emotions—sort them, separate them, and figure out which ones to address—but the answers aren't easy ones to give. I look around as we walk, examining the mingling dance of the blue and green and black in the horizon. Even in the sunlight and the blue skies, the road is an endless, depressing shade of black. Tucked between the greens, browns, reds, blacks of nature are decrepit buildings, falling apart at the seams, and broken pavement, the color faded and cement crumbled with age. Blades of grass peek up through tiny cracks, and I'm careful to step around them. To let them live as long as possible.

"We should stop here," Thorne says. His hand touches my arm, but then, as if he's remembering I'm something he shouldn't touch, he moves it away. I can't pretend it doesn't hurt.

Thorne plops his bag down on a spot of green grass under a tree and falls down next to it. His feet stretch out, much like an animal getting ready to sleep, and he looks up at me. I cling tighter to the strap on my bag and bite my lip. We're going to lose precious time.

"Are you opposed to stopping?" he asks, eyes resting on me.

It's not about the waiting; it's about the fact that we can't even have a conversation right now. "We haven't gone far. If we stop too much, we'll never make it in time."

"Where are we going exactly?" he asks.

"There's a plan," I say finally. I sit down with him. Not too close in case he doesn't want me there, but close enough that he could reach me if he wanted. Normally I would sit next to him, and our legs would dangle near each other, bump together occasionally. Not today. I don't know where the line is between us today.

Thorne takes a bite out of a big, green apple from his backpack. The crunch of it reverberates in the air, and I can't help but think how normal it is. How we could be in the Compound right now, him eating a green apple and me sitting beside him. How that life could've been mine if I would've wished for Thorne and nothing else. If I had never gone digging for information or fought or escaped.

If that hadn't happened, then we could just live and laugh and share kisses under the stars. He could fish with the boats, and I could step up to serve in my father's place without complaint. I would know nothing of the lie, have no question about my branding to Thorne, and be content. We could have a family and safety and simplicity. We could be those people who have everything they need, where life seems too simple and easy.

But it did happen.

And now I'll never be able to wish for a simple life with Thorne and have it be enough. I'll never be content to live in the Compound, especially not now. That can never be mine. They were transferring him. Even if we went back right now, it wouldn't change anything. I'd still be a pawn, a tool that the Elders want to use. Thorne would still be separated from me, still be altered. I'd never be free from the uncertainty because them taking him away doesn't help me understand what feelings are real and what feelings aren't. It would only make it worse because I'd miss him. I'd never feel complete.

I can't undo anything. I can't change what I've done, only where we end up. I can find the answers, save myself, save the people I love, and move forward.

That simple life is gone forever. I can't even wish it undone. And I don't know that I would if I could. Not if it means not being out here.

"Neely?" he says again. "Where are we going?"

"What do you know?" I ask. Xenith's words from that night echo in my head. I shouldn't tell Thorne anything, but now he's here and maybe the rules have changed.

Thorne's eyes search my face. "I only know what Xenith told me, which was pretty much that you were alive and you were out here."

"Why did Xenith send you?"

"He said I was a liability and that I felt you because you were alive, just out here. He said, 'You're annoying the hell out me anyway,' and I got out the next morning." He pauses and looks at me. "I couldn't handle living without you, in case you're wondering. That was the story Xenith wrote up before he helped me kill myself. I don't remember much after. We were beyond the barrier, and he pushed me in a car and told me I'd find you alive when the car stopped. Here I am."

Xenith betrayed me. He sent Thorne after promising to keep him safe. He let him travel above. Why did he get to take a car while I had to travel through the darkness of the Burrows for days? I had to fight to live while he was here. I watched all those people—innocent people—die. If he can break the rules, then I can tell Thorne something real.

"Xenith planned out a route of Remnant camps near some of the old cities," I say. The map that rests now in my pack flashes in my head, with each location and each bend and twist of Xenith's handwriting. "We're going through Texas and then over. The camps are all linked to Cecily and the Mavericks. When did you get here?"

"I slept in the casino for two nights," he says, eyeing me suspiciously.

"Why did Xenith help you?" Does Xenith trust him more than me? Does he think I'm not strong enough to make it?

"First tell me some things," Thorne says. Determination laces his tense expression, and that's such a rare thing for him that I nod swiftly and shut my mouth. "Why the Mavericks? Who are they?"

I examine the curve of Thorne's face, the spark in his eye, and the way his hair swishes away from his cheeks. He really doesn't know anything. He doesn't know why he's here. Why would Xenith send him?

"They're a group in San Francisco that has existed since the Compounds were created. Xenith knows the people there. I went to him after I found some information in my father's office, and he sent me to them."

Thorne's hand runs aimlessly through his hair. He stands to his feet and tosses the apple core across the green landscape. "And you just blindly volunteered to come out here and—what? Join them?"

"After what my father did to you, it's the only thing I could do," I say, standing to my feet, too.

"How is that logical at all?"

I can't believe I need to explain it. He should understand. "My father knows we're connected, and if he knows, it's only a matter of time before the Elders find out. They probably found out in the same instant."

"I know you think they did something to your father."

"I don't think it. I know. They're evil," I say. I've felt it since the beginning, but I never told him I found proof. "You heard what Cecily said they did to twins. We aren't some exception, and they would've done it to us. I had to leave to stop them."

"And you couldn't take me?"

I don't miss the betrayal in his voice, but Xenith's words are in my head. I'd asked the same thing once. "Killing us both at once would've raised too much suspicion. They monitor everything, and since we were on their radar, they would've never let us go. You were safer there where Xenith could keep an eye on you."

Thorne groans. "I don't need Xenith to keep an eye on me. You're supposed to trust me."

"I do!" He should know that.

"Then why are we here? You trusted Xenith enough to fake your death, but you don't trust me enough to tell me why."

I pause and inhale. "That's not fair. I trust you. I trust you with everything."

"You don't."

Thorne's jaw is tense, and a heated feeling of his anger attacks me from the inside. It's not a lot, but just enough to let me know that he doesn't believe me. He thinks I don't trust him. I've spent my whole life trusting him, and even though I have questions now, he's always been the only sure person in my life. Even if our love isn't real, if it is only exists because of the branding, I can't deny who he is to me.

"I read some of my father's files one night," I say. "Logs about experiments, twins, myself. I found information on how someone believed there was life here in the Old World and the Elders covered it up by killing him."

"What?"

I don't stop. He wants to know what and why then I'll tell him. "The branding isn't what we think it is. Everyone in the Compound is blocked by it. They can't ask questions or wonder. They have no free will. It's why they don't question anything the Elders command; the Elders have been altering us. They did something to my father's branding—that's when he changed, Thorne—and it made him completely vacant of emotion."

I pause to take a breath. Ever since I found out my father isn't himself because of the Elders, all of his actions make more sense. I still hate it all, but he's not doing it on his own. Why would they do that to him? What do they want with him?

"According to what I found, the Elders plan to transfer a number of families to a brand-new Compound and apply a new branding. They're calling it the Ultimate Compliance. The Mavericks know a way to remove it."

Thorne shakes his head. "The Elders wouldn't do that."

I sigh. I don't have any way to prove it to him. "They would and they are. I've read it. They would wipe out everyone like that." I snap.

"So you came out here to stop them and save everyone?" He stares at me like I'm an idiot.

I try to keep my emotions in check so I don't spill any of my feelings to him. I don't want him to feel my true anxieties. "Yes, and to save myself. They have a plan for me, too. I'd never get to live in the South as a teacher. I was set to be the next director, and I didn't want that. Especially not after I learned everything. I had to get out, to stop them. It is the only way to live freely."

Thorne is silent .

"Your family was going to be transferred to the new Compound. I couldn't lose you," I add.

His eyes snap to me. "My family?"

"Yes, and you. Staying there meant losing myself and losing you." I couldn't handle that. Losing him forever is too much to even think about.

Finally he shakes his head and takes my hand. "You could have told me that, Neely. I would've helped you."

"I didn't want you involved," I say honestly.

"It's my family," he says. His family. His.

"It's mine, too." The tension flows between us, and a breath hitches in my chest. He's not as angry, but the spinning confusion courses through me. "We should go."

"Why you?" The question takes me by surprise. His gaze on me is so intense that I want to look away. It's so hurt and worried, and I don't want to see it.

"What?" My voice is barely a whisper.

"Come on, Neely," Thorne says. He pauses and inhales. His hands squeeze into tight fists at his side. "If there's this whole method of communication like

Cecily mentioned, why do *you* have to go? Why not just send a message? Why did Xenith send you out here?"

I have to look away again. My head is spinning with Xenith and Thorne, with truth and lies, with deals and death and freedom. Thorne reaches out to me through the connection, but I block him out. He shakes his head and stares off into the distance. As soon he looks away, I change my mind and try to reach out for him, but he's blocked me out, too.

"This all started with me," I offer to the silence. "My father told me he was the one in control of everything, and I kept pushing him. I kept disobeying the rules and toeing the barrier and reading the books. I kept going to you after he told me not to see you. Then the Elders did whatever they did to him because of me. He hurt you because of me and found out about our connection. Someone has to make it right—that's on me, too."

"And Xenith has pure motives?"

"Yes," I say.

"But why you, Neely?"

"That's what I have to find out. Xenith said the best way to do it was to search for answers. So that's what I'm doing. If I can stop this, then I will do anything in my power to stop it."

I want to tell him the rest. That I need to know if our love is real. That I'm on this mission in order to stop the Elders, to find the truth, to fight for my own life, and to free myself from being a puppet to the Elders.

"This seems like a bad idea."

I cross my arms. "You don't have to be here. I didn't want you here anyway." This is all to protect him, and if he's here, then I can't do that.

Thorne's eyes are closed. His jaw is tight, and his hands are shoved into his pockets. I kick the ground with my foot in silence and look up at him. The boy I love. The boy I grew up with. The only one who knows me.

"Haven't you ever asked yourself why Xenith cares so much? Or what he *gets* out of this?"

I look up at the sky and watch the sun move to a different spot. Watch the world move around it. I can't look at him or he'll know just how dangerous that answer is. I don't want to see his face when he learns the truth about Xenith. Maybe he'll never have to. Maybe I can keep pretending I haven't asked that question a hundred times.

I pick my bag up off the ground and toss it over my shoulder. "We should go."

Thorne steps in front of me, and I'm forced to look at him. "Why do I feel like you're hiding something?"

I watch him, uncertain in where I should move, but the way he looks at me tells me this is a chance to come clean. I'm trying to protect him. I don't want him to be in danger or to worry, and after all we've been through, I need him to trust me in this.

With a sigh, Thorne yanks his bag off the ground and walks on in silence without looking at me.

XENITH IS LOOKING AT ME. *I've been trying to ignore his eyes for the last twenty minutes, but they almost look through me.*

"Come eat," he says to me again, but I shake my head. I leave the Compound tomorrow, and life's a little more comfortable behind these pages.

I glance over toward his kitchen from the top of the book I'm reading. "I don't want to."

"I'm not giving you an option," he says back.

We stare at each other, and the smell lingers in the air around us. It does smell good—and it's hard to tell when I'll get to eat a real meal again. We've loaded some food in my pack, but none of it is very filling. Xenith sets a plate in front of me. It's the version of mac and cheese that Sara's made since I was a child.

"Xenith," I say. I'm surprised. "This is my favorite."

He smiles at me. "I know. I found the recipe in my mom's stack. It may not be as good as Sara's, but—"

I find his hand. "Thank you." We both freeze until I pull my hand away.

I put To Kill a Mockingbird on the table next to us and silently take a bite. It's just as good as Sara makes it. He doesn't take a bite until I've taken three. He doesn't sit either, just leans against the tall table with his plate in his hands.

"That's one of my favorites." He points toward the book. "That line where he talks about courage." I lower my fork and study Xenith's face, the way his eyes close into slits like he's thinking. "How courage is more than a man with gun, and instead it's trying something you know you'll fail at before you ever start but doing it anyway."

"That's nice," I say.

"Nice?" He moves his hand from mine and crosses to my side of the table. "It's terrifying."

I shake my head, confused. I start to take another bite, but he's looking at me like I'm crazy, so I don't.

"Courage is terrifying, facing something that can ruin you. It's..." He stiffens next to me. "It reminds me of you, of tomorrow." Xenith moves his plate off the table and takes a bite, then moves to the couch and sits with his back toward me.

I keep my gaze locked in his eyes. "Why are you telling me this?

"As soon you stepped into my quarters to ask me for help, when you started snooping, all the odds piled against you. You don't know what you're facing, and you're still going. That's courage, and it's impressive. You aren't like anyone I've ever met."

Is that courage? Stupidity maybe. Only stupid people would challenge the Elders. If they find out I'm not dead, I'll have openly declared a war. I know it's stupid—and that I'm only slightly aware of what they're capable of. I leave the table and stand in front of him.

"Maybe it's surrender."

He looks at me while he chews. "Nah. It's courage," he says. He abandons his plate on the side table, and I fall into the chair beside him.

"If you'd surrendered, you'd still be up there staring out at the ocean and listening to every story they told you. But you're not. You're here. Soon, you'll be out there." Xenith jumps off the couch and motions around the room. "That's only a place for the courageous or the stupid." He pauses. "And you're not one of the stupid. I wouldn't let the stupid go out there. Stupid wouldn't survive two days."

I need some water. My mouth is dry, and my heart is racing. He's looking at me like he shouldn't, and I'm feeling something that I shouldn't. I ignore it, push it away, pretend I don't feel anything.

"It's all on me, so I hope you're right."

Xenith sighs, and his blue eyes search my face. "You can do it. You're not alone in this."

I look away and shake my head. "You said it was mine to carry."

He's beside me in an instant, kneeling so he's even with the chair. He puts a hand on my chin and pulls my face to his so I can't look anywhere else. "That's true. It is up to you, but you're only the main part. There are other people doing this with you. You've never been alone."

A tingle runs up my spine right to where he's holding my chin. His eyes are searching mine for something. I know what they seek, but I'm not going to let him see it. I don't want him to see it. It's easier to hide the things I shouldn't feel or want. These things only confuse me. I smile and look away. His hand falls down.

What do I say? What do I say? I should say something. I can't think.

"Thanks," I say. We both pause for a moment, a breath. I will not kiss him, even though the memory from days ago plays in my head. I clear my throat. "I think I'm going to turn in."

He nods and straightens up. "Night, Neely."

I stand and move away from him. The whole time I'm hoping my legs don't give out on me. Xenith's not usually so encouraging, and these brief glimpses into what's underneath are overwhelming. I'm almost to the bedroom door when I turn to him. "If I was crazy, I'd say you wanted me to succeed."

His eyes are mingled with sadness and surprise and something else. Something I don't want to see there. He shrugs. "I do want that. Most days."

"And the other days?"

He runs a hand through his hair. It reminds me so much of Thorne that I tremble at the movement.

"The other days I'm very selfish."

The words hang between us. I can feel them there even after the door closes.

XENITH'S DEEP GAZE, sneaky grin, and soft words of courage float through my mind, distracting me just as they have been the last few days. I try to shake the thought of him but I can't. I blame this place. From the last stop to here, there's been practically nothing to look at. Only sky, barren trees, and concrete, and none of them are entertaining. The trek through the desert has been the longest two days of my life.

Thorne hasn't said much, but sometimes I feel the pins and needles of his anxiety, mixed with pulses of excitement and piercing frustration as they seep through the connection. I can't tell if he's angry at me or at this place or Xenith. Maybe all of them. I don't know how to console him, especially when I can't make sense of this either. I don't want to feel my own uncertainty, let alone his.

The sudden changes remind me how quiet everything is. How even the birds don't make much noise. The world is still, allowing memories to come back. All the things I've done to get here, all the things that were done to me, all the things I run from.

"We should stop," Thorne says. "Find some more water and rest."

I shake my head. "We're almost to the camp, and then we can stop. The Remnants will help us. Cecily said they'd know we're coming."

I hope.

Thorne shakes his head as we walk. "But we haven't stopped since sunset."

"That's because *someone* overslept at midday," I snap. We've stopped enough already, and we have to make it. I don't care about sleeping or resting, just getting there. It's not really his fault, as he doesn't know, but there's no one else I can blame right now.

He glares at me because of the jab at him, and I know it was childish. I know he's worried about me. "Yeah, I did. And when's the last time *you* overslept? Or slept at all?"

"I'm fine," I say, waving him away. "We're almost to El Paso. It's only a few more hours, and then we can rest."

I pick up my pace and move away from him. I don't want to look at him right now and be reminded of all the things between us. As much as I want to fix things, it's easier to let him hate me; at least he's not worrying. His hand squeezes my arm, and he jerks me back to him. We stare at each other, neither one of us moving, and I barely breathe. The pull of our connection rushes through me, and my heart pounds, torn between wanting to taste him and wanting to run away from him, from the possibility of us. The possibility that I don't want to admit to him. I can feel his annoyance, see it taunt on his face and his tensed jaw. His hands are sweaty on my arm, and only an inch rests between us, between our lips. An inch that could easily be closed if either of us moved in. I want him to kiss me. I want to feel that connection again, have us be the way we were before.

"Neely..."

His fingers trail up my arm, and chills move with them. I inhale and silently count up from one. His warm breath is on my chin, and I close my eyes, ready, aching for him and the fire of our connection when we kiss. But all the things I left behind flash before my eyes: all the reasons, the faces of the people who died, and the plans that have changed everything forever.

A flash of heat rushes through me, and I'm suddenly angry with Xenith. How could he risk this? He broke our deal by sending Thorne, and I was a fool for believing him. I open my eyes and pull away, jumping backward a few steps. I hate him being here. If he dies, all of this is meaningless.

"Neely," Thorne says in a whisper.

I shake my head. The air is tense around us, as if the wind is holding its breath, too. Waiting to see what I do. Thorne looks at me, his eyes unsure and hard. He teeters, his weight on his toes. His eyes rest on me, and after a couple seconds, he shoves his hands into his pockets.

"We need to keep going," I say quickly.

In the stillness, we only look at each other. I don't like the way he studies me, like he's trying to figure out who I really am. Like I'm some kind of new species he's never seen before.

He's the one who starts walking first, his pace a little faster than normal.

"DOES IT RAIN IN THE DESERT?" Thorne asks softly. The sky is gray with clouds, and the wind changes enough to tell us something is coming. He walks past me. "We should find shelter."

Our pace escalates with the wind, and the sand scatters as it blows. The long stretch of road and sparse grass does nothing to ease our shared anxiety. A streak of lightning flashes across the sky. I look up as we walk and count the seconds until the crackle of thunder echoes in the distance, the same way I did when I was a child.

A bird dashes across the sky and lands on a rock near us. It's a raven, with long feathers so black that they have a dark, almost purple tint. It watches us with beady yellow eyes like it can't decide if we're friend or food. Chills form down my arms. Images from a book on Raven's Flesh flashes in my mind as the thunder comes again, crashing in the distance. We only saw a few pictures in the Compound, but they were enough to make an impression. People with darkened eyes, black veins covering their body, faces drooping and peeling away like dead skin. Sometimes it was bloody; other times it was murky. Every time, it was horrifying.

Twelve seconds.

The black bird jumps and flies toward a mountain. My hair whips into my face, obstructing my view. The bird cries out, as if it's talking and waiting for someone to answer, but there is no one. I bet that was how the people in the Old World felt: alone and scared and calling out with no answer.

"We need to find a place before the rain," Thorne says. His voice is calm but dissonant in the noise around us.

"There's supposed to be some kind of border into the city." A single drop of rain hits my forehead.

"What is that?" he asks. In the distance, the top of something dark and solid sticks over us in the sky. I can't see the whole thing, but it vaguely reminds me of home and of the walls that kept us inside the Compound.

"A barrier, I think."

The force of the wind around us makes walking feel more like running on a wet beach. The bird calls out again. It flies beyond my sight, and I strain my head to see. I make out large wings before it disappears completely. The sky flashes again, brighter than it has all afternoon. Almost as if the sun had returned.

The water pours after that. No other warnings, just pelting down on us from the sky. Apparently, it can rain in the desert. Chill bumps form over my skin, and within seconds, my hair and my clothes are matted to my face as we run through puddles of water.

13 DAYS BEFORE ESCAPE

I RUN THROUGH A PUDDLE and take notice of the dark color in the sky. It's not raining right now, but it will again.

It's the perfect day to die.

Part of me wants to tell Xenith that I've changed my mind, but I know I can't run from my fate and I can't hide from death. Not when I'm putting myself right in its path.

I move toward the docks, and my breath fogs up the air. The sun hasn't cracked the sky yet, but there's an orange tint to the sky that says it's ready. The fisherboats are off in the distance, and Thorne's out there with them. They've only begun their day. The whole Compound will be waking up soon, ready to start something new, and my day is almost over. Only hours left.

How many now? Twelve.

I shake the number away and watch the boats turn into tiny specks. It puts some of my anxiety at ease to know that Thorne's out there with them instead of here. If he somehow figured out my plan, he could stop me. Not now. Not when there are miles of water between us.

The sky is dark shade of gray. The sun must have decided it was taking the day off. Maybe it doesn't want to shine on us anymore, doesn't want to spread around any happiness. I eat lunch outside in the center of the courtyard. Three people pass by me with their lips turned down in a scowl and brows furrowed. They don't want me out here since I was locked away in the safehouse. My father did a good job of turning his people against me.

This is part of the plan. People need to see me, need to ignore me, need to believe I'm not important. All these things will add up in the end, will make it stronger, more believable—at least, that's what Xenith says.

I move from the table and bump into a woman with a small child. An apple rolls from her bag, and I catch it before it hits the ground. When I hold it out to her, she doesn't take it.

"I'm sure it's fine. It doesn't look bruised," I say.

She stares back at me. I'm the serpent, and she's the innocent girl in the garden. I'm tempting her, dooming her to lose everything just by taking it from my hand. I think that's how the story went. She looks as if she wants to, and her hand moves forward before she freezes. Then, she shakes her head and pushes past me. She doesn't take the apple. I stand, holding it out to nothing but air.

Ten more minutes. In ten minutes, Kai will knock on the door. He'll bring me a little envelope with a little white pill inside that has a red letter on it. I've seen it only once, the day that Xenith held it out to me in his quarters.

"This will be the thing that kills you and keeps you alive," he'd said.

I'd squinted my eyes. "That thing? It's small."

"And powerful."

I'm to take the little white and red pill when I'm on the beach. We decided that drowning was the most believable. The pill has the ability to keep me alive while making me appear dead—even to the most trained of Healers. It's a ruse, but Xenith says it will work.

Later, Kai will give me the cure while he's at the Healers' unit. He will save me before my body meets the traditional fiery tomb, and then they'll replace my body with another's. I will be dead and then alive again.

There's a knock on the door, and I swing it open too quickly so the door bounces off the back wall. Kai stares back at me, an envelope in his hand. He holds it out to me and steadies his gaze. "Are you sure you want this?"

I nod and hold out my hand. He places it there without any objection.

"Thank you," I say.

Kai hugs me, his movement sudden and tight, like he's afraid to let go. It's comforting to be in his arms. Then he leaves without a word, not that I expected one.

There's a note inside the envelope.

See you on the other side. - X

That could mean so many different things. I choose not to think about it and hold the little pill in my hand. It looks like a polka dot that's fallen off a shirt and landed in my palm. It doesn't look real, and it doesn't look like it can do what Xenith has said.

It's deceiving, as I'm learning most things are, but here it is. No second thoughts; there is no time for them.

TIME GOES SLOWLY IN THE RAIN. Each step feels as if we're not moving since the landscape doesn't change and the rain and wind pelts us as we move.

"There!" Thorne yells. He looks back at me and takes off in a jog. Ahead of us, I can see a portion of an abandoned building. It's small, with crumbling bricks stacked tall and empty space every ten feet. It doesn't look extremely stable, but hopefully it's dry. In the distance behind it, there's a huge metal barrier that's longer and taller across than I can see in the rain. The border keeping out Mexico—or keeping in America.

I follow Thorne into one of the openings. It's a small, simple room with a roof, floors, and mostly held-together walls. We both strip off our wet outer layers and spread them across the dry space. The blue color of my pack looks black, but luckily nothing inside is very wet. My eyes catch sight of the cover of Xenith's book, and I'd forgotten it was in there. It's not ruined. Good.

I peel the socks off my feet, and my toes are red. Blisters are starting to form, which is irritating with so much farther to walk. I look up in time to see Thorne pulling off his wet shirt, his muscles chiseled underneath. I forgot the way he could make my stomach do that flip-inside-itself thing. He shakes water from his hair and lays the shirt on the ground to dry. My eyes scan up his body, from his arms that are more defined from all the work on the fisherboats, to his chest and defined abs. It wasn't that long ago when Thorne didn't have abs like that. I feel my cheeks warm up, and then Thorne smiles, staring at me.

"Why, Cornelia Ambrose," he says, "am I making you nervous?"

I laugh, but it gets caught in my throat. Right next to my common sense and my nerve. I toss my other sock toward my pile of wet clothes. "No. Why would you make me nervous?"

He shrugs, the smile still playing on his lips. And my stomach is still jumping around, trying to escape. I'm wringing the water out of my hair, staring out into the beyond, when he turns to me and pulls me closer. My wet hair falls, forgotten. The surge of our connection pulses through me, and he's so close to me I can feel the heat of his bare chest through my layer of clothing.

"I miss us," he says. His voice is ragged, and he presses a chaste kiss to my forehead. "I came because I wanted to be with you. The fact that you left for my family only means I'm never leaving you."

"Thorne—"

He puts a finger to my lips. "Nothing you can say will change my mind. I'm here. You're not going alone, and besides, we are stronger together. I can help."

I lean into his body, still pressed against mine. We stand there, wrapped in each other's arms, silent aside from the wind and the rain and the thunder that crashes around us. In his arms, everything else falls away. The mission, the danger behind us, is forgotten. The world is ours. I feel better now that he's with me. Even though he's one of the questions I have, he's still Thorne.

His finger traces my cheek, and as he presses his lips against my cool neck, chills rush through me at the contrast of our skin. A cascade of longing passes through me—mine or his, I'm not sure—but he feels it too because his eyes focus on mine.

Our lips crash together. In seconds, we're entwined. The scruff on his chin scratches my face, and my heart pounds as wildly as the rain on the roof above us. A gust of wind rushes through the open spaces, cool against the heat of our bodies.

His kiss is fierce, purposeful. His hands run through my hair, tangling in the strands. My branding burns and my head spins and the hours wrap around me, but with Thorne kissing me, none of it matters. Nothing except the feel of his lips on mine and the fire of our touch. Through our kiss, I can feel everything.

I can't see what happened over the last few weeks, but I can feel the way he felt. The memory of them affecting him now. As if this kiss, this moment, was the only thing he'd been waiting to experience again, never certain that he would. Thorne's confusion at the way I'd been acting after learning about the placement testing, about the branding and the Elders and his family. His pain when he believed I was dead, such a deep sickening pit in his stomach that it made him want to give up. The joy and frustration when Xenith told him the truth. The second he saw me again. Those feelings all plague him, and with his guard down and us completely open, they seep into me.

How could I just leave him behind? I was so determined to find the truth that I didn't even think about what the truth would do to him. Even now. My freedom from our branding means his freedom, too. And even though I want it, I know he doesn't. He never has.

Thorne pulls away from me again, his breath raw and jagged. He runs his finger over my cheek, eyes wide. "What is it?" he says. "Something just happened. I felt it. You feel guilty about something."

I pull away from his arms, and I'm not sure what to say. I can't be weak now. We've got too far to go, so I look out the holes in the walls at the rain.

"How long will it last?"

Thorne exhales, presses a kiss against my neck. "Hard to say. But get comfortable. We'll wait it out."

I'VE BEEN WAITING ALL DAY. There aren't many people on the beach now because of the sky. It's still dark, preparing for an explosion. I look over the waves. They are harsh today—rapid. They seem to reflect the sky. I know they are two separate things, like Thorne and I, but they are so much alike. When one is reflected in the other, it's hard to remember they're different. How can things so different from each other be so similar? They were made to go together. They were made to be vast and infinite and mystifying. The way I used to believe we were.

I'm sure Thorne's out there right now, swaying and tossing on the ocean. He's probably pulling in a net of fish or cursing because he hasn't caught any. He's baiting hooks and swabbing decks and joking with the old men. They like him, and he's good at fishing, but it's not the life he wants either. He deserves more—we all do—and that's why I have to do this.

I walk along the shore for a minute because I want to enjoy it, but the little pill is a boulder. I need to take it. I need to toss it in my mouth and swallow it. I need to, but I can't. Dying is a scary thing, and I literally hold my life in my own hands.

I close my eyes for one last moment. The waves splash on the sand and make a sound as they fold over each other. Over and over. The sand swishes away with the tide. I hum along with it, like the forbidden song my mother and Sara used to sing as children. A song about love that Sara taught to me.

The water is up to my shin. I don't feel like I'm moving at all. The waves are wild, quickening in speed and intensity. I try to find the melody, but it's too lost in the waves. I move in deeper until the water's at my waist, beating and thrashing against me, warning me, telling me to go back. I don't go back. I keep my eyes closed and watch the waves move around me, pulling me forward and pushing me away. The sky is dark, the wind fierce. The waves respond to the movement, and I dive into them just as the rain falls.

My eyes burn, and I spit out the taste of salt. A wave is coming toward me, a wall of dark blue. I try to shove myself up, back to the surface, to the air, but my foot is wrapped in the seaweed, pulling me down. I gasp in one more breath before I'm swept over by water.

Suddenly, I don't want to die like this. I want out, but I can't find the surface. I try to reach up, to get air, but I can't and my breath is running out. There's a sudden rush of panic—panic that isn't mine—and I know Thorne can feel me, can feel this moment. I didn't think of him, of what this would do to him, and I want him. I thrash my head and body, trying to free myself because, even though this was the plan, I no longer want it. My brain screams for oxygen, but it doesn't come. There's only more water.

Then it's calm. The little pill must be working because my adrenaline fades. I feel calm, warm, peaceful.

I look up, hoping to see the glimmer of the sun, but everything is darkness and the pounding of the rain feeding into the waves. I instinctively open my mouth and breathe in water as if it is air; my lungs are nothing but liquid now. I think I hear some voices, but maybe it's the sound of the rain on the ocean.

My heart rate slows more, and I think of Thorne, of his touch, of his contagious hope, of his lips. My father flashes in my head next, a gentle man who left me notes every morning and spoke of Mother in a whisper. Now he's an evil man with hatred that the Elders have created. I have to save him. Sara's bright smile; Kai's laugh. I can almost see my mother with her deep red hair falling over me. Maybe she's waiting. I reach out to her, but she disappears into an endless void of dark water.

WATER DRIPS ON MY HEAD, and I shoot up from the ground, sticky with sweat. Thorne is staring down at me, completely redressed. The sun is bright outside again, but rain leaks from the roof.

"I tried to wake you," he says. I meet his gaze. "You were dreaming."

I bite my lip and pull my legs toward my chest. My shoulders are tense from the dream and the ground, and it's a silly thing to worry about but I run my fingers through my hair on instinct. Pull it back in a ponytail. I yank my socks up from the ground and pull the stiff fabric back over my feet.

"You kept yelling his name." Thorne's voice waivers a little. "Xenith's. You were talking about dying."

I feel his worry rush over me and pull at my stomach. When did I become the girl who makes him anxious?

I don't look up at him as I tie my shoe. "It was nothing. Just a dream."

"You don't say someone's name over and over in your sleep and have it mean nothing. Do you have feelings for him?"

I scoff at him. "That's ridiculous. Are we seven again?"

"I don't know happened between you two. You two have always been a little—"

"What?" I snap.

His gaze is as intense as fire, and he shakes his head. "You've always been quick to trust him and take his side."

My trust for Xenith is different. He understands me a way that others can't because we both feel like outcasts. Me for being the director's daughter and for my connection with Thorne. Xenith Taylor for breathing, asking questions, knowing whatever he does. I can't feel Xenith's emotions, can't predict his moves, and there's a security in that. An instinct. And if it's wrong, then that's on me. Being the only one making a decision instead of being told what to feel or what to want is exhilarating.

I meet Thorne's eyes from across the room. "I promise I have no feelings for Xenith. You don't have to worry." I smile the best smile I can. Sunny days, presents, and kisses—I think about all the happiest, most reassuring things I can and push them through connection. Thorne steps toward me like he wants to touch me. He can't touch me until my emotions have calmed down. One touch and he'll know I'm lying about how I feel.

"I can force it out of you," he says.

"You wouldn't do that." He's only done it to me once, after my father lost his grip on reality and bruised my arm. I wasn't going to tell him, but he pushed through our connection, past the lie, until I told him. It was painful for both of us, like fingers poking in my brain, and we've sworn to never do it again.

Thorne shakes his head. "No, I wouldn't." He sighs. "I want to believe you. Do you know how much I want that?"

"Trust me and you will," I say.

I feel his frustration rushing over me, swaying inside and building toward anger. He's conflicted. "Then tell me whatever it is you're hiding. I know there's something you aren't saying," he says. I look away from him. "Something that has to do with Xenith." I shake my head, tears forming behind my eyes. He reaches out and runs a hand across my cheek. "Tell me."

There's a silence around us. Thick and burnt. Suffocating. I can't handle not saying it. Not if we have twenty-three more days. It's just us out here. Just this secret and us.

"The branding affects everyone. I told you the Elders' plan, but it's also done something to us. Cecily said the branding caused she and her twin to share dreams, and I think it does that to every set of twins"

I pause for a breath and then recount everything I learned to Xenith. The files I found outlining experimentation on twins and about the Elders having a plan for the branding and me. The notes from Xenith's mom when she realized we shared emotions.

"What do they want?" he asks.

"I don't know that yet, but it's not good. And if they've really been experimenting on me, on us, then it makes me wonder."

"Wonder what?"

My mind drifts back to the conversations we'd had before. The times when I asked him if he wanted anything for himself, if he'd wondered what it would be like to be unconnected from me. He'd always said no, and I never had the heart to tell him that it was the one thing I wanted.

"I think our feelings for each other may not be real," I say.

Thorne's eyes get wide, and I feel his confusion and anger and sadness all at once. I close my eyes and try to ignore what he's feeling, but it's too strong. Too mixed with my own guilt and confusion.

"Think about it. If the branding causes twins to be connected—we can feel each other's emotions—who can say that our love is real and not manufactured? What if it's all a trick of the Elders? What if that's what they want from me?"

Thorne looks away from me, and he says nothing at first. He paces the floor, resting his hands on a window ledge with no glass, leaning in and tense. He's quiet for too long, and then he's looking at me again. His warm eyes bore into mine, and it's impossible to ignore the angry, determined rush through the connection.

"You don't love me." His voice is broken and unlike anything I've heard from him before. It pierces my heart because I do love him. That's what makes all this so difficult.

"I do."

"You just said you didn't!"

"I said what if it's not real. That's not the same as I don't love you. I do love you. That's why I need to understand what parts of our relationship are really us and what parts are because of the branding." Thorne runs his hand through his dark hair, and I try to keep my frustration in check. "I don't want to be their pawn. This is our life. It's not a game. Whatever they are doing, we have to stop them."

He doesn't move, doesn't seem to breathe. "You've always felt that way. That you wanted to be your own person." He looks at me, his eyes dark and glassy. "Do you think I somehow make you less? Because all these years, I thought we were one. There's a reason we're branded together, Neely."

"And you don't think that reason could be because of the Elders?" I pause. I know my words aren't what he wants to hear, but I have to say them to him. I have to be honest about this possibility. "I don't know the truth, Thorne, and I need to."

I don't look away from him because I need him to understand, but now it feels as if I have placed a wall between us where there never was before. I think he realizes that some of the questions I've had for my whole life, questions he dismissed, have been building up to this moment that neither of us were ready for.

"So it was never about my family or the other people in the Compound? It was about you and this quest."

I shake my head. "It's about all of that. It's connected. Can't you see that? Us and the branding. Them and the branding. The new Compound and the Ultimate Compliance. Whatever the Elders are looking for and why they want me. It's one thing."

"What's the connection?"

I shrug with a breath. I wish I knew. Thorne glances to the ground, thinking. I can't feel anything through our connection; he's blocked me out. I take his hand, even though he doesn't want me to. The wall between us is too jarring. It must come down, crumble.

"I love you, Thorne. I do. But I have to know. I know you can't understand that, but I have to. My whole future is on the line here," I say, and it's not just my future. "The Elders want me for something. They want you for another thing. They want to separate us, and they'll hurt so many people. They already have. Being out here has already made me see that. We can't trust them. Nothing about them. And this—" I say, pointing to the branding on his neck. The other half of me. "This is them. It makes us theirs."

He looks up at me, and his gaze is unfamiliarly painful, almost lost. I did that to him. My voice comes out cracked and broken, not my own at all. "I want to be us. Without them. Without this thing."

Thorne shakes his head. "That's the part that hurts the most, Neely. Without this thing, without them, who's to say we'd ever be anything? And you just want to—what? Rip it away? Stop it? Change us?"

"Thorne—"

"No," he says. His jaw is tensed, and heat runs through me. "You say you want to find out what's real about us. Well, I already know. *Everything.* And you say you love me, but what if you find out that our branding really is what makes you love me? And me, you? Then what?" I inhale. "You'll separate us. Just like the Elders were already planning to do. You'd be destroying us."

We stare at each other, and I'm not sure what to say to that. I would let them remove the branding, I would, and he's right.

Thorne sighs. "You're going to let the Mavericks take it away. It's not just a marking, Neely, it's a symbol of us. You're going to destroy it, and if you do and our feelings do really go away, you can only blame yourself."

"I get it," I say. Tears push at my eyes, but I don't let them out. Thorne turns away from me, and I watch his back move as he inhales. "You're right, okay? I'm no better than them, but if I have to destroy us in order to save everyone, I will. And I'll figure out how to live with that and be all right."

He turns so quickly to face me, and his eyes are brimmed in red. "You separate from me can never all right."

I shake my head because I can't speak. The betrayal and the pain in his eyes release the tears I've been fighting. Thorne sighs, and his emotions shift, suddenly more calm and sure. I feel some of my anxiety lift, and I know he's taken some of it from me.

"You and I are the real thing, Neely."

"I want to believe you," I say.

"Then trust in us more than you distrust the Elders." Thorne takes my face in his hands so I'm forced to look at him. "Trust in me."

"I do," I say.

He presses his forehead against mine. "Then we'll find out the truth together, and we'll decide. I wouldn't risk everyone at home either, but we are in this together. No more secrets, Neely."

I nod. "I just want us all to be freed from them. Completely."

"We will," he says.

Then he closes the space between us, and I am whole. Enough that, for a a single second, I let myself forget that I'm searching for a way out of this feeling, this wholeness. In searching for a way to make this completely real, I could lose all I know. I want to believe we are real. I want to believe in him and that his promise to free me means I can still, somehow, believe in us. I want to believe until there are no more days.

MY FAVORITE DAYS ARE Wednesdays. In the mornings, I have my placement, and I get to teach the smaller children. I like how hungry they are to learn. The alphabet is my favorite thing to teach them. To show them how letters form words and words build sentences and sentences create stories and stories are life. I stumble into the kitchen, already smiling at the thought of their faces when we learn F-J. I've thought of fun words. Frog and fang. Grapes and goats. Horses and—

"Morning, Cornelia," Father says.

I pause in the doorway of the kitchen at the sight of my father standing over the stove. He's never here in the mornings anymore. My eyes wander to the clock. It's seven.

"This is a surprise," I say.

He has this huge smile on his face when he looks over his shoulder at me. It always takes me by surprise when I see that glowing white smile on his face. In those moments, my father looks younger than he is and seems to forget the load he's carrying as the director.

"I wanted to be with you this morning. I know you have placement, but I've got a big meeting with the

Elders today and I'll miss dinner. So I rearranged some things," he says.

I smile. "I'm glad you're here, too, then." I move closer to the stove, and the smell that comes from it makes my stomach rumble. "What's all this?"

"Ah," Father says. He opens the oven door, and the aroma seeps out. "This was Amelia's recipe. Sara found it earlier this week in some old boxes of Richard's and gave it to me. This was always my favorite thing she cooked."

My eyes widen when I look inside and see the golden brown of French toast and maple syrup. Next to it is another dish that looks like eggs and cheese and peppers.

"They're delicious—trust me."

"I do," I say.

Father and I sit around the table, waiting for the food to finish, and he tells me a story about one of the first meals Mother ever cooked for him and how bad it had been. He laughs while he talks about her. He's being really open about her today and I'm not sure why, but I soak in the stories.

When breakfast is ready, he waits for me to try it with eyes wide. I nod in approval after my first bite of each. They are both pretty amazing.

"Why are the Elders coming?" I ask.

His fork freezes mid-bite. I study the tension in his jaw, the hardness in his eyes, and the way his fingers turn white against the fork. He hates talking about the Elders, especially with me. "I can't tell you much, Neely."

"Right," I say. "Sorry."

The Elders are a big mystery. They only come to our Compound to see my father. With six other Compounds to run, I'm sure they're busy. I've only seen them once, and I was two. They came when my grandfather died, so I don't remember anything about them except these big black hooded robes and how I clung to Sara's leg at the sight of them.

He pauses. "They're only coming to headquarters for a couple hours. They have a new method of practice to discuss with me. I'm sure it will be boring really."

I press my fork into the French toast and watch while the syrup falls out over my plate. The last time we talked about the Elders together was before my placement eight months ago, when they demanded that I begin studying for my role as director and I begged my father to let me teach. Just for one year and then I had to start my placement with the new session. I know it wasn't meant to be forever, but it could've postponed things. I won't become director until he dies or until the Elders tell me to take over, but I have to learn and train. I have to be prepared.

Father rests a hand on mine, and I look up at him. "What's wrong?"

"I only have four more months," I say.

He moves his hand and sighs. "I know being director isn't the future you wanted, but it's not one you can control."

"I know."

"I didn't want it either when I was your age," he says, lowering his voice. "Your mother was the one who helped me see that it was where I was meant to be, and then I accepted it. Maybe someone can show you that, too, and then you'll be ready."

I nod, but it's not the reassurance I want. I want him to tell me that he'll figure out a way to keep me from being trapped in a job I don't want for my whole life. I want him to say he'll work it out.

"You have four more months, Cornelia. And then after that, we can reevaluate."

"Reevaluate?"

He lowers his fork. "I can't change your position, but I can maybe get you some more time so you can keep teaching." I squeal excitedly. "No promises."

I launch myself from the table and into his arms. "I'll take it," I say.

My father hugs me against his chest. "I should go soon," he says.

Before I leave for class, my father is already gone. On the counter is a note, and I smile because I was sure he wouldn't leave one since he saw me this morning but it's a nice surprise.

I know you'll be ready for whatever comes—you get that stubbornness from me. It's a good thing and you'll need it because there's so much left to discover.

THORNE AND I DISCOVERED the El Paso Remnant camp from Xenith's map twenty minutes ago, and I have not seen a single person. There aren't many places they could be, and it's quiet, early morning. A few remains of buildings line the street.

"Hello?" Thorne calls out into the silence. There's no response. "This place seems abandoned."

"No," I say. "There's got to be something here."

We walk down the dirt road, through the old buildings and the overgrown plants. There's no movement. Everything is so silent. Too silent.

"Maybe we should go somewhere else," Thorne says.

Something moves behind him. I don't see what, but a bush sways from the sudden the motion. Thorne sends me an odd look when I move past him, my finger over my lips. He's right behind me as I walk, tracing my steps like a shadow.

I only take four steps before a shrill whistle pierces the air.

My stomach jumps in my throat at the painfully familiar sound. The Cleaners. I see them then in the sky. Large dark, metal machines. Thorne yells something, but I can't hear over the sound. I grasp his arm, ignoring the burn of the branding.

"Run!" I yell in his ear and pull him after me.

We both take off. It's almost like being at home, smiling as we run across the beach, sinking in the sand, the wind in our face. Only there's no beach, no sand, no smiling. There's only wind. It screeches around us with a shrill pitch, raging as it rips up broken buildings and tree branches. My legs pump as I go, and I clear my head, trying to tune out the disruptions. My muscles burn and ache, but I keep going, heart pounding. Thorne is beside me, moving with me. He's always beside me, even when he could run faster than me in his sleep. His breaths are steady in my head, and somehow, I hear his feet hitting the ground louder than the roar of the Cleaners.

I jerk to a stop, and Thorne nearly bumps into me. Fully visible in the sky are three large spheres that are bigger than a house. The sight of them is just as terrifying now as it was before. A chute protrudes from the bottom, and Thorne curses beside me, staring at them as it moves toward the ground. The Cleaners found something.

The chute moves around, freezes. The sound pauses before a tree—a whole tree—flies through the sky and into the tube, and the Cleaner makes a grinding noise before the whistling starts again. The whole process happens in a minute. Maybe less.

How are they here the same time as us? That's not a coincidence.

Thorne and I exchange a glance before he tilts his head toward the right. I follow his movement in time to see a bushel of blonde hair disappear behind a ratty, half-broken shed. I look back up toward the Cleaners in the sky as they move, the same sound accompanying them, but nothing from the earth is sucked up, no trees or houses. They're scouting the area, but then something black and small comes out of the chute. I haven't seen that before. Men—no, Troopers. More follow, dozens and dozens.

"Let's go," Thorne says, pulling me away.

Thorne and I take off in a run to the shed where we saw the blonde hair. But it isn't a shed at all. It's only a doorway, the entryway into another, longer room. I twist the handle, and it opens. We go inside and slam the door behind us.

"I'm sorry! I didn't mean for them to see me!" A little blonde girl points to us, crying. She must've been the one we saw run back here.

Another boy pats her back, a boy with big ears and a brown hat. "No tears, Delilah. I reckon it's safer for them with us than out there." He wipes a tear from her cheek, now dirty with a streak stain running down it. Her pink dress falls off her shoulders, too big, and the bottom is dirty from dragging on the ground.

"What is this?" Thorne asks.

The boy pushes Delilah behind him, like he's protecting her, and lifts a long gun right at us. "What's your business here? You one of them?"

"One of who?" I ask.

The boy cocks his head to the side. "Where you from? You ain't one of us. We don't need no yellow-bellied traitors in these parts. This here's a war."

"A war?" Thorne asks.

He raises his eyebrow at us but doesn't lower his gun. "A war here and everywhere. Them or us. Remnants or Elders. If you ain't a Remnant, you an Elder." The boy steps toward us with the gun.

Thorne raises his hands in the air. "We aren't here to hurt you. We were sent here."

"By who? People don't just come wandering in here at all hours in the morning. Not in the daylight and not when they're out there," the boy says, nodding toward the doorway.

"By Cecily," I say.

"Cecily sent you here? Y'all are the ones she was talking about in her message?" He lowers his gun, and Delilah peeks around his leg.

A door behind him bursts open, and two men in weird hats look between the four of us. One is tall and burly, with dark, unruly hair escaping under his dirty flannel shirt. The other is short and stout, a gray button-down tucked into his jeans that makes his belly seem enormous.

"What's going on here, Benny? What's the hold up?" The burly one looks us both up and down before speaking. "Who's this lot?"

"Cecily sent them. Them's the ones that escaped, the ones we supposed to help," Benny, the boy, says.

A piece of the roof blows off, and Delilah screams. The sound of the Cleaners seeps into the small room.

"Right," the burly guy yells. "Now ain't a good time. The Cleaners and Troopers are here. We have to prepare, relocate until they're gone. We ain't safe here."

"You got a gun? Any sort of weapon?" the other asks. He's a teapot with legs and speaks in a squeaky voice. We both nod. He looks surprised. I have the knife in my pack and Thorne has the gun from Cecily, but I'd never planned to use either of them. "Then you may make it. Come on."

We follow them through the doors, the girl looking back at us as we walk. Thorne watches everyone as we pass by, each one dressed in scroungy clothes. There are lots of people—hundreds of them, all ages, packed into a gathering hall. They huddle across tables, in corners. Babies cry around us, old women cough, and men stare at me. I don't look at any of their faces. I don't even want to see them in case all this ends badly, too.

We learned about wars in school—about the way greed and technology made everyone crazy. Made them kill each other. Before the fall, the president blocked off borders. No one in and no one out. They built these huge metal walls across Mexico and Canada, and only a few years later, the fall happened. It's part of the reason the Old World couldn't recover from Raven's Flesh, the reason no other country would help us and why they still won't. Not that they know there's even anything else here to save.

At least, according to the Elders. None of that was probably true.

"This ain't the time for pleasantries," the burly guy says. He moves around a table, picking up guns and clicking them into place and passing them along to a line of men nearby. Benny, who has really blond hair with his hat off, whispers in Delilah's ear.

"What is that thing out there?" Thorne asks, looking through a small crack in the covered window. I didn't realize he hadn't seen one before. I guess that's a good thing.

Teapot smiles at Thorne. "That thing is a Cleaner. It'll rip your legs plum off your body if you try to stay where it don't want you."

"The Cleaners are what you should be the least scared of," a woman's voice says. I didn't see her step up. She sweet-looking, with big brown eyes, and pregnant. Tan skin. A little taller than me, but still short. Her hand rests on her belly, and my eyes dart away. I can't look at her. Not after the last one died in the fire, one that I can't shake the Elders caused.

Big Burly steps in the center of the room. Everyone looks at him immediately. The chaos around us quiets except the noise outside.

"We gotta run, folks. Everyone knows where we're going. The hole is about a mile west of here. There are Troopers everywhere. Cleaners. It's risky, but it's our only hope. Go to the center. I love y'all. We'll meet where it's safe. And if we don't..."

"We'll meet on the other side," they all say in unison.

Then it's silent inside the hall. The people trickle out in small groups of ten or fifteen. I move to the window near us and watch them run. The first group is out of sight when the second starts running out the door. It goes that way, another group leaving the hall every forty seconds—or however long it takes to get to the edge of some trees—then another goes.

Delilah pulls on my arm, her blonde curls falling around her dirty face. "Do you run a lot?" she asks. Her blue eyes are wide, awaiting my answer.

"I run sometimes." I say. It's true. Down the beach usually, when the morning air is salty and brisk. But lately, a lot more than that. "How old are you?"

"Seven," she says, scrunching up her nose and looking back out the window. The next group is heading outside, still undetected. "I'm real fast. I've been goin' since I was borned. My brother Benny taught me that there be two rules survivin'." She pauses and looks at me. "I can tell you if you want to know 'em."

I nod. She presses her lips together. "Rule one: Don't stop runnin'. If a Trooper gets you, hit 'em real hard and keep goin'. Don't ever show 'em where we hide though—go anywhere else, but never stop if you're bein' tailed."

I repeat it back to her. Never stop. Burly Guy calls for the next group. The Remnants around me start moving toward the door. "And the other?"

Delilah cocks her head to the right. "Run fast."

Benny calls her over, and she doesn't look back at me until she's at her brother's side. Thorne's arm brushes against mine as our group readies at the door. Run, run, run.

I should be good at that by now.

There's a yell, and then people are pushing past me. Thorne practically pulls me out the door before I realize we're out, and then I go too. The shrill sound of the Cleaners is more vibrant out here in the open. Inside, I almost forgot the sound of them and the way the wind seemed to still and spiral at once. Outside, I can't even pretend.

The pregnant woman is on the ground. She's fallen only a few feet from us, and by the way Thorne looks at me, the way his eyes meet mine and dart away toward the woman, I know he wants to help her. People seem to be rushing around her, ignoring her even though she's obviously injured. I move toward her, but Thorne reaches out for me.

"I'll get her. You keep going. Stay on the mission."

"I can help," I say. I want to stay with him. The thought of him not making it is enough to paralyze me. What happens when a Cleaner takes you? Where do you end up? Do you even survive that?

Thorne shakes his head. "Together, right? Go. I promise I'll find you," he says to me.

I nod. I believe him. I want to believe him. He kisses me quickly, then he's gone. Swooping up the woman so she can lean against him while they walk. He tosses me a look before he disappears from my sight. There's a yell behind me about the Cleaners, and I turn to look while I run. They're approaching at a rapid speed, sucking up trees and buildings and who knows what else as they move toward us. They're close enough that they block out the rising sun, and I move faster.

But they're not alone. Just as the last group exits, Troopers dressed in black uniforms with shiny guns jump out of trees. Appear in the air. Come from behind things. They're everywhere. A sea of men in uniform. A black sea of death.

Don't stop running. Delilah's voice echoes in my head. I turn and take off as quickly as I can, trying to find Thorne or someone I recognize in the crowd of people. It's impossible to see anything. The Cleaners move around us, blowing up dirt and leaves and debris. People are going in every direction.

Someone cuts my arm when they pass by, and I scream at the sudden pain. It's a fluid movement, and then my arm is bleeding, drops falling into the trampled, dying grass. I trip, catch myself before I fall, and hear a scream. Somehow I hear her scream over the crying and the whirring shrill of the Cleaners, the breaking noise as it chomps up whatever it's found. I hear the scream as if it's tuned just for my ears. And then I see her being dragged behind some trees by a Trooper.

I'm not sure how I move against the fierce wind of the Cleaners—adrenaline, maybe—but my feet act as wings. All I know is I'm there, standing in front of a wooden house that's held together by poles and beams. Delilah is with a Trooper, who's bloodied and beaten and probably not in his right mind. Not if he's cornered a child with a knife. Surely, he won't kill her. Surely. She's crying, begging him, trying to wriggle out from his grasp.

"Let her go!" I shout. He looks at me, confused. She's still fighting his hold on her. "Please let her go." I squeeze my good hand around the wound on my arm. It's a deep cut, but not to the bone.

He does it. He lets her go, just like that. I step toward him, and then he falls over, dead.

Benny stands behind the dead Trooper and pulls Delilah into his arms. I look down at the fallen Trooper, and when I look up again, Benny and Delilah are gone.

I run back to the main path where the Remnants are still rushing toward the hole. Cleaners screech in the air, covering the sun and making it look darker. I watch them, searching and waiting. For what, I don't know. The whistling pauses before a Remnant gets sucked up into the air toward the Cleaner. His screams aren't heard, but his limbs fly around, trying to find land again, and then he disappears inside the tube. There's a chomping sound. Someone else is dead.

I need to find Thorne. All the Remnants are running toward the center, toward the hole, so I follow them and push everyone and everything out of my mind. I don't want to see them being hurt around me. I just want to find Thorne and get out of this.

From the corner of my eye, I see him. I think it's Thorne. I yell his name, know he can feel me through the connection, but then the figure disappears. As does another person. It's the entrance into the underground, and I've made it.

It's only forty feet away. That's nothing. I let myself smile. This part of the nightmare is almost over.

Then something pierces me, and I fall to the ground and scream.

A sharp pain courses through my leg. A Trooper steps into my vision, looking down at me. I'm crying and screaming, I know I am. Searing fire burns through my muscles, and it's all I can think about. I see the Trooper's gun. I pull up my hand from my wound, and it's covered in thick blood. The Trooper is over me, and he repositions his gun to my head.

I wonder if this is dying, if this was always the way it was supposed to end. I stare up at the Trooper. There's something about the way his nose curves and the point of his chin that reminds me of my father.

There's a sharp blow to my head, and everything is dark.

THE SKY IS DARK TODAY, which is fitting since there's a funeral. They don't happen often since the dead aren't celebrated in the Compound; they are barely remembered. There are stories that the dead used to get whole days to be remembered, have parties and dances. We don't do that. We have a simple service held four times a year for all those who have died—unless it's someone important to the Compound, like a director, and then we have it immediately. Our funeral services are the exact same for everyone: The people gather on the beach, men in black, women in white. The names of the deceased are stated, and the survivors toss ashes in the sea. Then we all move on.

My father is home today, waiting for me to dress. There are few occasions lately that we go out into the Compound together, and aside from our weekly dinner, I rarely see him anymore. He's never here. But this is a big event in the Compound, an act of unity and oneness, so we must appear to be a picture of father and daughter. He is the director, the leader of everything and the example. I am expected to be at his side.

Father knocks on my door.

"Come along, Cornelia. Even the dead don't like waiting."

I glance at myself in the mirror and open the door. My father's eyes—blue like mine, the only thing I got from him besides his stubbornness—are wide as if he's seeing a ghost. We stand there in silence until he clears his throat. He walks toward the door without saying a word, and whatever is going on with him, I hope it ends soon.

Outside, the sky is overwhelmed with darkness. Around me, people are stirring. Little houses are busy with life. Children cry, and smoke from hearths billows up toward the sky. House after house is the same.

As we walk through the center of town, a little boy named Jacob runs past us, his black pants covered with specks of gray from the gravel dust. His mother yells after him, but Jacob doesn't stop. Not until he sees my father. Then he freezes, and his chest heaves.

"Jacob Teem," my father says. His voice is rough and loud. It's always rough and loud lately. "I believe your mother is calling for you. Tell me, Jacob, what is the punishment in your household for disobeying your parents?"

Jacob's eyes expand three sizes. He gulps, and the freckles on his face seem to dance in trembling fear. "Director, sir, we must spend the day on trash duty throughout the Compound for each account."

My father nods. "How many times did she yell your name?"

Jacob doesn't answer. My father bends down toward him, and I swear the boy is about to pee his pants. Father whispers in the boy's ear. With a nod, Jacob flees from us and back to his mother. I hear her say his name in the tone that mothers get. I've heard Sara's voice change that way many times.

"What did you say to him?" I ask.

My father stands, straightens his shirt, and we walk on before he answers. "I told him the Elders were looking at his records, and if he continues to disobey, they would send him North to be a servant."

"Father!" I say.

He doesn't even look at me. "He will listen now. These are the cards we must play to teach the children right and wrong."

"But you're scaring him. How does a child running constitute a warning such as that? Since when is running forbidden? You aren't teaching him. You're threatening him."

Father stops and looks at me. His face is contorted and red, very unusual for the way he's always so composed. I miss his smile. Where is his smile? "I will not have my own daughter questioning my authority in public or in private. You should learn to tame your tongue, Cornelia. It will get you into trouble."

And then, he keeps walking. I inhale and push away my anger before following him like a good little girl. If he can act like this, then I can too.

Thorne's family is already on the beach when we arrive. Sara waves as I walk by, and I smile back at her.

"Cornelia," Father says. He waves me over, and I join him toward the front of the forming crowd.

The head of each family lines up along the edge of the ocean. Silver urns glisten under the sunlight. I know all these people. Sam the grocer. Hank the mill worker. Henry the Healer-in-training. Jane the teacher. There are about sixteen dead to name today. We haven't had a ceremony since the winter.

The matron has already stood up in front of us to begin the service when I see him saunter up. Xenith Taylor is dressed in black, head to toe, and carrying his father's urn from a few months ago. The matron gives him a disapproving look, and then she continues with her ceremonial words.

Xenith catches me staring, and I look away toward the water.

I NEED WATER. I pointlessly run my tongue over the cracks on my lips and reach out for Thorne, but my hand hits the ground. That's when I remember. I'm with the Remnants, and we're running from the Cleaners. My heart races, and I freeze with panic, waiting for the sound of the them: the shrill whirring or chomping, the sound of death and crying. There's nothing.

My head is spinning before I even sit up all the way. There's a hot, thick liquid on my left arm that reminds me of the sand when it's wet and warm.

Where's Thorne?

I survey the empty place. No, not empty—the Trooper who shot me is here. He's dead. Blood seeps from a gaping wound in his head. There are other bodies, too—children and men and women—but Thorne is nowhere near me.

I need to find Thorne.

I stand, a sharp pain piercing through my body, and the sky above me is moving so quickly that the dark clouds seem to dance. I look around as the breeze picks up. The trees billow in the wind and my stomach churns with my surroundings, but I don't dare close my eyes. If I do, I will fall over and never stand again.

There's a pull through the connection, a dull throbbing that's familiar and diluted. It felt that way before—when Thorne was far away and I was pretending to be dead, hiding out with Xenith—and it would seep through despite the block. He's in pain; I can feel that, too—the pressure of worry and anxiety and fear. I've felt it before when my father tortured him, and it's not a forgettable emotion. Thorne must be nearby.

Each step is a thousand knives in my body, but his pain is undeniable. He's here somewhere.

I move slowly, past pools of blood and too many bodies sleeping on the ground. Sleeping. They have to be sleeping. Pretending they are asleep makes this easier, something other than the bloodbath that it was. Sleep is not as final as death. Death that I caused by coming here when the Elders are obviously tracking us. Tracking me.

After a few feet, I pass another dead Trooper. There's a shimmer of metal in his hand. I lean down and notice that he's probably just a little older than me. How did the Elders get to him so young? Where did he come from? Did he have a family?

His eyes are open, bloodshot red with dark brown irises. I pry the gun out of his cold, stiff fingers, which stay in position, still clutching a phantom weapon. I close his eyes before I move away from him and toward the hole in the center of the field, toward where Thorne could be.

Everything is my fault. *Because I killed my mother. Because my father is insane. Because I loved Thorne. Because of the secrets.*

My arm is crimson, and my stomach lumps as I step over a body. The blood from my arm drips on her. Her. A girl that looks younger than me. I step over her like trash.

Because I escaped. Because he followed me.

I am so close to the hole, to where the connection is leading me. It's only a few more steps before I see a man on the ground and hope it's not him. That it's someone else.

Because I am selfish.

I wipe my hands on my tattered pants and cover my eyes with my hand. As if all of this will be gone when I look again. But it isn't. Choices have been made and can't be undone. This field littered with dead is all the proof we need that the Elders are somehow following me. So many people have died for me in this journey. People I can never thank or know or repay.

I bend down to the dead man. I try not to look at his eyes or his shape. Or the color of his hair that matches Thorne's. I look for one thing.

My hands find his neck, and I try to wipe it clean. The blood is dried already, caked to his skin like it never wants to leave his body. Heart racing, I peel it off with my fingernails, and the dried pieces become part of me. His skin is soft, like Thorne's, but cold with death.

I look down, and there is nothing. Just skin: creamy, perfect, white skin. There is no branding. It is not Thorne. I half-cry and half-scream. I'm thrilled that someone else has died who's not Thorne.

It's not Thorne.

But I was still led to a man who isn't Thorne. I still feel the connection pulsing through me. The pressure in my head and the nausea in my stomach tells me that he's alive and nearby. I ease myself back to my feet and start to move away. The ground shifts, bounces. I freeze. Step. Another shift. I lower myself to the ground again, searching for something. I'm not sure what until my fingers find a crevasse. They slide into it, and the ground moves up. It's a door.

I slip my hands under the dead guy's stiff body so I can move him off the door. I push him and scream as my arm stretches and the blood flows. The dead guy has barely moved, but I try again.

Heat rises within me, and everything feels off-centered.

When I'm calm enough to move, I try to push the guy with my legs. I pound and pound at the door. Thorne's name tears through my throat. Again and again it burns my tongue, tasting of desperation and despair. I'm so close to him, yet I can't reach him.

I can't move the guy off the door. He budges a little, but not enough.

I'll never get to Thorne.

I'm going to die out here.

Then I hear voices, and someone pounds back up at me through the door. I yell, but I'm not sure what I say. Exhausted, I curl up on the ground. Noises move under me and around me. Everything is spinning. Green and red and blue whirl in my brain, and I can't separate the colors.

"This is her?" a voice calls.

"She's injured," a different voice says. "Get her inside."

Hands are on me, voices grow around me, everything is fuzzy, and someone says, "You're safe now."

Safe.

"YOU'RE SAFE, NEELY. Open your eyes. It's okay. You're safe." I stare directly into Xenith's cobalt eyes, and get lost in them. It feels as if I just saw him yesterday.

"Take a breath," Xenith says.

I do, and the air fills my lungs quickly. I gasp it in again, fill up with it, and then cough out the air I've craved so much. The last thing I breathed was water.

My hand squeezes his as I inhale, slowly this time. He's staring at me intensely, so innocent and concerned. I keep gasping, even though I can breathe now. It was just a dream. A nightmare.

Xenith strokes my hair. My head is pounding. How long have I been asleep? I'm on Xenith's couch, so that means the plan worked and they saved me. Him and Kai. It worked; I'm dead.

Then I realize I'm holding his hand. I drop it and pull my legs underneath me.

"What time is it?"

"Just after six," he says. He's still sitting on the end of the couch. The chair near me has blankets on it and a stack of books, an empty plate, a cup of water. I look at Xenith. His blond hair is messy, and his clothes are wrinkled. He's been waiting for me to wake up.

"Everything went okay?"

"Perfectly now that you're awake."

His gaze hangs between us. I have to break away, to look somewhere that's not at him, so I look past him toward the wall. "What day is it?"

"Wednesday," he says it like it's supposed to mean something. I shake my head. My hair feels strangely stiff against my neck, and I probably look like a monster.

"How many days are left?"

"Eleven." Xenith taps the side of the couch, a rapid tick tick tick. His hands still for a second, then play with the edge of my blanket. The fabric slides between his slender fingers like water. He drops the cloth when he notices my gaze and clasps his hands together. "Are you hungry? I can make you some breakfast before I go." He moves from the couch and picks up his drink.

"Go where?"

He takes a sip, peering at me over the rim of the cup. "Your ceremony."

"It's today?"

"In an hour."

"My own ceremony?"

"Your father deemed it so. Rumor has it that the Elders are coming."

The Elders are coming here for my ceremony. They never come here.

"That's bad isn't it?"

Xenith shrugs. "It's something."

I look away from him, search across the room for that familiar glass globe with the Old World. I stand slowly, knowing that Xenith is watching me. My legs are like jelly from not moving for so many days, and the first steps I take are a little shaky. My feet are wobbly and the sudden shift between sitting and standing causes the room to be unstable, but my fingers reach out toward the globe, tread over it. I'm going to be there soon.

Xenith is watching me when I look back at him. "Who are they really mourning at the ceremony?" Because it's not me, not when I'm really alive.

"Just some girl," he says quickly.

"Some girl. Where did she come from?" I say. The cup is in his hand, and he's at the counter—the same place he stood the first time I came to his quarters. I expect him to put up a fight with the information, but he doesn't.

"Kai and I had to sneak into the restricted part of the medical ward to switch your body with someone else's, in two hours and without being caught." He jumps up on the edge of his counter, pulls his feet under him, and takes another sip.

I look at him from across the room. "Sounds simple."

"Typical Tuesday night with the boys."

"You have boys?" I say.

He gets quiet. I'm stupid. Of course he doesn't have boys. He's Xenith Taylor. He doesn't have anyone.

He clears his throat. "Not usually."

I avert my eyes for a second and try to think of something to break the small awkward tension between us now. "Kai was helpful?"

Kai was Xenith's idea. Since he's a Healer, he already has direct access to the building. It took a lot of convincing and explaining why he couldn't tell Thorne any of this. Xenith met with him in private, and I don't know what was said, but eventually Kai agreed.

"People are surprising," he says. He stares at me when he speaks. I'm suddenly unsure about all of this. About what I've done and where I am now. Not that I can change it.

"Who was the girl?

"An Unclaimed," he says. He jumps off the counter and tosses his mug into the sink. Xenith picks up a few things as he walks across the room and disappears into his room.

An Unclaimed is in my urn. The Unclaimed are the bodies that have been frozen since the Takeover. They were kept by the Elders. Kai told me once that it was a strange sight, these people who are frozen and waiting to find peace.

"I never understood why the Unclaimed were there. Do you know why the Elders keep them?" I say into the empty room.

Xenith comes back with a black dress shirt and coat in his hand, tosses them on the couch. "Those frozen souls are research—two hundred years of research."

"Research for?"

"Why do you think we don't get sick?" he asks me. I never thought of it. "There are others down there that are more recent than the Takeover. New diseases could develop, and the Elders never want us to fall victim—" He scoffs as he says that word. "—to the same things that destroyed the Old World."

Xenith pulls his shirt off, and I can't help staring. I'm pretty sure my mouth might even be hanging open. His arms are chiseled, abs more perfect than I expected. He keeps talking, as if it's the most normal thing in the world to stand half-naked in front of a girl. In front of me. My cheeks burn. How do I look compared to him, with my rat's nest of hair and wrinkled clothes? I hope my hair isn't as bad as it feels.

He keeps talking, and it's kind of hard for me to think straight.

"Sometimes people wander too close to our barriers. The Troopers take them out on sight and stash them away. After proper research, they are disposed of in the night. They have to do it like this. If everyone knew there were others, the leaders would lose predictability, stability, and order. They have to be consistent no matter the cost."

He slides a tank top over his chest. I should be glad; I shouldn't be looking at him like this. Still, I can't stop.

The shirt covers his chest but accents the lines and curves of his arms, displays the muscles there until I'm aching to be wrapped up in them. I shake my head, force those thoughts away, and bring my attention back to our conversation.

"There was one down there who passed for me?" I ask, keeping any disappointment out of my voice— it shouldn't be there anyway—when he pulls his black dress shirt on.

"Number Fourteen. I knew she was there. My father was the one who found her before he died." Xenith buttons his shirt, his fingers moving deftly over each small piece of metal.

"Who is she?"

He shrugs. "How do I know? Number Fourteen. Just a girl. She looked like you. Same hair. Close to your height. She looked as if she'd drowned, bloated from the water in the same way you would've been."

He stands close to me. His scent is intoxicating, and his hand sweeps a piece of my hair behind my ear. The whole action makes my stomach jump into my chest.

"What about my branding?" The words come out breathless.

Xenith reaches out for my hand, warm fingers pressing against my palm, and pulls me close to him. His fingers trail up my neck and linger over my branding, tracing it as he talks. "Just a few minutes and a little rod that makes the same ink print on the skin. That was all it took. No one looked that closely."

I pull away from him. I can't have him that close to me. "How do you have that?"

He tilts his head and smiles. "I can't reveal all my secrets, now can I?" He steps away from me, plops down on his chair. "Just enjoy being dead."

I'm dead. My ceremony is today. Everyone's saying goodbye to Cornelia Ambrose. Will they be upset that

I'm gone or grateful they were spared from the fever and the Raven's Flesh?

"Which one?" he asks, jolting my thoughts away.

Xenith's across the room now—how does he move like that?—and holds up two ties, one black and one purple. I point to the purple one, and he smiles, tosses the other aside. "Anyway, after the switch—you for her and her for you—I carried you through the back of the medical ward during the night shift's lunch break. They don't care as much. Kai walked out the front door, same as he came in. It was done. Brought you back here." He loops the end of the tie through the top. "Kai questioned my motives. I told him what he wanted to hear." He pulls the fabric tight, his eyes not moving from my face. "Is it straight?"

I reach out and pull the tie a little to the left. Xenith leans into me, his breath warm on my face. He touches my hand before I can move it. Have his eyes always been the color of the ocean?

"Then I gave you the red pill with the white letter and waited through the night for you to come back." He pauses. "And here you are."

We stand there for what feels like hours but is probably only seconds. He removes his hands from mine. Bounces back away from me and dresses in a black jacket.

"You'll wait here for a few days, and then you'll go to the Old World. Only the four of us will know." Xenith spins around in a circle. "How do I look?"

"Four of us?" I say.

He nods, touches my cheek. "You, me, Kai, and Fourteen."

FOURTEEN TIMES I ASK to see Thorne. I can feel him, but it isn't the same. All I feel is his pain. It's masked, like he held some of it back, but it still impacts me. They don't let me go to him.

I'M IN AND OUT of sleep for two more days before they let me see him. He waves at me from the other side of a window. A little ragged, a little bruised, but still the same.

THORNE SITS NEXT TO MY BED and stares at me. He still looks weak to me, but he smiles and puts my mind at ease. Even if I know he's pretending. We're both getting too good at that.

"What happened?" I ask. "Help me up."

Thorne doesn't take my hand. "Doc said you couldn't walk yet. The healing needs a few more hours before you can put weight on your leg."

"I don't care," I say.

Thorne shakes his head. "Be reasonable. You need your strength."

I cross my arms at his gaze. If he's walking around, I should be able to, too. His injuries were worse than mine, and I don't feel bad at all.

"Fine, don't help me."

He doesn't. I manage to get out of the bed on my own and stand up. I don't put a lot of pressure on my right leg, just let it touch the ground and stand on my left. I ease the weight down, and it only hurts a little. I'm standing tall, strong, and on my own. And then it hurts a lot and the pain shoots up my leg, and Thorne catches me when I fall over.

"Damn it, Neely," he says. His words are breathless, and I know catching me hurts him, too. He sits on the side of my makeshift bed. "Did you hurt yourself?"

I shake my head. "I'm fine."

"It's good you bounce back quicker than me."

"So what happened?" I ask after too much silence.

He sighs and rakes his hand through his hair. "The guys from the first day have spoken to me a little. We've all been waiting for you to wake up. They have Healers here who fixed us up. Joe said those attacks happen every few months. He said the same thing about them being quiet for months the other day. So they took a chance and went aboveground to live. They've been up there for a while. Then, all of a sudden, someone spotted a Cleaner, and we came along. Joe said some people think it's connected."

"Who is Joe?" I ask.

"The big guy."

"Joe thinks we brought them?" I don't need an answer. I wondered the same thing when we arrived. It can't be a coincidence.

Thorne shrugs. I clear my throat. "How did you get down here?"

"I got a shot in the stomach. It was bad, Neely. I don't even know how I got here. I know I wasn't far from the entrance when I got shot, and people were coming this way. Maybe I followed them?" He looks at me. "They told me you broke in."

Did I? It's kind of vague in my memory. I remember the dead guy and trying to get him to move off the door. Was that breaking in? It's fuzzy.

"I felt you in pain, like before." I pause, thinking of Xenith and the deal that Thorne doesn't know about. "Thorne, we should probably ta–"

"I see you're up and about this mornin'," a man says. I look toward the door at a short man with gray hair and a beard. He has small, round brown eyes and rosy cheeks, and he withdraws a metal board from the foot of my bed. "You couldn't keep her in the bed?"

Thorne shakes his head. "She's impossible when she wants to do something."

The man chuckles. "I'm Doc," he says. "Everyone here calls me that, so I reckon you should, too."

Doc has this way about him that puts me at ease. Or it would if I let it. He's nice enough, maybe too friendly, but he did save Thorne. And me. He turns the pages on the metal board and writes down something about me.

"Thank you for saving us," I say.

He looks surprised. "You're welcome."

"When can I leave?"

"What she means is how long until she's able to walk on her own?" Thorne corrects me. I hate when he does that. Doc starts to speak.

"No, I mean when can I leave?" I shoot Thorne a look, and he sits back in his seat. I have to get to San Francisco.

Doc takes a breath and puts the metal board back. "I'm not in control of when you leave—that comes from higher up—but your leg should be good soon. We've got some pretty advanced medicinal treatments here. You'll have to keep a cast on it for a few more days, though, just to be sure."

"But I'll be able to walk?"

He runs a hand over his beard and makes a clicking sound with his tongue. "You'll be able to walk."

"So who do I talk to so we can leave? It needs to be soon."

"That'd be me," Big Burly says, lingering in the doorway. "I was waitin' for ya to be ready." He stands next to Doc and looks between Thorne and me. Teapot and Benny are with him, standing silently in the back.

They all look at me like they don't trust me.

"Reckon it's good you're awake. Your boyfriend here was real worried." He clears his throat. "We didn't have much time to talk last time we saw each other. I'm Joe. That," he says, pointing to Teapot, "is Ty."

Doc scoots out of the room in silence.

"Why are y'all here?" Ty says. "We don't get a lot of folks coming through."

"It's the timin' that makes us wonder," Joe says. "It's some strange odds that two strangers arrive in tune with an attack force. Real fishy."

I cross my arms and look to the white-blond boy. "We told Benny."

"We done talked with him and with your boy here. Now I'm askin' you."

We have a stare-off, a battle of wills. Mine is strong, even if it's tired. He reminds me of my father: sly words, a cunning smile, and charm that oozes off him. It will not drown me; I can swim.   .

"We just want to leave," I say.

"It don't work that way," he says. "We survive 'cuz we don't give nothin' without gettin' somethin'. We helped you. Now, surely you can answer this li'l question."

"Xenith Taylor sent word to Cecily. She said you would be nice enough to help us out."

The three men look at me, eyes wide. "I heard 'bout that," Ty says. "Why'd you come out into this world? Whatcha after?"

Thorne looks at me, his eyes sharp and questioning. How much am I going to tell them? Just enough of the truth. "We're going to the Mavericks," I say.

The men shift, suddenly unsure of me and Thorne and our presence. Unsure of Xenith's name. Unsure of everything, perhaps even themselves.

"Them things was chasing you," Benny says. It's the first time he's spoken since he came into the room. His voice is low, and he repeats it, his eyes shifting around the room. "If y'all left the Compound, then they were after you. All our people died 'cuz of you."

"Benny," Ty snaps.

I don't say anything, but I think he's right. I play it my head. The Cleaners found me right after I left the Compound. The fire happened when I was about to leave the Burrows, and then the Cleaners tracked us here to a place they hadn't been to in months. The Elders somehow knew where we were.

"But all them people is gone 'cuz they led the Elders right to us!" Benny yells.

"Benny!" Joe yells back, his face red.

Benny huffs, slams the door against the wall as he stomps out of the room, and we're all quiet. All unsure of what to say. Of what it means. How could they be tracking us?

"We can help you," Joe says. "Get y'all out of El Paso. On to somewhere else. We have a trader truck leavin' soon for 'nother camp west of here. I'll send word that y'all are coming. That's all I can do for ya."

"Thank you," I say.

He nods, and then, "I reckon it was only a matter of time anyway."

Someone screams from down the hall, and it echoes in the silence that has fallen between us. Ty scoots to the doorway and out into the hall. He's back in a matter of seconds, too short to count.

"The baby," he says. "It's time."

Joe runs a hand through his short, cropped hair. He nods his head and exhales. He takes two steps before he looks at Thorne.

"Thank you," he says. And he's gone. The other two follow him out the door, and I can't stop looking at Thorne.

I look at Thorne and remember the woman who fell. He saved her, and now she's having a baby. They both could've died, and now a new life is about to exist.

For the first time, I'm grateful that Thorne is with me. My best friend. The boy I love, real or not. The one who saved that pregnant woman. A life has changed forever. It will never be the same. Not for us and not for Joe and not for that baby.

I take Thorne's hand and feel the steady buzzing between us through the connection. Contentment. We're quiet and still, listening to the noises down the hall. Yelling. Screaming. And, after a long period of silence, crying.

A baby is here because we were here, one that could've died. Or maybe would have never been threatened if we weren't here. A tear falls from my eyes, too. A baby. A single moment of joy in all this terror. Acknowledgment that nothing is as bad as being alone, that life goes on and we must keep fighting.

"Happy birthday," Thorne mutters into the air beside me.

I LOVE THE AIR IN THE AFTERNOON, when all the
placements are finished and everyone has time to do
whatever they want. It's my favorite part of the day
because I get to go to Sara's after lessons. Kai is home
before dinner and Thorne laughs and we are all together.
It's more like before.

I run there, ready to see them and ready to steal
kisses from Thorne. But when I get there today, Sara
and Kai are sitting together, whispering back and
forth. They both look up at me and stop talking. I shift
awkwardly. Ever since Thorne and I started dating
officially, it's been a little weird. I've always been part
of their family, but it was unspoken. I had a place that
didn't need a definition. I was daughter, sister, friend
here. Girlfriend is something else.

"Neely, I'm glad you're here," Sara says. She pats the
seat beside her, and I sit down. Kai and Sara exchange
a look.

"What's going on?" I ask.

Kai plays with the necklace around his neck. Ever
since he cut his hair short for Healer training, he does
that. "Thorne had his test today. He didn't make it."

My heart drops. Thorne's been looking forward to
being a Trader since we were children. As far as jobs

go, it's one of the best ones a person can have—sorting through Old World artifacts for new uses. Thorne's good with people. He's organized, stable, calming. He's everything they look for. How could he fail?

Sara looks older today. I can see the lines deepening under her eyes. "I tried to talk to him, but he said he was fine. You know how he can get," she says. Thorne rarely retreats, rarely hides, so when he does it's serious. "I wanted to warn you."

"Maybe you should talk to him," Kai says.

I meet his gaze. Sara has no idea about our connection, but Kai does. He discovered it when we were ten and Thorne broke his arm. I screamed like I was the one with the broken arm. Kai made us promise not to tell anyone, and we didn't because, even though he was only three years older, Kai knew more than we did.

"Where is he?"

"He said he was getting some air," Kai answers.

Thorne is hidden under the docks, exactly where I expected him to be. We discovered this place when we were little, and we used to come here and watch the fisherboats unload. When we were children, he used tease me about the fish, say he would toss me in with the catches. I poke my head down, and Thorne sends me a weak smile. I take that as an invitation and lower myself next to him. His hand runs circles in the sand, so I reach out and take it in mine.

The connection pulses through us. He's tense, but more than that, he's lost. I've never experienced Thorne this way: confused and deflated. I take a breath at the sensation, at the weight he's carrying around now, at the bleakness. Thorne tries to pull his hand away, but I don't let him. He's always there for me; I can be there for him. We need to be there for each other if this is going to work. I inhale and connect to his emotions. They hang between us, like a thread, and I reel them in. He exhales as some of his pain, frustration, and sadness seep into me. The sudden addition of them is a little overwhelming, but I won't tell him that.

"What do I do?" Thorne asks. His voice is heavy, wary.

I kiss the back of his hand. "I'm sure you'll find something. You're good at everything."

He shakes his head. "That's you. You're the one good at everything, so determined to do what you want."

I sigh. I don't know about that. The one thing I want is to teach, and my father doesn't know that yet. Pursuing that is walking away from the director role. And I don't even think the Elders will allow it.

"If you could spend your days doing anything, what would you do?"

Thorne looks at me for the first time, a wicked smile at the corner of his mouth. I feel his excitement right before his lips press against mine one, two, three times. I have to push him away, but I'm laughing. "Besides that."

"You weren't specific," he says with a laugh. I raise an eyebrow, and he looks back out at the water. "I like the ocean."

I follow his gaze to the gray boats, three of them loaded with fishermen. They haul nets onto the shore, yell undistinguishable words across the deck. "A fisherman?"

"Why not? Those old men tell good stories."

"You don't want to do that." Thorne is more than a fisherman.

"I would do it," he says, and I believe him. The tone of his voice, so certain and determined. It's times like this when I'm reminded why I love him. Thorne is special, amazing, smart. I love teaching, but my fate has already been decided. I'm only delaying it, but Thorne can pick. I don't want him to settle.

"You said anything," he adds. I stare off into the distance. Maybe I can talk to my father, see why he thinks Thorne was passed up. Being the director of the Compound has to matter somehow.

"I meant it," I say. Thorne smiles, but it doesn't reach across his whole face.

I'll ask my father tomorrow.

TOMORROW WE'RE LEAVING WITH some guy named Len, but this morning I get to watch the sun rise. I shouldn't be aboveground, but I've been under it for too many days. Asleep for too long. I had to go outside, to sneak up here just for a second. Colors dance across the sky, over the outline of hollow buildings lined like disfigured teeth. Alternating shades of red, pink, orange, yellow. It's a disarray of perfection and melancholy.

"See that over there?" a child's voice calls from behind me. I look around and tilt my head to listen. "My brother says that's the *real* El Paso."

I shift on my good leg, lean in on the wooden crutch that Doc gave me, and turn to look for Delilah. I have to search for her face in the trees before I see her blonde curls peeking out from behind them. If not for the curls, I wouldn't notice her at all as she's completely masked to blend in with the woods.

"This is the fake one?" I ask her. She walks up behind me. It's only a second before I feel her fingers on the bottom of my neck, reaching toward my branding.

"Did that hurt?" she asks.

"No. I've had it my whole life. It's just there."

"What does it mean?"

169

"Everything." I look back out over the horizon as Delilah stands beside me. "So that's not real?"

She scrunches up her nose and eyes at me. I can see she wants to tell me by the way her face creases and her mouth opens slightly—and then she clamps it shut. "I can't tell ya. We don't do somethin' for nothin'. It's against the rules."

Right. Rules. Survival. I need the info, and I make a decision.

"How about I teach you to read? At least the basics. We only have a day so we can't do much, but I can at least teach you how to spell your name. And you can help me learn about Old El Paso and the Remnants. Deal?"

Then she nods. "All the camps are fake, and we're close enough to the real cities so we can 'member." Delilah steps out toward me into the sun. Under the golden rays of morning, her hair practically shines. Her clothes are brown, black, and green: the perfect colors to hide in.

"Do they teach you that in school?"

She looks confused. "What's school?"

"You know, where you go to learn things. Reading and writing, counting."

She shakes her head and walks around me, bending toward the ground and picking up dirt. "We don't have that. We has stories that the others tell. I can count though. I learned that 'fore."

"How old are you again?"

"Seven." She digs in the ground quickly, pulls out a worm, and stuffs it into a small jar she has in her pocket. It wriggles around the bottom.

"And you can't read anything?" Her shoulders move up in a faint shrug as she slides the container away. "Do you know how to spell your name?"

She shakes her head and wipes her hands off on a leaf. In our silence, she practically fades into the background. I stare out at the real city. The sun's beams bounce off the remains, and it almost looks like it's still glistening, still trying to live.

"I can't wait to learn."

And I can't wait to teach her, to feel like life is normal again.

WE START AFTER BREAKFAST. I ask Delilah for some paper, but she doesn't know what that is, so I explain.

"It's something you can draw on. What do the kids draw on?"

She brings me a piece of a broken wall and shows me how it works. She uses dried berries—or, at least, that's what they look like—and scribbles brownish-red lines on the slick piece of plastic. Then she wipes it away like a chalkboard.

"Are there a lot of these?" I ask, pointing to the small, round berry. She nods.

I teach her how to spell her name first. She already knows what it sounds like, how the letters go together to make a word, but not what the letters look like written out. Her eyes follow my hand as it moves around the board making letters. She doesn't look away until I say the sound of each letter and put them together to form her name.

"That's my name," she says, smiling.

I nod and talk through the sounds of the letters with her. Once she remembers them, I move the board so it rests in front of her. Her small fingers graze mine when she moves for the berries.

"Can I try?" she asks. She copies the letters I wrote. Her hand is shaky, but she gets it on the first try and squeals with excitement.

For the next two hours, I teach her names, and then we start on letters. She finds something else I can write on, something more permanent, and I write out the whole alphabet on a flat piece of white wood. I even teach her the Old World song Sara taught me, the same tune I know so well and sing to myself all too often. It don't know all the words, just a melody and a few lines about holding a hand. Delilah sings it back to me as if she's known it her entire life. The whole day feels simple.

IT'S THE SIMPLE THINGS THAT MATTER, *like when my father leaves me a note. Except today there isn't one. For the last two months, he hasn't left anything for me, and I think maybe one day I will stop waiting for them to return. But I do, and I wait for him all day to say a word to me or come home and he doesn't. I never see him. He's gone before I'm awake and home long after I'm asleep. If he comes home at all.*

I keep hoping that I'll run into him at home, but I haven't and I want to talk to him about Thorne.

This morning, I'm going to see him.

The Compound is alive with morning errands, with trips to the grocer, with teens going to placement and kids going to school. I have an hour before my class this morning with the ten-year-olds.

On Tuesdays, Father usually spends his morning on the docks with the fishermen. They give him an account of their needs, the time spent on the ocean, and the catches they make. When I get there, he's just about to leave. The fishermen are all boarding the boats to head out for the day, and a few of them wave when they see me. I've been here a lot this month to visit Thorne. That's how I know my father is here.

He turns when some of the fishermen call my name and walks toward me.

"Cornelia, why are you here this morning? Come to work with me?"

I shake my head. "To talk with you actually. Do you have a few minutes?"

Father looks at his watch, his eyebrows furrowed. "A few," he says.

I expect him to say something else, to reach out and touch my arm like he used to do, but he doesn't. He barely makes eye contact. His gaze explores the horizon of the beach.

"We really need more security out here," he says stiffly.

I love the beach for that reason exactly. It's the one place where the Elders don't watch us. Where would we go for any sort of freedom in this place?

"Father," I say. He looks down at me, and there's a coldness in his eyes that I don't like. It doesn't fit him. "Are you all right? I haven't seen you."

"I'm fine, Cornelia," he says. "It's been busy."

Father starts walking, and I follow after him, rushing so I can keep up. I should just say why I'm here. He doesn't seem to be in a good mood.

"I wanted to ask if you knew why Thorne was passed up for Trader? He's been studying for that position for years. You know that and encouraged him, so I'm confused."

My father stops suddenly and whips around to look at me. "Is Mr. Bishop complaining about his placement? He chose fisherman, did he not?"

"Only once he failed—"

"And you are here to do what? See if I can overturn the Elders' decision? I do not question them, Cornelia, and neither should you."

Since when? "That's not what I meant."

"You were very clear in what you meant. The Elders have a reason for everything, and it is not up to us to question or seek understanding in their reasons. It's up to us to accept them."

I shake my head. "Are you okay?"

"Perfectly," he says.

I've never heard my father talk that way. He's always been a believer in the Elders, but he's never spoken this way of them. With such a devotion. "Are you sure?"

"Cornelia," he says sharply. "If that boy is leading you to question the Elders or myself as your leader and guidance, then perhaps you should reconsider your stance next to him. The Elders do not ignore threats to life or livelihood. I'd hate to see you led astray."

Tears bite at my eyes. What is going on? This is not my father. He would never talk to me this way. What happened to the father who left me notes and told me stories and laughed so brightly it could fill a room? This can't be just because he's tired.

"I believe you have placement in a few minutes," my father adds. "You shouldn't be late since you only have a little more time left there."

And with that he leaves me. I watch him walk up over the beach, and this deep concern settles inside me. Something is happening, and with every instant that passes, I feel more unsure.

FOR SOMEONE WHO'S ONLY SEVEN, Delilah is more sure about life than most people I know. Probably even more than I know. There's something about her that I like. She's got spunk for someone so young, and that seems to be what keeps the Remnants alive out here. She's mastered A–I already. She knows how to write them and match them with words or people or things I don't understand.

A low-sounding, guttural hum rings through the room. I jump up quickly and knock the chair to the floor. Is that a warning? Is someone here in danger? Delilah laughs. The sound is high and melodic. "That's the lunch bell!"

I slowly follow beside her on my crutch through the darkened tunnels lit by torches along the walls. My leg feels better, but she insists I use the crutch until she gets to the letter "N." I told her she had until dinner, and then I was ditching this thing.

"Real El Paso were one of the first cities destroyed," she says as we walk. "In the story, it smelled like rotten eggs."

The same way the Burrows smelled before the fire reached us. If the Elders destroyed the city and it had that scent, then they really did start the fire. But how?

"How do you know that?" I ask.

"I'm li'l. People say a lot of things when I'm 'round," she says.

We enter a room full of makeshift tables and seats created from half-broken Old World items and tree trunks. It was never like this at home. We ate meals in our own houses, complete with our own real tables and chairs. The Remnants stand in some semi-formed line, but it's not straight and it's more clomped together. We join it at the back of a line of Remnants carrying trays for food. Delilah stands beside me and slides her hand in mine. It's so small. Hard to believe we were all that small once. All that innocence, warmth, and friendliness.

I feel a sudden wave through my stomach and inspect the line. I find Thorne immediately, only a few people in front of us. He smiles at me, and I smile back. He's been with Doc all morning while I was with Delilah.

"Do you love him?" Delilah asks me.

I look down at her and then back at Thorne. "Yes," I say.

Saying it feels right, but once again I wish I knew what the branding was really doing to us. I can't imagine my life without how I feel about him. If it's not real, if it's all manufactured, then what does that mean for me?

"He should sit with us then," she says.

She hands me a tray that's gray and white. There's a large crack down the center, and it's missing a corner. I have to let to go of her hand to take it and balance it with my crutch.

"Out huntin' today, Delilah?" one of the cooks asks her. The woman is thin with bony, pale arms. Her lips are a straight line, and there's no life in her eyes. Even her hair seems to be falling out. She puts some food on Delilah's tray.

"I was trackin' this morning. Found two rabbits," Delilah answers with a giggle.

The cook laughs. It's short and forced, but her faces changes a bit. Gets a little rounder at her smile. "Two? That's more than Miles found. You'll have to tell 'im. That boy hates when you beat 'im!"

Delilah smiles at the woman and leads me through the line to the end where my plate of food awaits. I carry a plate and balance on my crutch as we walk toward the back corner of the room. There's a small, lone table here that's brimming with people. Too many people for such a small table. One of them is an older man with a crooked hat and a bushy black beard.

"That there is Pete," Delilah says. "He knows all about Old Paso." She steps away from me with her plate, and I follow. She puts a hand up to stop me. "Let me go first."

I watch her skip over to the table, all charm and smiles. The people around Pete separate for her and one even gives her his seat. She talks to him silently before every set of eyes at the table drift toward me. My stomach feels sick when she waves me over. Thorne walks up behind me, his breath on my neck.

"Want me to take that?"

"I can do it," I say back.

He looks at me and then follows my gaze to Delilah. "You two having fun?"

"I'm teaching her to spell," I say. Thorne nods. He knows how much I love teaching. "How was Doc?"

"I'm good as new," he smiles.

Delilah calls my name and waves me over. I look at Thorne. "Coming?"

"For what?"

"Some answers," I say. Thorne and I move over to the table across the room.

"You must be Neely. Little Lilah said you was nice," Pete says. He waves and someone moves for us. I lower myself into the newly emptied chair next to Thorne, still warm from the previous man. "You teachin' her how to read and write, so I reckon I'm supposed to tell ya 'bout how we work."

"That was the deal," I say. It comes out a little snappier than I mean it to.

Pete raises an eyebrow. "Whatcha wanna know?" I move the food on my plate around with my fork, bite my lip. He laughs at me, a loud guffawing laugh. "Don't even know the questions!"

A few awkward moments pass us by in silence. What do I want to know? Where do I start? I want to know everything. How they died. What the Old World and the Preservation were really like.

"How do you survive out here?" I ask. Pete shifts in his chair and says a quick word in the Remnant language. Delilah stares at the man until he sighs dramatically. He shoves a bite of the white mush into his mouth. Some of it drips into his big, bushy beard.

"We survive 'cuz they didn't. We know how it works. We use whatever leftover resources we can find from before and build things new. That's how it works if others go 'bove at all."

"How many camps are there?" Thorne asks. I look at him but don't speak. This can be a way for Thorne to learn some of what I know and for both of us to understand some more.

"More than I know I reckon. See, them Elders tried to destroy everythin', but they can't do that. People's always going to survive and adapt. That's all we've done—adapted. 'Course, I reckon it's different everywhere. Who's to say new camps aren't set up every single day? I just know the people we workin' with, and I'm sure it ain't everyone." Pete rips a corner of some bread off with his teeth.

Beside me, Delilah swings her legs in her chair while she eats her white mush. She looks from me to

Pete and back again. I pick at the peas on my plate, then stuff a few into my mouth. They taste like nothing.

"San Francisco is the only place where they live above and below. The Mavericks took it way back durin' the Preservation after the Elders abandoned it 'cuz of the earthshakes. It's some kind of headquarters, a place they run things from, I reckon. None of us goes there."

I shake my head and dip my bread into the mush. I chew it quickly so I don't have to taste it. "Why do the Elders tell us everything is dead? It's not dead."

Pete gawks at me, his eyes shifting between amused and frustrated. He opens his mouth, shuts it, opens it again. "There's a war between us and 'em. You think the war ended with the Preservation? The Elders want all the land, and they want all of us off it. We're nothing to them. So the Cleaners come out ev'ry few months and suck the people out. Right after they toss somethin' over them. A bomb, a poison, somethin'. Sometimes its stuff that's been out in the Old World forever, but the Elders are waitin' for the right time to use it up. Best way to get rid of vermin is to keep sprayin' for bugs."

The fire. That's how they started it. They'd already had it in the Burrows, and they activated it to kill me. They really did all die because of me. I lower my fork, no longer hungry. So many people are dead. Someone walks by and speaks to Pete. He stops talking to me and answers the other woman in the Remnant language.

"Where was I?" Pete asks, clearing his throat and taking a long swig of water. "The network keeps us informed. We share everythin' with most of the other camps because it's all we got. Goods, food, news, deaths. Got some real smart people in other places, too, done rigged up some of that technology that destroyed the Old World. We got it now ourselves somehow, and we use it."

"Like the cars and guns?" Thorne asks.

He nods. "We got to be careful. That's why we call ourselves El Paso, even though it's right over yonder. If they think that's where we is, that's where they gonna go. It's safety. We move around. This is just one of our places in this area."

"Tell her 'bout San Francisco," one of the guys with us says.

Pete eyes us both suspiciously and pushes his plate toward the center of the table. "The Elders lived there 'fore the ravens, 'fore the States fell. They were three rich men who wanted the States to be a good place again, who wanted to flourish 'emselves. They'd been looking for a way to live forever when Raven's Flesh happened."

"No one can live forever," Thorne says. His tone is completely even, but I can tell that he's struggling. No one can live forever, but maybe they have succeeded.

"So you think," Pete says. "The Three had lots of scientists, and after the cure, one scientist realized them others was lyin'. He tried to make it better. That's what you have to do when you realize somethin' isn't what you think it is."

I feel off-balance as Thorne listens, his face twisted in confusion. He looks at me and sees my lack of surprise, which makes him more confused.

"What did the one scientist do?" I ask Pete.

"He had two sons and a daughter in a Compound. Story goes that he saved one of them, and they started the Mavericks. The other son stayed in the Compound, and we never heard what happened to him. The girl was a spy, relayin' information to her father." Pete stops just long enough to eat his food. That must be Xenith's family. He told me that they started the Mavericks. This whole time he's been connected to the outside in some way.

"In the Old World, everyone thought San Francisco would break apart—all them earthshakes they had at the end—but it's there still." Pete looks between us. "The Mavericks are there. They're good people. Saved a lot of lives. Gotta know how to find 'em though 'cause they're on the move a lot."

"Is that how the Elders haven't found them?"

Pete pauses, and a smile spreads across his face. "The Elders are always lookin' but they don't build on this side of the map anymore. They send the Cleaners sometimes, but we're all careful. They believe all of it's dead, but really, all of it's full of Remnants trying to rebuild."

I don't think that's what the Elders believe at all. I think they are waiting.

I WAIT AS LONG AS I CAN *before I have to go visit my father at headquarters. This isn't a pleasure trip. I need his signature so I can keep participating in teaching lessons to the younger kids. At this point, everyone my age is doing the thing they will do forever. I don't want to do anything forever, especially not what they've assigned for me.*

Director.

I've known all year, all my life, what my fate would be when I turned eighteen: Assistant Director Cornelia Ambrose. It's the one thing I don't want, but I'll never be able to avoid it, not entirely. This is a delay tactic. We haven't been on the best of terms, but it's all I have. I'm still his daughter, and that has to count for something.

The hallways here always put me on edge. I don't like being able to see myself in the floor, to hear my shoes as I walk. The walls are so white and the lights too bright. I feel like I'm out of place, and everyone is watching me contaminate the space. Plus, I know what's underneath the shiny layers of tile and laminate: the dead. We keep them in the basement until it's time for the ceremony we have four times a year. Months and months, the dead wait below the floors. It's creepy.

Father's office is in the far eastern corner of headquarters, so I have to pass by the Healer unit and the Troopers station before I make it to his quarters. I try to block out what lies beneath me and beside me.

"Cornelia," Mary Jenks says. She's my father's assistant, though I'm not sure what she assists him with. She's a short woman with blonde hair cut to her shoulders, and she's always wearing black dresses and shiny shoes.

"I'm here for my father."

Mary flips the papers on her clipboard, her brow furrowing. "You're not on his schedule."

I put on my best innocent, doting daughter face. "He's so busy, I know, but it should only be a minute."

She smiles at me, eyes darting around before landing on me. "He should be back soon. You can sit in his office if you'd like."

I thank her and go inside. My father's office is dark. The walls are brown here, unlike the rest of headquarters. One bookshelf covers the back wall of the room, filled with the history of the Compound by ledgers from previous directors. There's a couch the color of the tide and two chairs that are near his massive, disheveled desk. If not for the floors that still shine under my feet, I wouldn't recognize the place.

I take a seat in my father's chair behind the desk. When I was little girl, it made him look so big and powerful. Now, sitting here makes me anxious. I don't want this life. This job. It's changing him, and I don't want that either. I look down to his desk and see a ledger open on the surface. I shouldn't—I know I shouldn't—but I look at it.

The script is tiny, hard to read. I have to squint to make out the small letters. The top is dated 2336. My great-grandfather was the director then, in our two hundred and twentieth year of Preservation.

5th day of March, 2336

Another survivor found his way to the barriers today. Where are they coming from? This is the third one in a month. The Elders have declared a new way to prevent them. They will scour the Old World for more and stop them before they get to us, clean the world of what remains. This world needs more perfection, so they tell me. We need to keep the Raven's Flesh at bay.

Ever since Nicholas Taylor, the Elders have been on edge, more determined to stop any malicious activity. I must agree that the timing is too suspicious, as it was only a month ago I wrote of his confrontation with me. The Elders wanted to remove his family, but in the end, they didn't. I can't blame them for wanting to remove Nicholas. The Taylor line has always questioned too many things. It is the cause of their deaths far too often, and it all started with the scientist in the Preservation.

Perhaps I should have been more cautious with him, but he was a good friend to me, someone I trusted. He claimed to have proof—proof!—that the Elders were up to something unkindly. That they could not be trusted. As a friend, I heard him out, but it all seemed to be the ramblings of a madman, and as a servant of the Elders, I did as they commanded.

I was told to end the threat. I did so with remorse at the loss of another founding family. I discovered the proof he spoke of, and I hope it is safely kept away. The Taylors have always been and will always be a threat to our life as long as they continue to exist within our walls.

If anyone in the Compound learns of the world that exists out there, centuries of work will be lost, and we will be no better than those who were destroyed. We were saved for a purpose. No one must ever know the truth. Neither the truth beyond the barrier nor the truth within.

During our meeting after his death, the Elders used the words "experimental ultimate compliance." I'm not certain exactly what that means, but they say I will be the first. It's a new technique to save those, like the late Nicholas Taylor, who question things they should not. I explained that I believed our people to be satisfied with our way of life, completely, but they disagree.

Apparently, I am special. The Elders tried to get me to understand, but I'm not completely clear on their meaning. Whatever they are looking for among the survivors, I have it. I am honored to set my family apart. Unlike Nicholas Taylor, I trust in them completely.

My mind is reeling, and I jump when I hear my father's voice just outside. I dive toward the chair on the other side of his desk and stare up at him when he steps in the door. My heart pounds inside my chest. Can he hear it?

"Cornelia, this is a surprise," he says. "Your face looks pale."

I shake my head as he walks toward his desk.

"I need you to sign this," I say quickly. The words tumble over each other, and I thrust the paper at him. There is life outside.

He raises an eyebrow in my direction and takes it from my hand. He pauses as he lowers himself into his chair and glances from the open book to me. He closes it, then reads the paper. The walls suddenly feel smaller, like they're pushing in on me.

"I wanted to speak with you about this. It's my wish that you should start training for your future," he says. "It's time to move on from this."

Survivors. Outsiders. Barriers. Old World. The truth. What does it all mean? Are there people outside? Life? There's more than just the Compound. There is life outside.

"Cornelia," he says. I look up at him. I can't believe they've lied to us.

"Actually, I'm not feeling well," I say. I move from the chair and toward the door.

My father lays the paper on top of the book. I stare at it, at the red siding and the words inside. Outside.

"You should go to the Healers on your way out," he says.

I nod and say nothing else.

There is life outside.

My feet chime against the floor as I run down the hall and past the Healers. Past the Troopers. Out the door.

THORNE WATCHES FROM THE door while Delilah and I go over the rest of alphabet. She's mastered all the way to "N," just like she said she would. I feel Thorne's eyes on me, and then irritation seeps through our connection. Not at me, but at the things we learned earlier.

"We need to talk," he says when I meet his gaze.

I look at Delilah, who smiles up at me while copying my "P." "You keep practicing. We'll be back," I say to her.

Thorne jumps to his feet and is standing by the door before I finish the sentence. He leads me through the door and takes my hand. The storm of our connection heightens. We move down the underground corridors under the pale light of lamps and torches, drifting through hushed conversations under the dim lights. A few people stop talking and look at us like the intruders we are. The tension Thorne's feeling flows into me and makes my own muscles tighten

We finally stop in a small, circular room.

"What is this?"

Thorne pulls a torch off the wall, lighting up the room. "Joe brought me here this morning. We were talking through some ideas to get Remnants actively involved in safety patrols and productivity." He pauses. "He showed me this."

He shines the light on the floor, and below my feet is the symbol of the twin branding, the same one we have on our necks. Dozens of them. Painted in the same colors that Delilah's been using on her letters. Under them are names. Emma – Laura: bodies. Jonathon – Samuel: moving. Hannah – David: thoughts. I glance over as many as I can see in the low light, and finally I see, Cecily – Deanna: dreams.

I kneel and touch the writing on the ground. "What is this?"

"Joe said the Mavericks had operations here decades ago, and the scientist's family was spying for them. These were the twins born that decade."

Why would they write the names here? What's that other word mean? I read them again, and the pieces start to form in my head.

"The Elders were looking for clues with the twins, something special like Cecily and Deanna," I say. A connection. Dreams. Cecily and Deanna shared dreams. This is a map of the twins the Mavericks were aware of and what they could do.

Thorne moves across the room, taking the light of the torch with him. I follow him over to a desk, and he points to a paper with writing I don't know. It must be from the Remnants. "Joe said the spy informed them of the twins' birth and of any abilities or reactions. I guess the Mavericks thought everything would be obvious."

Whatever the Elders are after, they are willing to go through a lot to find it. "If the Elders were really trying to obtain immortality, why would they need a special trait? How would they get that from twins?"

"I don't know," Thorne says, running a hand through his hair. "All of this is a little overwhelming. I don't want to believe it, but I can't not believe it. If what Pete said is true, all of that, then this is way bigger than our Compound. It's bigger than us."

"And what are they really after?"

Silence falls between us. I look around the small room. The walls are made of dirt and stone with more of the markings in the familiar berry ink. I wish I could read it, figure out what it meant.

"It's Xenith's family, isn't it?" Thorne asks suddenly. "They're the spies. You said his family started the Mavericks, but really, they helped start everything."

I nod. "And we're going to help end it."

Thorne is quiet again. Then, "I've been thinking. The Benny kid was right. The Elders know we're here, and every second we stay, we put them all in more danger."

"I know," I say. I've thought it, too. "We have to find whatever they're looking for and keep the Elders from getting it."

"It's all connected. This proves you were right all along." Thorne meets my eyes, and I know he wishes he didn't have to say that. That he wishes I was wrong because that would mean none of these dangers exist. That the possibility of our relationship being manufactured didn't exist. We can wish all we want, but I know neither of us will be content with the lies. Not now.

If this is the truth, or leading us to the truth, then nothing is what it seems. Not the Elders, the Remnants, our lives, or even us. My father was only the beginning.

MY FATHER FELL ASLEEP ON THE COUCH, papers spread across the floor and himself and the kitchen. Asleep, he looks so much like who he had been a few months ago that I almost feel bad for avoiding him. Ever since I read that journal in his office, I haven't quite known what to say or how to act. Everything is different now.

It's crazy, and that's what I keep telling myself, but it feels right. Like a missing piece has been put back into place. It's been three hundred years. Of course there's life outside. And if the Elders are trying to stop it from coming in, then it's no wonder they aren't involved in our lives here. They're trying to be everywhere. The question I can't understand is why no one asks about the Old World. Hasn't anyone else wondered?

I stare at my father and the papers littered across our house. I should walk away, go back to bed, and pretend I never saw them. But what if there's more information? What's the outside like, and why is it a secret? Why would the Elders lie?

I start in the kitchen, furthest away from him and the easiest place to lie about should he wake up. I fill a mug with water and set it on the table. My cover. I was thirsty. Without another second of thinking, I leaf through the papers. My heart starts pounding, but I focus on the words.

At first, it's nothing except procedures and rules and bylaws. Things I've known all my life, but it looks like the Elders want to change a few of them. Phrases are crossed out and replaced with red lines and messy handwriting. The slightly curved, thin letters are the closest I've ever been to seeing the Elders.

The only thing remotely interesting I see is one line: THIS WILL PROVE USEFUL FOR THE LARGE MOVEMENT IN THE FUTURE.

But there are no context clues as to what that means exactly.

Time passes. Occasionally, my father moves on the couch, and I freeze in place, afraid to breathe. He always goes back to sleep, and I continue reading until my eyes hurt. Until I work my way off the table and am nestled on the living room floor.

There's nothing here. This is all a waste of time.

I throw the pages down, and then I see my name.

This part of the page isn't typed; it's handwritten in the Elders' writing.

CORNELIA AMBROSE IS THE PLAN.

I reread the line, and a knot forms in my stomach. What plan? Why me? I have nothing they could want. The rest of the page is useless. It's scientific words that might as well be another language. I'm the plan for what? My eyes scan the page, and at the bottom, I notice a four. This is page four.

I search through the stack on the floor and find the rest of the pages. They are out of order now, but I can't worry about that, about what he'll do or say, in the morning. Right now, reading this information this is more important.

Starting at page one, the notes outline an experiment from years ago that the Elders started at the formation of the Compounds with the branding. The details are very direct and offer no explanation or back information.

THE BRANDING PROVES AN EFFICIENT TOOL IN KEEPING QUESTIONS AT BAY; TEST SUBJECTS ARE NOT INJURED BUT ARE OPEN TO WHATEVER IS BEING TOLD. THEY THINK FOR THEMSELVES AND STILL MAKE DECISIONS, BUT IN A CONTROLLED ENVIRONMENT, THE DECISIONS ARE INTENTIONALLY OPTION A OR OPTION B. THERE IS NO OPTION C, NO DEVIATION. THIS WILL BE USEFUL IN THE FUTURE.

The branding does something to everyone who has it. All of the people in the Compound. It stops them from asking questions, from seeking anything beyond what they are given. That explains why no one has ever wondered about the Old World: there's no reason to wonder.

I turn the pages and keep reading. It's more of the same, outlining people who were test subjects before the Preservation and their reactions to the branding. How they altered it so it wasn't noticeable to the person that they were being forced to do something they didn't necessarily want to do.

The Elders manipulated genes together, creating marriages that would produce the most genetically appropriate children for the Elders' needs, and this leads the next page to twins.

THE ETERNITY SOUGHT IS TO BE FOUND. TWO PEOPLE BORN OF ONE OFFERS THE BEST OPPORTUNITY TO EXAMINE GENETIC SPLICING. THE STUDY OF THE WAY A CELL FORMS AND DEVELOPS CAN BE IMITATED IF THE TESTING IS STARTED FROM CONCEPTION.

IDENTICAL TWINS ARE THE IDEAL STUDY SUBJECT, THE MOST LIKE CLONES THAT THE UNIVERSE CAN CREATE. THESE TWO HALVES ARE STRONGER THAN ONE WHOLE; IN STUDYING THEM CLOSELY AND EXPERIMENTING WITH DATA COLLECTED, THEREIN LIES THE POTENTIAL TO LIVE FOREVER—EITHER ON ONE'S OWN ACCORD OR, SHOULD THE SEARCH FOR TRUE IMMORTALITY FAIL, IN A REPLICATED FASHION. THE PROMISE OF STRENGTH FOUND WITHIN FRATERNAL TWINS IS NOT TO BE OVERLOOKED. WHILE THEY DO NOT POSSESS THE QUALITIES OF ETERNITY, THEY COULD BE THE KEY TO SURVIVAL IN STRENGTH, SKILL, AND OTHER REASONING, AS THE BOND COULD BE MADE UNBREAKABLE IN ALL CIRCUMSTANCES. PERHAPS ALSO DEATH.

The Elders were studying twins? They wanted to live forever? To prolong life and rebuild themselves? Why would someone want that? How could they do this? What happened to all the twins? But there are no answers on the pages. Only more disturbing facts and experiments outlined. Test subjects with no names.

Between the branding and the twins, I can't shake the feeling that the Elders are up to something incredibly dangerous. I toss the paper down and scan the last one. The one with my name on it.

It talks more about twins before it mentions me.

EXPERIMENTS ARE CONCLUSIVE. THE TWINS WHO RECEIVE THE TWIN BRANDING ARE NOT ALTERED IN THE SAME WAY AS OTHERS. THEY HAVE NO INHIBITION WITH FREE WILL, AS THE OTHERS, BUT HAVE SOMETHING MORE POWERFUL THAT COULD DESTROY ALL THAT HAS BEEN BUILT. THIS IS AN UNFORESEEN CONSEQUENCE. IT SHALL BE REMEDIED AND STOPPED.

I think about the other people in the Compound. Thorne and I are the only ones here with the twin branding. There are no others. Is this what they did—removed twins?

THE TRUE IDENTITY OF CORNELIA AMBROSE LEAVES MANY QUESTIONS, AND TO START, WE MUST DETERMINE HOW THE TWIN BRANDING HAS CLAIMED HER AND THORNE BISHOP. LIV TAYLOR WILL EXECUTE THE EXPERIMENT.

The next entry says, CORNELIA AMBROSE FAILED. That's the end.

I lower the page back to the floor and close my eyes. The room spins, from exhaustion or confusion, and I realize that the life I know is completely false. There's nothing here that's my own. The Old World does exist. The Elders are manipulating everyone, lying to everyone, and no one even knows it's a possibility.

And if they are lying about all this, what else are they lying about?

I pull myself up off the floor and move toward my father. When I look down at him, he doesn't look calm, like himself, anymore. He looks tortured. The Elders have betrayed him, used him, and he has no idea. I take my father's hand, and even though he's asleep, I'm almost positive he squeezes it.

DELILAH SQUEEZES MY HAND tighter as another call for lights out sounds around us. Her board full of letters is completely finished. It's half her size. Some of the letters are big and some are small. They're all crooked, but that doesn't matter. The point is, I taught her that. I taught her something lasting.

"Will I see you again?" Delilah asks me. The warning call fades through the camp, but I think another one only follows it.

"We're leaving at dawn," I say. I don't look at her. I can't look at her because she melts me.

She digs in her pocket with her free hand and pulls out a small, folded piece of paper from a book. The words on it are typed and perfectly spaced on one side.

"I wrote a note for you," she says. She kisses my cheek quickly and whispers "I love you" in my ear. Another bell echoes, and Delilah pulls her hand from my own. I smile and look down at the paper. There, written in the margins, is her name spelled in crooked letters, and the word thanks, but the "N" is missing.

IN MY DREAM, I'M DROWNING. It's the same feeling of the water surrounding me and pulling me under. I'm relaxed and devastated all at once. I move my legs, my feet, my hands. I try to swim. Try to kick. Try to scream. There's only more water. Only more water filling up my lungs.

His face is the last thing I see—Xenith's—and he's telling me words that I can't hear.

"Neely, wake up," Thorne says, his voice tired. He keeps shaking me, pushing on my shoulders, his gruff voice calling my name in my ear. "You're dreaming again."

I open my eyes to find Thorne staring down at me. "You okay? That was intense. What were you dreaming about?"

I shake my head. "It's nothing. I'm okay." He reaches out for my hand, but I don't take it. His shoulders tense and he turns his back to me, and I know he's waiting for me tell him that I'm scared. But I can't say it, so I stare at the ceiling in the darkness and wonder when all of this will end and I will wake up.

"NEELY, WAKE UP," Xenith whispers in my ear. He shakes me, and I jerk at his touch and sit up, panting. His blue eyes peer back at me. "You were dreaming again. You were yelling his name."

I pull my legs in toward my chest and rest my chin on my knees. "I keep having the dream."

"The drowning one?"

I nod. "I keep feeling it. All of this is going to come crashing down on us, Xenith, and then what?"

"It won't."

A pause. "I don't think I can do this."

"You can."

"Not without Thorne," I whisper.

Xenith sighs heavily. His arm is too close to mine. His chest is too bare and his body too warm, so I force myself not to look at him. "You have to. You're going to destroy the blockade I built if you keep calling out to him. It will only stop so much from getting through to him in the connection."

I nod silently. Xenith gave me an injection right into the branding that numbs a connection, like putting it to sleep temporarily. If I use it too much, it will break. He's never done it before, so we're not sure how long it will work.

"I feel like the wrong girl for this."

Xenith brushes a piece of my auburn hair behind my ear. His gaze is so intense on me that I can't look anywhere else.

"You aren't," he says.

I stare at him. Four days together and I still can't figure him out at all.

"You have me. You can call on me if you need me."

"I know."

"I'm right here. I'll be right here," he says, his voice as deep and dark as the night around me. He doesn't leave until I'm asleep.

THE MORNING AIR IS MOIST with humidity. Joe and Benny stand next to us, Joe with his arms crossed over his chest and his hair ruffled from sleep. Or lack of sleep. Benny stands with him, but neither say much to us as we wait in the silence. I expect something to happen. Noise or crickets or birds. There's nothing aside from breathing and the slight rustle of the wind.

Thorne won't look at me. He hasn't met my eyes since we woke up, and he's blocking whatever it is he's feeling. Where did he learn to do that so well? A month ago Thorne would've never hid anything from me, but I wouldn't have either. Yesterday we seemed to be in a good place, like we were on the same journey. Today? Today it feels like yesterday didn't happen. We are further apart than ever.

The sound of a gunshot echoes in the air. I jump. It has to be a Trooper coming back for us, but there's no sign of movement. No whistling whir of the Cleaners, and Joe doesn't look alarmed. Just down the road, a vehicle moves toward us. As it gets closer, the sea-green door of the truck stands out against the dark blue of the rest. It jerks and sputters before stopping.

A man jumps out, hugs Benny, and shakes hands with Joe. They talk back and forth in the Remnant language, and I pick up a few words of it here and there but not enough to completely understand. Thorne and I stand there in awkward silence, unsure what to say. The new man is short and scrawny, dirty. His hair is gray and pointing in all directions. I notice one of his teeth is missing when he speaks with Joe. He nods at us.

"This is Len," Joe says. "He's goin' to a camp in Phoenix for a delivery. He'll take you with him."

That's all that's said about it. Joe says goodbye to Thorne and thanks him for all of his help. Thorne was always better at people than me. When he turns to me, he simply says, "Be safe." Then he steps back and nods at us. "Best of luck to you both."

"And to you," Thorne says. "Good luck with the baby."

Joe smiles at us, beaming at the mention of the baby.

Benny holds out a hand to Thorne, who shakes it. Then he snaps his fingers and digs around in his pocket. "Delilah wanted me to give this to you," he says, reaching out to me. He opens his hand and drops a small green band into my palm. It's thin, no bigger than a piece of wire, and made out of some sort of plastic. I saw her with this on her wrist, so I slide it onto mine as well.

"Thank you," I say.

He nods, and then we watch him and Joe disappear underground. Len stretches behind us and lets out a groan.

"Reckon we should get going. Can't stay in one place too long. There's a seat in the back the girl can probably fit in. She's small enough."

I maneuver around the front seat and squish my feet up in the cramped space of the back. I exhale, grabbing the side before the truck starts to move forward.

"What's your names?" Len asks after we've barely started going.

Thorne says his name first and doesn't offer mine. In the silence, I tell him.

"Them are weird ones. Lots of weird ones nowadays," Len says. "Hope you don't mind the music. It's a long drive."

WE'VE BEEN DRIVING FOREVER. Len stops a lot, dropping things off from the back of his truck to people who appear out of the trees, out of the ground, out of nowhere. We stay in the truck and don't move when he makes stops. He doesn't want anyone to see us.

Len isn't so bad. He likes to sing loudly while he drives to some funny song called a *show tune*. My leg is cramped up in the back seat, and it reminds me of the safehouse. Thorne says something to Len that I can't really hear because of the music. Whatever the question, the response is a scowl and a snort.

We're silent again. The bump of the truck on the road and the rhythm of some lady's voice fill the air. We move on that way, none of us wanting to be where we are, for the next hour of our trip.

I listen to the girl sing about freedom. The music stops sounding so strange after that.

THORNE'S HEAD RESTS AGAINST the window, slightly bobbing as we move. We're about four hours into the eleven-hour drive, with no more stops scheduled until we're there, when Len finally turns off the music. Thorne's not asleep, but he's quiet. I'm quiet, too, feeling the hours slip away from me. Eighteen days from my deadline and we're not there yet. The pressure is starting to grow.

Len groans and hangs a hand out the window; the wind rushes back into my face. "You two sure are a silent pair," he says.

"It's better that way," I say after it becomes obvious Thorne isn't going to speak.

He laughs. "I used to think so, too. When I was a kid, I never said anything to anyone. I just walked around with a dazed look on my face and tried to figure it all out."

"Figure what out?" Thorne asks.

Len looks at him with a smile. "Exactly." I can't see Thorne's face, but I can imagine it, furrowed and hinted with frustration. He hates answers like that. I should know. Len chuckles. "Everything, you know? It was all a mystery. This world is so full of things that a little kid can't understand. It's not right, the way we live."

"You've got it better than some," I say. I think of the ones who died in the Burrows. Of Delilah. I turn the little piece of green plastic around my wrist.

"I reckon," he says. He looks at me through the rearview mirror. "I never said anything. Not 'til I was five. My parents and brothers thought I was a little off, but then I opened my mouth and said a whole sentence. A few of them. Nothin's stopped me from talking since."

Thorne laughs. It's light and half-pretend, but it makes me smile. I want him to laugh again like he used to. I need it to feel like it did before everything happened. I know he's just as lost as I am, and that's all because of me. I want him to find himself again. Maybe when he does, I can, too.

"What business do you have in Phoenix? There ain't much there anymore," Len says.

Thorne looks at me through the side mirror. I feel his question just as loudly as I hear Len's.

"Just passing through."

We don't have a plan, only a dot on a map and the memory of Xenith telling me it's off the road. Telling me I'll know it when I see it. But I'm not even sure what I'm looking for. "A place you have to stop. It's part of history," was all he'd said.

Len grunts back. If he knows I'm lying, that I have no plan, he doesn't say it. He simply nods his head in reply. I look out the window to evade any more glances.

XENITH AVOIDS MY GLANCES and ignores me when I talk. It's been like this for days. He barely looks up. We were paired up to complete a presentation for our Old World history class. By "paired up," I mean I volunteered to work with him. Since his mom died a couple months ago, no one else has really wanted to be near him. Thorne wasn't happy when I raised my hand, but it's not fair. Xenith never asked to be different. Thorne and I should understand different more than anyone.

I stare at Xenith while he scribbles on some paper in black ink. Our project is to outline the movement of Raven's Flesh. Each group has a different aspect of history to explore. From life before to destruction to the disease and the Preservation to the Compounds. We have the progression of the disease.

"Why are you looking at me like that?" Xenith asks.

"Like what?"

"Like I'm going to break."

"Your mom just died—"

"It's been two months. I'm fine."

"You can talk to me, Xenith. I'm your friend."

"Really?"

"Yes. I always have been."

"Neely, everyone you know tells you stay away from me. Maybe you should. Maybe I'm dangerous."

"Please." I roll my eyes. By "everyone" he means Thorne, and that's because they don't like each other. Though his closeness is odd. I can smell him, mint and musk all rolled together. I've never noticed it before.

"So, Raven's Flesh..." Xenith pulls away. He slaps a picture of the sun on the map we're making. The sun represents the heat of the fever. "It manifested in humans like a common cold—sniffles, coughs, warm temperatures, fatigue, nausea—and within hours, the skin started to change."

I write as he speaks, listing each of the symptoms out on the page. "Seems like a horrible thing." I say. Xenith only huffs. "What?"

"Nothing."

"You don't think it's horrible?"

He avoids my question. "Then they found a cure, the Solution." He picks up the plus sign picture. "Which changed those with the Raven's Flesh to become flesh-craving hunters. Book says the whole thing was an unexplainable accident."

"Xenith—"

He huffs. "Can we just do our project?"

"No," I say. I reach out my hand to cover his. "What's going on?"

He pauses, looks at my hand. "Maybe I don't believe what everyone tells me to believe."

I jerk my hand away and cross my arms over my chest. "Like I do?"

"Yes, just like that," he says. He leans in to me. "Maybe I care about the truth."

"This is the truth."

We stare at each other. For fourteen years, I've defended Xenith. Partly because I saw how lonely he was, how sad. Even more because of this side of him— this piece that questions everything. It's only grown since his mom died, like somehow her death rooted him in the certainty that everything else isn't what it seems.

"Everything okay here?" A Trooper stops by us, staring at the papers spread across the table.

Xenith doesn't look away from me. "It is. We're just having a little debate about the best way to do this." He looks up at the Trooper. "Red or blue paint?"

The Trooper nods and walks away without a response. I take a breath and stare blankly at the project.

"You should be careful what you say. It could get you into trouble."

"Trouble's in my blood," Xenith says.

"What's going on with you two?" Thorne asks. Xenith nods toward him and leaves me at the gravel corner of the courtyard.

"He's just a friend, Thorne," I say. The words taste a little bitter around Thorne. He'll never get it.

We take a couple steps. "I don't like the way he looks at you."

I move to stand in front of Thorne so that he has to look at me. "How's that?"

"Like he knows your secret," Thorne says. He frowns. "You haven't told him about us, have you?"

We start walking again, rocks crunching under our feet. We made a deal that we'd keep our connection a secret. I hadn't broken it yet, and I didn't plan to. "I wouldn't."

Thorne nods, and we walk down the road in silence.

WE'RE STILL ON THE ROAD, desert and sun all around us. The sound of Thorne's laugh drifts back to me. I keep my head down. I don't want to be the reason he stops.

"No way that happened," Thorne says, amusement flickering in his voice.

"I swear to you it did. Hung right there on the rope, britches clear down to his head," Len says.

His chuckle fills me with warmth and something that's too close to hope for comfort. I lean up closer to the seat so I can hear it better. It's the quiet kind that keeps coming softly when you want to stop, but you can't yet because the memory of it continues to play on.

"Yer awake," Len says, smiling. Thorne turns to look at me, and his smile fades, taking away whatever hope was forming within me. When did I become the person who makes him frown? Why is he so mad at me? I say hi lamely. Len chuckles at it; Thorne just glances away.

"Perfect timin', too. We gotta stop," Len says. "We've got a couple more hours. Get out and stretch them legs."

Thorne opens his door and jumps down. He doesn't hold the door open for me. I try to reach him through our connection, but there's nothing. I just wish he would yell at me and get it over with. I push my way out and stumble when my feet are solidly on the ground. Thorne's back is to me, but I feel his irritation come through the connection in short snaps of tingles.

"What? What did I do?" I ask. My voice is a little louder than I intend.

He shakes his head at me. "If you have to ask, then nothing. Never mind. You did absolutely nothing."

"Thorne Bishop!" I yell, stalking after him across the dirt. "What the does that mean? Tell me something here."

He turns back around, and I wish he hadn't. The look he has is so unfamiliar and cold that it makes me hurt in every cell of my being.

"What did you do?" Thorne says back. He's yelling without raising his voice, and it's the same tone Sara got when we were children. It's worse than screaming. I can handle screaming. I can't handle pain and disappointment. Not from him.

"What happened with Xenith?" he asks.

There's a lump in my throat that I can't swallow away as much as I try.

"I know something happened." His voice is a little lower than before. More pained. He looks at me, waiting. "Why do you keep calling out his name in your sleep?" he asks, raising his voice.

I blank. I didn't know I was. "I don't mean anything."

"Every time you close your eyes, it's like he's here. Last night you called for him, and I came and you kissed me, Neely. You kissed me thinking I was him, and I felt how much you..." He pauses, looks away from me. He doesn't have to tell me what he felt last night because I remember it. The curiosity of Xenith when I wasn't connected to Thorne. How much I wondered what it would be like to kiss someone else. "And earlier in the truck, you cried out his name. You aren't telling me something, and I want to know what it is. We said no more secrets."

"There's nothing to tell you, Thorne."

He shakes his head. "I saw the book, Neely."

I shake mine back, confused.

Thorne pulls my pack out of my hand and digs through it until he finds whatever he's looking for. I wait, annoyed at his insistence that there's something going on. There's nothing. But then he pulls out the book. It's a little torn from the travel and I'd even forgotten that I had it, but there it is. I don't have to look to know the page he's opened to. I know that page. I know there's a quote about courage and what that means underlined in blue. I can hear the words again as Xenith reads them aloud, as he adds his own weight to them, his own simple meaning that is anything but simple. Especially when paired with what he'd said.

The other days I am selfish.

"It doesn't mean anything. It's just a book that he gave to me before I left. You're making something out of nothing," I say. My voice cracks, the confidence in my own words gone. It's not only him I'm lying to.

"Then why cry out for him, Neely?"

"Because when I cried out for you, he was there. Okay?" I say it harsher than I mean to, but there's no gentle way to say hard things. He shouldn't be here anyway, and if he wasn't, he wouldn't ask these questions or be hurt by them. Thorne's face falls, brows crinkled together, and a blast of heat flows through me from his anger that switches into a weight in my stomach. I push through it. "Because I drowned, Thorne, and it haunted me. I may not have really died, but it was real. I had nightmares about it for days, and when I cried out for you, he was there. Not you."

His face is torn. He wants to comfort me, but he's angry. That's what I feel the most: the heat of his anger inside me. He wants to hold me, and he wants to run. I can see the battle, feel it inside him as strongly as I feel my own. His frustration, the longing to hold me close. It's overwhelming, trying to balance this, trying to guess which side will win.

"And whose fault is that?"

Anger wins.

Thorne walks away, leaving me standing there. An ache forms in my head and my stomach. It clouds around me and pulls at my nerves. Len looks on as if he didn't see the whole thing.

NEITHER OF US HAVE SPOKEN for the last hour, so the music is back on. Thorne's still angry with me—angry and frustrated and worried. It's a tornado of emotions, strong enough to destroy everyone and everything in its path. And it lives inside of us both.

Thorne won't look at me.

There's no way this is just about me saying Xenith's name in my sleep or me kissing him thinking it was Xenith. It's that I wondered, that I felt whatever curiosity about Xenith I was feeling. I don't know how to explain that to him. Me wanting out of our branding was always just me, never Thorne, and he won't understand it. Especially when it comes to Xenith. If *this* is Thorne's reaction to only this part of the truth, what will he do when he finds out about the deal I made with Xenith? The trade of my life for Thorne's? And that I don't even know exactly what that means. Nausea rises in my stomach.

I've made a mess out of this.

"Did I tell you the story of Lulu?" Len asks. He flicks off the music. Neither of us respond. "Lulu was the girl I loved more than anything in the world. I met her before I decided I wanted to start talking. The other kids made fun of me, but Lulu didn't. She said I had nothing to say, that was all. She was always my friend, even when no one else was."

Len laughs to himself. "When we were older, I went up to Lulu and asked her out. She had a boyfriend—everyone knew that—so she said no. I asked her out every day for a month. Finally she said to me, 'Why do you keep asking me out when I keep saying no?' Do you know what I said to her?"

We're both still silent. His story isn't helping much.

"I said to her, 'I figure now that I can talk, I should say everything I want to say. You can't leave things unsaid in case you never get the chance to say them. So, Lulu, I think you're the most beautiful girl I've ever met, and you're kind and smart and everything I'll ever want. I love you, Lulu Demiss. Won't you please go out with me?'"

Len stops talking. I wait for him to continue but he doesn't, and we sit in silence for a few minutes before he reaches for the radio.

"What happened?" I ask.

Len looks back at me in the rearview mirror. He glances to his right at Thorne. "She died. The boyfriend of hers got them both snatched up by the Cleaners."

The silence is returns, thick and tight. I have that lump in my throat that prevents the words from coming out of my mouth like they should. Thorne sighs.

"That's a sad story, Len," Thorne says.

Len nods his head. "It is. But she died knowing I loved her—and I lived knowing she knew it. Ever since then, I make sure things don't get left unsaid. If you've got something to say, it's best to just say it. You never know when it's all gonna be gone."

Thorne glances back at me through the side window, and my heart races.

MY HEART RACES WHEN THORNE calls my name. I turn around with a smile and hold out my hand, and he moves toward me, waves lapping over our feet. I look up. The sky is lit with small, golden flecks shimmering above us. The world is so big, so much more than the Compound. People in the Old World used to go up to the stars, before the end of it. What was it like up there, swimming between stars?

"What are you doing out here?" Thorne asks, coming up behind me.

"It's like they're dancing," I say, pointing to places where a cluster of stars twinkle.

He nods, and I can't help smiling. We're both still, staring up at the sky. It's peaceful, just the two of us with his hand in mine. Everything around us is moving: his heart, my heart, the waves, the wind. Was it only six months ago when we first kissed? It feels like he's been part of me forever.

Thorne pulls me close, so close that our bodies are touching and electricity practically buzzes between us. He wraps an arm around my waist and starts swaying with me.

"What are you doing?"

"Dancing," he says. He presses our bodies closer together. We move, slowly, in tune with the waves, and he presses a warm kiss against my forehead. His breath lingers over me as he hums along with the waves and moves us around the beach. For the first time in my life, it's just me and Thorne. I already can't imagine it any other way. Here on the beach, the one place where the Elders don't have eyes, with my head on his chest, I'm complete. He is, too. I can feel it.

"I love you," I say.

As soon as the words come out, he freezes. I meant it, but I probably shouldn't have said it. He drops his arm from my waist. God, he doesn't feel the same way. I focus my attention on blocking my emotions out as I turn away from him. I shouldn't have said that. I ruined everything.

"Don't," he says, reaching out for my arm. "Don't block me out, Neely."

I can't handle the look of worry in his eyes, and the branding burns my skin with his hand wrapped around my wrist. I shake my head so the tears won't fall. It takes all my energy to keep my emotions from flowing out to him. He pulls me closer and cups my face in his hands.

"I love you, too, Neely."

There's not a jolt through my body, so I know he's not lying. He does love me, even if we'd never said it before. I shake my head anyway. "You don't—you don't have to say that just because I did."

Thorne kisses my lips gently, and I feel my worry slip away. "I didn't. I love you. I think I've always loved you. I'm sorry. I was shocked—I always thought I would be the one to say to say it first." He smiles at me as a tear falls down my cheek. "I thought I would be the one wallowing in wait."

"Why?"

"You don't like to let people in. Even me."

"You know every part of me, Thorne. I don't know if I could keep you out, even if I wanted to. I love you," I say again, braver this time. It's freeing, more freeing than I imagined.

"I love you," he says back.

His lips meet mine, more sure, more passionate than I think they ever have. My heart is pounding, and all of my emotions are flowing into him. All of his are part of me, and I know he's real and true. That we are real.

Somehow we end up on the ground, and everything is a blur except lips and fingers and goosebumps. The sand seeps between my clothes, into my pores. My heart is racing. His body is on mine, and he can't be close enough. His fingertips wander across the flesh of my stomach, and I gasp. He pauses, but I kiss him harder.

I don't need the stars. So many feelings are pounding, pounding, pounding, pulling between us, leaving me restless.

OUR ARRIVAL IN PHOENIX leaves me restless. It's quiet, abandoned, and dark as far as I can see. But I know this is the place Xenith wanted me to stop. He said I would know it, and I'd know this anywhere.

"You sure you want me to drop you off here? I can take you further near a camp," Len says.

I shake my head and look out the small backseat window. Len gives a disapproving huff and puts the truck in park, watches us as we maneuver out. It's a little tricky since my legs are shaky from not moving all day, and Thorne, now that I see him again, looks paler than I remember. More tired. Thorne shakes Len's hand. Complete stillness surrounds us.

"Be careful out here, especially with lights. Don't want any Snatchers to come for you," Len says, his eyes locked on mine, too wise for my good. I don't ask what a Snatcher is. There are some things I don't need to know anymore. "I hope you make it to wherever it is you're going."

He doesn't wait for us to respond. We both watch the truck until it disappears and leaves us standing in the stillness.

Thorne follows me, and there is no sound, not even of animals or crickets. It seems as if even the stars have decided to hide from us since there don't seem to be any in the sky.

A gravel path that leads us to a large building with no fences, not anymore. There's nothing here that should make this place seem like anything, but even in the starless, gloomy night, it's familiar. I tap into the connection and find Thorne feels the same way: there's a peacefulness here. The gravel levels out into a large circle. Decayed, dismantled wood rests in various spots on the ground. In the center, the building sits. It's the largest one here, just like it is at home.

This Compound is exactly the same as ours. I lead us to the center of the circle, just to the right of the building, and look out. Dark blotches of shadow spread around us in the near distance. If I tried, I'd be able to see them as they are in my memory of our Compound: perfect and uniform in shape, size, and spacing. Lined with white fences, exactly fourteen feet from the front door. Four porch steps. Two windows on each wall. Slanted roofs. But here, even in the darkness, I can tell they aren't perfect.

That's how I know it's dead. The Compound is always perfect.

I move around the courtyard, my foot scooting against a broken piece of wood. These used to be tables. Once, we ate lunch here as children. Once, Xenith and I did homework here. Once, my father stood atop one and demanded attention from the people. It was hundreds of miles away from here, but if I closed my eyes, it could be the same place.

Thorne's beside me again suddenly. "This is one of the Compounds the Mavericks took down."

The center building in the courtyard is a market at home. I follow Thorne inside through a broken window, and it's so eerily the same. That is, if everything at home was left behind like this. The metal shelves are empty and rusted in some places. Grains, spices, and broken glass jars plaster the floor like a warning. We find a few random packages—a can of soup and some sealed bags with no labels—and stuff them into our packs.

Beyond the courtyard, we walk along the wooden fences. Some of the posts are broken in half while others protrude into the air, as if they are reaching out for something to hold on to and failing, falling back into place, misshapen and broken.

I count as we walk past the houses. When we were children, we had to count how many houses stood between us and the courtyard so that we didn't go to the wrong one. It happened one time, and we went in during someone else's dinner. Sara never let us forget it.

"Fourteen," Thorne says, stopping in front of the house. Fourteen steps away. The fence is split here, open and waiting for us to enter. Thorne and I exchange a glance, but he goes in ahead of me. I wonder if it's the same inside as well.

Thorne steps up four overgrown stairs, and they creak a bit under his weight. The white paint that covers the outside isn't white anymore. Now it's yellowing like sickly cheese, and everything is peeling away to reveal the rotting wood underneath. The red front door is locked, wood warped, slightly bending and splintering. He kicks at the door a couple times before it bursts open, releasing dust into the night air. I follow him inside and see the paint on the door is faded, alternating in shades of lighter pink and darker red from the corrosive heat of the sun.

The house smells of something rotting and stuffy. Despite the smell, the entryway is still put together, a small, rounded room with doorways on either side and an angled staircase in front of us. The wallpaper is a faded shade of blue, but when I look closely, I notice the patterned swirl of flowers still fighting to be seen.

The entryway leads to a small living room off the left. The walls look gray but that could be the lack of light, and the floors are covered by dirt and a moldy piece of carpet. There's an old couch, simple and sturdy; two small tables; a fireplace with a mantel; and a chair. Everything even rests in the exact way it does at our house. At every home in my Compound.

"Thorne?" I call out.

My voice echoes back to me before he yells that he's upstairs.

I can see Sara everywhere in the exact same way. Except here, the floor is covered in trash. Broken glass. Pieces of paper. Trash. A splintering chair. A plate that's cracked in half. There's even the top of a toilet on the middle of the floor.

"Neely, come up!" Thorne yells.

I do, and I already know where I'll find Thorne.

He's in the third door on the left in a drafty room with no lights or candles. There's a single large bed with a disgusting mattress, a desk to the left with a lamp, and a window that's boarded up. It smells musty in here, like dirty socks and mold. Thorne sits on the edge of the bed, looking out the window. When I come in and lean against the door frame, he glances at me for a moment and then looks away again.

"I hate the thought of you with him," Thorne says with a pause. "I hate all of it."

I sigh and tap my fingers on the splintered wood of the door. "There's nothing between us."

Thorne's eyes snap up to me. "You keep saying that. I have so many questions. I don't want something to happen and us never say the truth to each other."

I move and sit next to him, taking his hand. I steady my emotions and wait until I can feel his worry form a lump in my throat. I want him to know that I'm not lying. I can't lie while I'm touching him or he'll know. This feels like the only way.

"If you ask me, I swear I will tell you, but make sure you want the answers, Thorne. Because I love you. I want you trust me."

He pauses. "Only because of the branding?"

"Maybe," I say. The connection doesn't change, and he nods softly. "But also because I know you completely, and that part is real."

Thorne pauses. "Did you kiss him?"

I pull my hand away. "Do you really want that answer?"

He takes it back. "Yes," he says, and I feel the steadiness again.

"Yes," I say.

Thorne curses and stands. I touch his arm, and it's only half a second but he lets his guard down. I feel it—everything. More emotion that I knew he could ever feel at once. He wants to yell, to punch someone, to break something. The anger he feels toward Xenith, not even toward me, is overpowering. He wants to forgive me, to be okay, to kiss me and show me that he's the one I'm meant for. He feels like he needs to prove himself, to prove us. I've hurt him in ways that he can't place, and then there's something else: disappointment. In me. In the fact that I don't trust us, even though I trust Xenith. And at the thought of Xeinth, he comes back to hatred, to anger, to all the reasons I'm a fool for trusting him.

"Thorne, I'm—"

"Don't say you're sorry, Neely, don't. That doesn't change anything."

Thorne sighs. He runs a hand through his hair, paces around the room. I know what he feels, but I have no idea what I feel. His gaze snaps back to me, and he takes my hand to feel the connection.

"If they can take the branding away like we heard, do you still want them to?"

"Yes," I say.

"For Xenith?"

"No. For me," I say quickly and shift toward him, making sure to keep my hand in his. "You understand that it's not about you, right? Or anyone else. It's about me finding my own way."

"And then what?"

"I don't know."

"Do you feel anything for Xenith?"

I think about Xenith. The boy I knew since we were children, the one who never seemed to fit. He brought me here, and he lied about Thorne—but I did, too. When we were alone, he was something else. Someone kind and challenging, someone who was always there. I liked his kiss, his presence, but he wasn't Thorne. He didn't have what we have. But what if all we have is because of the branding? If it was gone, would we still feel so passionately? Xenith is far from normal, but he's not like me and that is something I long for since I don't know who I am without the branding.

"I don't know," I say. "Maybe?" I exhale. Thorne does, too. "I'm sorry. All I can say is he's not you."

"But you don't even know if you trust what we have is real."

I pause. "But I trust you."

"Okay," he says.

"I'm sorry I never told you about it from the beginning. I thought I was doing what was best. You have to know that."

"I do," he says, and then he drops my hand and heads into the other room.

6 DAYS BEFORE ESCAPE

XENITH'S IN THE OTHER ROOM, bent down so all I can see his head. I look back at my book. Xenith has amazing books from the Old World that I've never heard of before. There's nothing else to do aside from plan and wait, so I read.

"Are you going to shower?" Xenith calls.

I don't reply, just keep reading. This story is written in old English, but I like it. Girls wore big dresses and had dances. They were stronger than most of the girls I know, dealing with marriage and no wealth and lies.

"You," Xenith says. I look up from the book, and he's staring at me.

"Me," I say. "I'm reading."

He shakes his head. "You're taking a shower."

"I did."

"When?"

I pause. "Yesterday."

He smiles and pulls the book from my hand. "Don't lie to me, Neely. It's time. You're starting to smell."

"I am not!"

Xenith crosses his arms in front of me. "Now. I will drag you there if I have to."

I shake my head, and then he's got me over his shoulder. He's carrying me into the bathroom, and

I'm kicking my feet, begging him. The water is already running, filling up the bathtub, pouring from the top spout. The sound of its sloshing shakes my nerves. He sits me down on the sink, and tears start to run down my cheeks. I'm shaking and sobbing. It's not totally because of the shower; it's because of everything. It's leaving and dying and living. It's being here with him. It's what happens in a week.

The air is warm and sticky with steam. He wipes away a tear from my cheek. His hands are on my chin, forcing me to look at him.

"You have to do this, Neely." His voice is soft, as if he's talking to a child. I guess I'm being one. "This isn't something you can be afraid of. Not you. Not now."

"When I close my eyes, I can still feel the waves."

Xenith wraps me up in his arms and pulls me in. I let his arms cover me and hold me closer. I let his words whisper in my ear. I let his hand run through my hair. I let myself inhale his earthy, minty scent. Maybe it's the steam that's building up around me or the sadness I feel about being alone, but my brain starts to make my body do things on its own.

My lips press against his warm neck, trace up to his jaw. He pulls away and looks at me like he's lost, too. Everything I see in his glance matches the way I feel. I say his name softly. Seconds pass by, each of us staring at the other. Then his lips touch mine. Our kiss is hesitant and innocent. Then it's not. Our bodies crash into each other. My mouth is not my own, not the way it's pressing against his. My hands run along his back, and he pulls me in to deepen our kiss. Our lips and our tongues are searching for that lost thing, hoping to find it in the other person.

Everything is right in this moment—so right and less alone that I sigh into his mouth. My hands slide under his shirt and pull it over his head. He doesn't stop me. He kisses my neck near my branding, and I forget everything. I don't know what this is or why I'm kissing Xenith right now or why I don't want to stop. My fingers run across his warm back. He stiffens at my touch.

Xenith jumps and pulls away from me, backing up against the wall and looking at me like I'm some kind of ghost. We're both panting, and my skin is sticky from the fog of the shower. He runs a hand through his hair, and it's so Thorne that my heart skips a beat at the betrayal.

"Take a shower, Neely," he says. It's almost a whisper. He closes the door and leaves me with the water and the steam.

I stare at myself in the mirror until the steam deforms my face. I slowly get under the water, and it takes everything I have not to scream. Tears push out of my eyes, mingling with the water around me. By the time I make it out of the shower, damp and shaky from crying until I had no tears left, I go to Xenith's bedroom. I want to apologize or make it better. I was wrong for kissing him.

But Xenith is already asleep.

THORNE'S BEEN ASLEEP for twenty minutes. I should sleep. I should be asleep. My brain won't shut off. All the possibilities, the worst cases, play on repeat. I have to tell him everything, and I don't know what will happen.

I want to curl up in his arms and lie here. Time can pass us by. I wish I could let it.

I turn over and watch Thorne sleep. Listen to him breathe, peaceful.

I force my eyes shut. I just need to sleep, so I count sheep. One. Two. Three jump over the fence. Four goes to meet them. Five. Six. Seven...

THE DOOR BUSTS OPEN.

I scramble up in bed, Thorne next to me. Light shines in from outside, pouring over my face and in my eyes. A shadow stands there. Even from the outline, I know it's my father.

"I warned you," he says.

The sheets gather around us as Thorne's arms wrap around me. I cling to him so tightly I'll never let go. My father steps closer, into the darkness, and I can see him now more clearly. He has that look on his face, the one that says he's in control. It's evil with a twisted smile, and when I look into his eyes, they are empty, cold.

"We found you," a deep voice booms from the doorway.

My eyes shoot back to the door, and three figures stand there. I can only see their silhouettes—no faces, no eyes. The Elders have come.

"We will not be disobeyed," the second figure adds. That voice is high-pitched, but there's a power in the way he speaks.

"We will take what is ours," the third adds in a breathy, scratchy voice. I can't see their faces, but I don't need to. Fear passes through Thorne, strangling me, and the Elders move. Troopers pour into the room and rip Thorne out of the bed.

"Don't take him," I yell. I dig my hands into his skin, but the Troopers are stronger. I yell over and over, but no one's listening to me. No one is listening.

"Neely," Thorne yells as the Troopers pull him out of my sight.

I scream and run toward my father. "Please bring him back! Don't do this!"

He doesn't respond. He can't respond. The Elders move in the sunlight.

"Take her," one of them says.

My father latches on to me, and the Troopers close in around me.

"Neely!" Thorne yells. I sit up in bed. A dream. It was just a dream. He's beside me, looking at me, his hands on my face, and I wrap mine around his forearm. The fire courses between us. I take a deep breath to calm myself.

"It was a dream," he says, wrapping me in his arms. "Just a dream. It's over."

It's over.

Except it's not.

If they found us, it would be so much worse than that.

I CAN ALMOST MAKE OUT the small patterns on the walls. Maybe they're more of a memory from my own life. I stare at them until my eyes get blurred and then look back at my watch. 3:06 AM.

There's never enough time. It moves too quickly, signaling the end of everything. The end is the thing I fear the most. Eventually, though, all things end. Days. Nights. Life. Even love. The fear of this loss is greater sometimes than the truth. Thorne lays here beside me, breathing, his arm resting over me. That truth is undeniable. Everything else falls apart, life slips away, and still Thorne is here. Safe. I cling to that truth as much as I can.

The truth. They can still find me—they will—and on that day, time will be quick and slow at once. Time will be my enemy. My captor. My peace. My end. If it doesn't find me, then death will. But I will fight the whole way. I will fight until I can't anymore.

3:07 AM. Another minute wasted. We should be moving, not sleeping. I know that too well. The dream plays on in my mind. Any second the Elders will catch up to us, and if they don't and we succeed, then what? What happens?

"Hey," Thorne whispers. His arm shifts off my chest and toward my neck. His finger runs down my face, groggy, sloppy, still asleep. "Why are you awake again?" His voice is rough, still exhausted. I'm exhausted, too.

"Can't sleep."

He smiles at me, his eyes glossy and his smile weakened by the daze, but still beautiful. Still perfect. "I'll get up," he says with a pause. "We can go."

His leg moves away from mine, and I reach out for him. He should rest. Even in the darkness, I can see the white pallor of his skin, the circles under his eyes. We need to stay. He's more tired than I am.

"Go to sleep," I tell him.

His leg brushes mine again, and my heart pumps louder. Of course it did. It always does. Always will. Our hearts are the same. I've forgotten that lately. I've been so caught up in everything else, in the questions and the lies, that I forgot the truth of him.

"I love you," Thorne whispers. His hand is focused this time, angled directly to caress my cheek. I grasp his in mine and smile. I don't want to smile. I want to pout, to cry, to worry, but I can't help myself from happiness in despair. And he is that reason. It's selfish and I know that with every fiber of my being, but I can't change it.

"I love you," I say, lowering his hand to the empty space on the bed between us. His movement is quick, and his lips are on mine before I realize his intentions. I cave under the heat of the kiss, of his lips on mine, on the sparks that ignite something deep within us both. Whatever exhaustion I saw in his eyes before is replaced with desire, for me, for us. I see the hungry glimmer when his dark eyes peer over at me. I touch his cheek, kiss his jaw, and shake my head. He sighs heavily and joins our fingers together.

"I'm with you," I say.

But for how long? The closer we get to the Mavericks, the harder everything feels. I hope I'm strong enough to stop it. Thorne's hand falls limp in mine, and I know he is asleep again.

I lay my head back against the pillow, and now my arm is crossed over my body in an awkward twist. I won't let go of his hand—I won't, even if it hurts.

IT HURTS TO THINK THAT I'm going to be dead in eight days. That I have eight days left to walk on the beach, to stare at the only picture of my mother, to spend with Thorne. How does that even happen? Didn't I walk into his quarters yesterday? Where does the time go? I don't know what waits out there, and part of me doesn't want to. I fear the end of this place, even as I long for it.

"Cornelia," my father yells, opening the door.

I roll my eyes and cram the picture of my mother under my pillow. His thinning hair has wings from where his hands were undoubtedly running through it. I don't say anything to him, and we both freeze in an awkward stillness. I wait for him to speak, to be himself again. I'd give anything for that.

"What was that?" He looks tired. The lines on his forehead have deepened, and there are circles under his eyes. What else are the Elders making my father do? It seems to be taking a toll on him.

"Nothing," I say. I evade his gaze and look around the room, playing it off. He doesn't buy it. He moves toward the bed and pushes me out of the way. I fight his hand, try to keep it from stealing my only memory, but he wins. He pulls up my pillow and, with it, the picture of my mother. I cry out, and he looks from her to me.

"Where did you get this?" I don't respond. He grabs my chin in his hand and forces me to look at him. "Did you take this from my office?"

I don't answer again. He lets go of my face, and I lose my balance. "The boy?"

"His name is Thorne, but I didn't get it from him." I did get it from Thorne, but I'm not going to tell him that. I got it two years ago as a birthday present. He traded Xenith for it. I never asked what it cost him, and he never would've told me. "Give it back to me." I hold out my hand like the disobedient child I am. "Now."

My father's face is expressionless. He looks at the picture once more and holds it in the air between us, ready to hand it over.

But he doesn't.

He rips it down the center, through my mother's smile. He rips across her deep green eyes and shreds her red hair into strips. He rips it until it's nothing but confetti, and then he throws it in the air. I lunge at him.

My hands are pulling, punching, gripping onto any part of him I can touch. He's holding me back, but not successfully. Blood fills the space under my fingernails.

This is not my father; this is only a monster.

He hurls me to the floor. My chest is heaving and my face is flushed, but my father stands there and bleeds on my carpet. He smiles, too. One of those devious smiles that makes my stomach jump to my throat.

"That, little girl, was a mistake you will pay dearly for," he says.

"You can't hurt me."

He squats down to me. His cheek is bright red, three marks down it. My marks. They look less human and more animal.

"I can do everything to hurt you," he says. "Don't you see that?"

I shake my head. "You won't."

"Why won't I?"

"I'm your daughter. If the people see you hurt your own daughter, they'll never trust your lies. They'll start to question you." I lean toward him, and even though I know it's impossible that they'll question him, I can play the cards anyway. My father doesn't know that I know everything. "You don't want them to ask questions, do you, Father? To doubt you or the Elders or this place?"

He meets my gaze before he stands. He looks in my mirror and wipes away the blood on his cheek with his hand. "Cornelia, you're wrong. That would never happen." His voice is soft and smooth, less like an evil tyrant and more like a person talking to a baby. No piece of my father remains. This man is something else entirely. The way he's looking at me, I know I've made a mistake.

"And if it threatened to, I now have an example."

Me.

THORNE WAKES ME UP with a kiss on my cheek and a spread of breakfast in front of me. It takes me a second to pry my eyes open, but when I see it, I realize I'm hungry. I've gotten used to eating less, but the plate of dried berries and vegetables, of nuts and grains that'd we found before.

"What is that?" I ask, pointing to the other substance. The jar we took from the market outside is in his hand and the yellow, half-liquid, half-solid form is familiar to me.

"Peaches," Thorne says. His smile is half-cocked on his mouth. "They're not bad."

I sit up so he can sit beside me on the bed, and together we eat. It's the most normal thing we've done since we've been outside, aside from sitting in an abandoned replica of the Compound while we do it. I sigh and let all the other pressures fade away, until Thorne breaks the moment into pieces.

"You had another dream last night. What was it about?"

I push the peaches back toward him and wrap a thread from the blanket on the bed around my fingertip. "My father and the Elders." He stiffens beside me, exhales. "They found us here."

"You're hundreds of miles away," he says. His words aren't as comforting as I want them to be or as he means them to be. We both know distance won't stop the Elders, even if we aren't saying it. Benny had no problem saying it, and Cecily had no problem with the fact that the Elders know exactly where we are right now. Maybe the Remnants are better with the truth than we are.

Thorne moves from the bed and puts the lid on the remaining peaches. He stretches his arms over his head as he sets the food on the dresser. I look away. Sunlight explodes into the room through the windows, bright and warm.

"We should go," I say.

I stand up, and Thorne's in front of me, hands on my hips, holding me in place. "I just wanted to say one thing," he says, then pauses and lowers his forehead to mine. A breath, a nervousness, flows through our branding. "I get it."

"You get what?" I ask.

"Xenith," he says. "I know you used to believe in us, and then one day you didn't anymore. One day you had all these doubts. I felt them, and I never mentioned it because it didn't matter. I believed enough for both of us."

"Thorne—" I start.

"Let me get this out, okay?"

I nod softly, and Thorne exhales. "I get that he knows things, and I guess you could talk to him about all the things you'd spent your life dreaming of, wishing for, and though you didn't feel you could to me for some reason—"

"That's not—"

"—I was there, Neely. I was right beside you, and you were so busy protecting me or hiding the truth from me that you didn't see. I don't think you wanted to. But you don't see with Xenith either. You don't know what you feel, you don't know why you kissed him, and you don't know his real motives. When you do, I'll still be the one who's here." All of his emotions surge through me again. The anger, the frustration, the disappointment, the sadness, the longing. "Whatever the branding means for us, I'm still going to be here."

I don't have time to process all the emotions before he's pulling me into a kiss. His body melds against mine, and the branding is fire. His emotions are swirling within me, a big mess of power, and mine are rushing, too. I don't know what is his or what is mine. He can't be close enough. I can't be close enough. I want to be his clothes, his skin. We tumble down to the bed, and he straddles me. The connection rushes through, makes me want more of him. All of him. It's different than any kiss we've ever shared. More desperate and more passionate. His lips greet my cheek, trail down my neck, trace my stomach. Each place he touches creates a small fire that builds up in my body. My hand entangles in his hair, and I pull his mouth back up to mine.

I know it's not forgiveness, but it's something like forgetting. At least for now.

WE SEARCH THE OLD COMPOUND for food before we leave. We raid the houses, and I try not imagine the people from home, even though this place reminds me of them. There isn't much here that we can take, but we find a little more than we had before and it's better than nothing.

"Ready?" Thorne asks me. I shake my head, and we walk toward the exit. Thorne moves with a new determination.

WE HAVEN'T GONE VERY FAR, and we already have to stop. The sun is mercilessly hot, but we manage to find a place to rest. I lower myself to the fallen tree trunk and stretch out my legs, sip some water. Thorne doesn't sit, even though I know he's tired. He stands and keeps a look out.

There's not much to see. There are some trees, but the ground is mostly dirt, covered in dust and branches of debris. This part of the Old World is barren.

"Hey, look over there," Thorne says. I stand and look with him.

In the distance, I can see the outline of another Remnant camp—or maybe a real city instead of the shadow. The buildings are spread all over, and it's a shell of a place, or so it seems. They are old structures. Some have fallen in, others only frames. They must be from before, more depressing reminders of what was. From here, it is as if I could hold this whole view in my hands. They are merely tiny toys. I could break them if I stamped my foot down.

"We should try to get there. Could be a good place to spend the night."

"Sure," I say. I take a sip of the water in my bottle. It's almost empty. We need water under this heat.

We could make it maybe a day without it. The odds are stacking against us the closer we get, and though Pete said the Elders don't come out this far, if they are following me, if they're desperate to stop me, how long will it be before they catch up?

"Don't look so worried," Thorne says, bumping my shoulder with his. A smile plays on his lips, but that doesn't fool me. I can feel his anxiety. He's pretending so I'll feel better.

"I'm just tired," I say.

I didn't sleep well with the dreams of my father. And somehow, Thorne knowing everything is more exhausting than lying to him about it. He's letting me in, talking to me, and that means some kind of progress. It takes everything I have to keep him out of my emotions, but now I don't know what he'll do. I'm not even sure I know how loss or desperation can make a person behave.

He smiles at me again, weak and uncertain. The concern plays in his eyes as he digs through his pack. "We'll rest here a minute and then keep moving." I nod and take some of the nuts from his hand. We're both silent as we eat.

Everything is jumbled inside me, and for once, I wonder if I made the right decision. I'm risking myself, the others in the Compound, and the people I'm trying to save. And for what? If the Mavericks have as much power as Xenith said they have, why are they doing nothing to stop the Elders?

It all made sense before. It was the best thing for everyone. For me. But if we don't make it, then it's a waste. If we don't make it to the Mavericks and back home in time, then I've failed everyone.

"Neely."

I look up at Thorne. He's so gorgeous. His eyes light brown specked with gold. The way his dark hair falls in his face and hides the scruff on his jawline. His smile, his lips. He's perfect.

He touches my face and pushes a loose piece of hair behind my ear. His hand is warm against my chin. "Are you with me?"

I nod my head and put my hand into his empty one. "I'm always with you."

He smiles and pulls me off the ground. "Let's keep walking then," he says, and he picks up his pack.

MY FATHER PICKS UP THE BROKEN pieces that once formed my mother and stuffs them into his pocket.

"Example?" I whisper.

"Oh, yes," he says. His dark eyes find me. "Rules are rules. They are for our good, and everyone, even my daughter, must obey them."

I stand while he speaks, even though part of me wants to stay where I am and surrender. If my father was a kinder man, one who treated a daughter like she ought to be treated, I would run into his arms and cry in them. He's not that person, though, and I'm not foolish enough to think of him as such.

"Perhaps it's what you need. The rules are absolute. No kissing in public, no sneaking on the beach, no lying or plotting. You are not to question our ways, and there are no second chances. Regardless of you being my daughter, there are no second chances." He turns to face me. "I told you to stay away from Thorne Bishop."

"I have been."

His look is disgusted, shocked almost. "You're a liar."

"That's you," I say.

My father slaps me, and I fall to the floor. I was so unprepared for it. I cover my face where his hand met my cheek. It burns, and I can feel it swelling.. The tears slip through my eyes, even though I will them not to come out. He pulls me to my feet by my hair and doesn't let go.

On the way out the door, he pushes a button. The bell to gather the residents of the Compound. He release me until we're outside in the center of the courtyard I'm the example, and they're all coming to look.

"LOOK," THORNE SAYS TO ME. He takes my hand and directs me to hide behind a rock. Outlines of large signs hang twisted in the air, but whatever they were before is long gone. Like most other things, it's just the skeleton.

"I think there are people over there." He points between two of the mountains where a small line of people stand around a few yards away from us. Another Remnant camp?

Someone grabs me from behind, and I scream as a hand clamps over my mouth. More hands hold me in place, tightening a grip on my arms. Thorne pulls the gun out of his pocket. It looks ineffective when up against three other guns.

"Put the gun down, kid."

The men are dressed in brown clothes that match their bronzed skin and dark hair. They aren't huge, not too tall or too short, but they've got more muscle than Thorne and I put together. The one who holds me has a good grasp. I would never be able to force my way out of his arms. All three of them bear a resemblance to each other, and each one makes me nervous. I feel a burst of Thorne's heat through me, and I reach out through our connection and pour as much peace into

246

him as I can. Underneath the anger, I feel the prickling sensation of his anxiety. He can't lose it on them. They're way bigger than us.

Thorne examines the four of us quickly before his eyes rest on me. I feel him level out.

The one who holds me presses his gun into my back and twists my arm around, and then my own fear pushes its way to the surface. It bubbles up, and tears press behind my eyes. Thorne takes some of it from me, and then he's lowering his gun to the ground and raising his hands to the air. One of them captures him almost immediately.

"Pretty little girl," the guy holding me whispers in my ear. He smells like onions. *Stay calm*, I tell myself. "Don't get many pretty girls."

"Don't touch her!" Thorne yells.

The guy turns to him and knocks him in the face. His lip bleeds.

"Let's take them in. I bet we'll get extra for the pretty girl."

They laugh before they push me along through a patch of trees toward the small gathering of people.

IT DOESN'T TAKE LONG *for the people to gather. My father hasn't released me. Instead, he's only held on tighter. I can't see his face, but I wonder if it hurts as much as my head aches from how tightly he's holding it.*

"As everyone knows, the Compound operates on a system," my father yells over the crowd. He's got his voice on—the one he hides behind when he's leading them, the one that makes him appear to be stronger, more trustworthy. "There are rules, requests, responsibilities. The societies of the past have all collapsed and died because they failed to follow these three simple formulas."

I search for soothing, familiar eyes in the people I've known all my life, but only find Xenith's in the back of the crowd. I avoid them and look around at all the people I have known all my life. People who are looking at me with judgment. They looked the same way a few months ago when I kissed Thorne out here: with disgust and disappointment. I hate that this is happening, that none of them know why they respond as they do or what they are really feeling. That all these emotions and all this disapproval is because they have been trained to feel it.

Sara's eyes catch mine while I scan the crowd. Kai stands next to her, and between the two of them, I feel lost. Concern and worry are etched on their faces. None of us know what this man who used to be my father will do next.

I know it's not really him, but I'm still angry. I feel my resolve for him crumbling, even knowing what I know, and I clench my fingers into fists to hold back my anger. It's good that Thorne is on the water today. If he was standing in the crowd, I know he wouldn't be as calm as I am trying to be.

"We have the rules for a reason. We are taught them from birth, and the rules apply to everyone, even my daughter," my father yells. The others all nod. "My daughter has forgotten her place in our home. It seems she believes she is above the rules. As our bylaws indicate, there is a consequence for every action and every person." He sounds like a recording, a machine that someone's turned on.

"What has she done?" Sara asks.

My father glares at her, and the others mumble because no one questions. No one. They aren't able. How is Sara able to question? I've never wondered that until right now, but there must be a reason. She has the branding, too, so she shouldn't be able to.

My father looks at me. There is a flash of uncertainty in his eyes, but only for a moment. I know he's going to lie to them. "Cornelia Ambrose tried to leave the Compound."

My heart stops beating. I search for Xenith in the crowd. He looks confused, and I've never seen him like that. My father can't know I'm trying to leave when I haven't even done it yet. Has my father been tipped off somehow? Do the Elders know of my plan?

"She tried to swim off-shore." My father's voice stays calm and steady, despite his false words. He's mastered lying so well that it can't be anything but perfect.

"Fisherboats found her in the ocean, near death, in the night. She claimed that she was running away."

"That's a lie," I yell, thrashing in this hands. Troopers surround me and hold me back, pulling me from his grasp.

"I would not be dishonest with you," he says to the crowd. "My daughter is unwell. She told me she hates all of you." His words spread in murmurs through the crowd. Through my people. My friends. "She has been corrupted to believe that this place is evil and that everyone in it is evil. I fear she may have the fever."

The fever. The way the Raven's Flesh started.

"We must contain her and make her well," he says.

The murmur is louder, uproarious. I shout over them, tell them it's not true, tell them he's lying. They don't seem to hear me. They don't seem to know I'm there at all. They only see my father, the tear in his eye, the scratch on his face from me. They hear his lies and they believe him, a façade that they don't know they shouldn't trust.

I hate him. I hate him and the Elders.

"As much as it pains me," Father says, and the people are quiet as soon as he speaks, "the Troopers are going to escort her to the safehouse. She will be there for a few days. I only ask that you forgive her harsh words against you. She is not in her right mind, but she must receive the punishment for her lies."

I scream when they pull me backward. "This isn't true!" I yell. I fight against them, but they're stronger than me. Frantically, I look around to the crowd. "It's not true!" In my search, I watch Kai pulling Sara into the house, and then Xenith disappears. The crowd comforts my father. They don't look my way at all.

The last thing I see before they lock me away in the safehouse is the beach. The waves are out of control, thrashing and beating against each other and against the sand. They're so fierce they could wash over the shore and straight into the Compound. They could pull everyone and everything out to sea. The hatred rolls off of me in waves like that toward everyone. It rushes and traps the unexpecting in the undertow and drowns everything. Them. This place. My father. Myself. Everyone. There are no survivors of the wrath. There is no absolution. No redemption. No hope. There's only lies and hatred, both things the Elders caused.

If I wasn't so angry, I'd almost be glad they were locking me away. The Troopers drag me from the courtyard to the outskirts of the boundaries and the inhabited spaces. I hear a Trooper laughing as they lock me in, as they wander back to headquarters, back to the center.

I've never been to the safehouse before, but it's horrible. It's not safe at all, but a place for punishment. It's as small as my closet, a dark room with a small, barred hole. It's big enough to fit a hand in or out, maybe some food. Three of the walls are covered with nails, barbed wire, and broken glass. The ceiling is the same, jagged and deadly. The other small wall has the window, and a bench where I can sit is across from that. The window looks out at the ocean, too far to smell or enjoy but close enough to haunt.

I can't do anything but stare out at it, wait for sunrise, and listen to the waves escort me to freedom.

THE THREE MEN ESCORT US toward the buildings until we're in closer range to the people we saw. Except they're not real people; they're statues. A ploy. They are shaped like people, from nose to feet. Up close, parts of them are chipped and discolored with age. The man that smells like onions pushes me through some doors, and all I see is stairs. Hundreds of stairs.

I try to struggle away from my captor, but he's still got a grip on me and his fingers dig into my arms. They push me forward to keep us both going.

When we make it up the stairs, the doors lead us back outside, but we're high up in some sort of mountain fortress. It's a whole complex of small holes, like windows and doors, and Remnants move in and out them. They've built their camp in an impenetrable location.

My captor tosses me down on the ground. Thorne follows, and we wait. I catch as much breath as I can and watch as a gray-bearded man comes out of the crowd of Remnants. He's tall, rail-thin, and his beard looks too heavy for him, as if he may fall over.

They all speak in their language, eyes drifting over to us. Thorne is as close to me as they will allow, but he feels closer as our emotions flow together. We each carry some of the other's and offer reassurance however we can. I scan the area. The Remnants all watch us back, eyes raking over first us and then the men who brought us here. I notice a boy standing behind his mother's leg, and when he sees me look at him, he cowers. They're afraid of us.

One of the men who dragged us here leads me by my hair. He's too strong to stop, and my body is twisted around so everyone can see the branding on my neck. Someone gasps in the crowd. A word is yelled, but I've heard it before and I know it means: Elders.

The gray-bearded man looks appalled, then pleased. His eyes meet mine, and he nods before turning away. The ones who brought us follow the man into one of the houses. More men jerk me to my feet and Thorne to his.

"We'll get out of here, Neely!" Thorne yells. His voice is frantic as he's pulled in the opposite direction of me. I fight the men who hold me back, who pull me somewhere I don't want to go, but it does no damage. Thorne's worry rushes over me, and I do nothing to hide mine. We can't be separated. But we are, and they shove me into some kind of room with no windows and a small space. It reminds me of a bigger version of the safehouse.

In the corner, there's a bundle of sheets balled on the floor that I don't plan to touch, let alone sleep on. A slot in the door opens, and a bucket appears. Who are these people? Why have the Remnants captured us? They were supposed to be on our side. Safe. The Remnants are supposed to help us, not lock us up.

I pace around the four walls of the room, looking for a crack, a door, something to show me some light or some reason for hope or explanation.

There isn't one.

THE SUN MUST BE SETTING because warm golden light fills the cell. A silhouette forms in front of my eyes.

"Food," the silhouette says.

It's hard to see her in the light, but I hear the sound of china clattering against each other and then against the floor.

"Where's Thorne? What are you going to do with us?" I ask.

Her feet moving across the floor echoes back to me. She sighs, hesitates near the door, and hides the sun from my view.

"It will all be over soon," she says. The door creaks closed, stealing the light with it.

I make my way to the door and pound my fists against it. Pound, pound, pound, and yell, "What will be over?" No one answers me except silence.

I sink to the ground and pick up the metal tray of china. There's a chipped bowl filled with something brown. It sticks together like porridge, but it doesn't smell like anything at all. A piece of bread. Some water. I pause and tune in on Thorne. Feeling him, wherever he is, has been the only reassurance of this place. We're both alive.

I nibble on the bread and take a sip of water before dipping the spoon in the brown dish. It's tasteless, but I eat all of it in case they decide not to feed me again.

It's only minutes before I feel wrong. Before my stomach starts to whirl and I'm so tired.

The room tilts, and no matter what I do, I can't fix it. My head spins. All I want to do is lie down.

I don't even make it to blankets on the floor.

I lean my head against the cold rock wall and slump. I know Thorne can feel this wrongness, but I can barely notice whatever he's sending me. Instead, I hear the song. The soft song in my head and the melody like the rolling waves. It's vague, but I know it from a dream—or a nightmare.

I hum along with it in the darkness until everything fades away and I forget.

I FEEL FORGOTTEN OUT HERE. The sun has set, and I can't see anything beyond my hand. I know the stars are up, shining on the water. I can't see them from my angle, though, which only adds to the loneliness. Thorne must be home now. His anger billows through our connection. I want to comfort him, but I know if I reach out to him now, it will only upset him more.

"Neely," a voice whispers. I jump from my seat at the sound. My heart speeds up, hoping. A light shines on me. I have to squint, but then I see that it's Xenith. All my hoping ceases, even though my heart surprisingly doesn't. "Are you okay?"

"I'm fine," I whisper. But I feel completely lost, overwhelmed, angry, upset.

His face appears in the little hole. "I thought you might be hungry," he says. He slides me a bag of food. Bread, water, cheese, crackers. "It's not much."

"It's perfect."

I tear off a piece of the bread to quiet the ache in my stomach. Xenith stares at me, not speaking. The light still shines in, and he looks over my face. His brow furrows, and creases appear etched around his face. Is that worry? Concern?

"Is it bad?" I ask.

Xenith shrugs. "Not really." But there's more emotion in his eyes than his words. Something in the way he tenses says otherwise.

"I'm the example. He told me that before he dragged me outside," I say. "Do they all think I hate them now?"

"Some." Xenith stares at me, oddly quiet while his eyes pour over me. I shift and take a bite of a cracker.

"He ruined our plan," I say.

"He didn't," Xenith says. "He made it stronger, as did you by yelling about the lie."

I shake my head. "But our plan will make his lies look like truth."

"Or his lies have made our plan look more believable," he says again.

I'm quiet. He's right. My father will be esteemed because of my death, but our plan won't be questioned. Who would question the death of a girl with the fever? No one.

"I'll stay with you for a while," he says.

Part of me doesn't want him there, but the other part doesn't want to be alone in here. I try to get more comfortable. I can't lean against the walls, but I can sit on the floor and rest my head against the bench. Shards of glass embed into my legs, but I'm so exhausted it doesn't matter. He tells me stories about his parents, about the Mavericks and the Old World.

At some point, I ask him how long I've been in here now. He says it's better not to know.

The next days pass the same. I watch the sun rise and set, and store away the loneliness as much as I can. I try not to think. Eventually, Troopers pull me out of the safehouse without a word or a glance. They hold back my arms and drag me across the beach. My legs won't work since they haven't moved in four days. I've eaten every day—Xenith brought me food in the night, and the Troopers in the morning.

They aren't gentle when the thrust me into a metal seat. I know we're at headquarters. I recognize the scent of musty sweat and the low whir of the machines, the white walls and the dim lighting that somehow illuminates my father in the corner.

Lucian Ambrose looks well-rested. His cheek is healed, the scratches I left on him gone. He probably cheated and went to the Healers for medicine while I rotted in a hole. He has a mug in his hand and a large plate of pancakes. Those are my favorite—and he knows it. That's the reason he's smiling at me.

"Hungry?" he asks. I shake my head. Right. I should be hungry. No one should've fed me while I was trapped. No one knows how to cross the outskirts, and if they did, they never would. Except Xenith. He raises an eyebrow in my direction, hopefully at my constraint. Maybe he will see this as rebellion. Rebellion I can play.

"I'm hungry. You're the one who made me hungry," I say. "I won't eat it. Not from you."

He moves toward me and slides the plate down the table. It lands promptly in front of me. He's probably had lots of practice. "Why on earth not? I'm your father. I'm looking out for you."

I look at up at him. "You're not. I'm the example. Examples don't have fathers."

He clicks his tongue. "Oh, Cornelia, you are so dramatic." He touches my forehead. "I do hope the fever is gone if I'm releasing you."

"Releasing me?"

"Of course. You're my daughter. I think the message has been received, don't you?"

I hate him. I hate him so much I can barely stand to look at him.

"You should eat that before you leave. I want you to make it home safely."

I don't pick up the fork or move toward the food at all. The smell is sweet and bitter, the perfect mixture from the coffee and the syrup. I don't look away until the door closes and a Trooper comes in with my shoes. He sets them on the table and looks past me at nothing. When he leaves, a gush of cool air tickles across my skin.

SOMETHING COLD PRESSES against my forehead, and when I open my eyes, Thorne is staring down at me. His eyes are rimmed in red, glassy. His hair is a ratty mess, sticking out in different directions, and his face is covered in dirt.

"Thank God you're awake," he whispers, pulling me against his chest. Everything aches. The world around us is still spinning slightly, but his hand is on my face, his lips on my cheek, grounding me. I start to speak, but my throat is dry. He hands me water and I sip it quickly, but then I'm thirstier and my hollow stomach growls. I try to stand, but Thorne stops me.

"Take it easy," he says. "No standing yet." He leans me up against the wall. He's saying I should feel weak, and though I'm thirsty, I don't feel weak. Somewhere in my brain I feel like I should.

"What's happened?" The question comes a few more times, quickly and on repeat. I glance down at my watch, and there's only twelve days left. Twelve days...

Before he can answer, vaguely familiar light devours the room. A woman enters our slab prison, dressed in a long, thin, brown robe that touches the ground. Her hair is pulled back from her face, tied together, and she carries a small jar and a big bowl decorated with black spots. She sets them both on the ground and looks at Thorne. By the time her eyes make it me, leaning in the corner of the room, they've doubled in size and her face is pale.

"Awake," she says.

Thorne puts a finger over his lips, as if to silence her. "Please..." he whispers.

She watches him for a second, then her gaze drifts toward me again. And she races out the door, yelling the word over and over. Thorne curses.

"What's going on?" I ask.

"I was hoping you would stay out through the day so they'd be stuck with us."

"Stuck with us? What?"

"We're a pair. They won't separate us," he says.

"A pair of what? What is this place? How long–" I look back at my watch. Twelve days. "Five days have passed?"

Thorne looks at me, his voice dripping with something regretful. "Neely."

I shake my head. This can't be happening. We've lost five days.

"We have to go!" I yell. "We have to leave!" He pulls me up in his arms so I can stand, and I try to fight away, to not need his support, but he won't let go. I'm yelling, and my head has an ache again. Things are spinning, and vomit builds up toward my throat. And then, I feel better. Ready, energized. Like I could run forever and never stop.

"Calm down," Thorne says. He pulls me away just far enough and looks in my eyes. "I promise, I *promise* we will get where we need to be. They won't keep us here. I have a plan."

I rest my head on his shoulder. He promises, plans, whispers his love for me, vows to get me there. I don't hear his words. I hear the clock, ticking in my head, matching the sound of my heart. Five days I was asleep. That leaves us with too few days now. Twelve days. That's not enough. It doesn't feel like enough. We're too far away for only twelve days.

The door opens again, and the same girl from before points toward me. Her lips quake, as if she's afraid, and then behind her is the gray-bearded man. He's taller now that I'm standing on his level, his limbs long and lanky like his beard. He leans on a stick, and his steps make a *click, scratch, tap* noise as he trails along the room.

"I see she is awake. How fortunate for you, young sir," he says. His eyes rest on me. "Your boy was nervous. *Demanded* to be put with you. Offered to throw himself off the top of this rock if we denied him."

I look at Thorne. Offered to what?

"Wouldn't have been necessary if you hadn't kidnapped us and poisoned her." Thorne's arms tense up around me. Poisoned? I was poisoned? Why would they do that?

"Such a strong word, poison. I call them necessary measures, especially when we get people who are a little too wild, like yourself. We can't afford risks in times like these, but we didn't assume she'd eat all of it."

Click, scratch, tap. Around the room he goes, watching us with each step. The frail, paper-thin appearance of his skin puts me edge. He steps toward me, and Thorne pulls me behind him a little more.

"Pretty girl," the man says. He reaches a hand out to me and puts it on my chin. "Thank you for falling right into our trap." He smiles and steps away. "A pair of enemies. That gets us a good profit. He asked for one, and he gets two."

Click, scratch, tap.

Click, scratch, tap.

And the door closes behind him.

I stare at Thorne, at the rise and fall of his chest. He's panicking. "What does he mean by profit?"

"Those men who took us? They were Snatchers. This whole camp thrives on trade."

"And they're trading us—selling us?"

"To the highest bidder."

"Why did he call us enemies?"

Thorne touches the branding on the back of my neck. The branding. Is this because of the Elders? They must think we're a threat. "Do you think it's the Elders who want us?"

"They'd take us, not buy us."

Thorne walks across the room and listens through a small crack under the door where the gray-bearded man exited. He puts a finger up to me and presses his body flush with the door. In the stillness, my head pounds. We have hundreds of miles that stand between us and San Francisco. How long will that take? What if this person who's buying us never lets us go or worse?

There's a crash as Thorne trips over the bowl in the floor. His face is white, and he stumbles to regain his balance. He can't hide his emotions quick enough. They course through our connection, and his nerves rush over me. It's more than that. It's fear. He's afraid.

I gasp and look at him. "What is it? What did you hear?"

His eyes meet mine across the room. "They said your last name."

"How would they know that?"

The words of the gray-bearded man flash in my head. *He asked for one, and he gets two.*

"Did they mention my father? Or the Elders?" I straighten up and move toward Thorne. "Did they?"

His eyes give me the answer.

Suddenly, I can't breathe. We have to escape. We have to.

"It doesn't matter," Thorne says. "We're going to get out of here."

"HELP!" I SCREAM. I pound against the heavy stone door. It's eleven minutes before someone responds. I don't recognize the man who opens the door, but he's there, looking at me. My eyes flood with tears, and I point to Thorne.

He's lying face down on the ground. His shirt's wet with sweat and blood. I sob over-exaggerated tears, heave in breaths of air. The man bends down to Thorne, looks at me.

"What happened?"

I only cry. It comes so naturally that stopping isn't going to be easy.

The man pushes me against the wall, crumples up my shirt in his fist. "Tell me!"

I don't need to respond. Thorne whacks him over the head with the large bowl. When the man bends over, Thorne steals his club, and the sound of it colliding with the man's head echoes through the room.

Another voice yells from outside and comes toward us. Thorne hides behind the open door, and the new gaunt, dark-skinned man looks confused. He rushes inside, toward me and his friend on the ground, when the door closes from behind. Thorne's there again, attacking the new man with the club. He ducks and Thorne misses. The man punches Thorne, making him fall over. I freeze, not sure what to do.

Then I remember my knife.

My pack is across the room on the ground, and I dig in the pockets for the little knife. I don't know why they left it, but right now isn't the time. It's not much, but it's all we have. Without thinking of anything else, I charge toward the man and stab the knife into the back of his neck. He stops kicking Thorne and crumples where he stands.

I killed someone.

Thorne stares at me, gasping in air, and I move to help him up. We don't say anything about the man or the blood pooling on the ground. We just go.

THORNE AND I TRY TO BLEND in with the others as we traipse around in gray robes that are too long, and I trip as we walk. We don't know which way to go, but we're following the other men in the robes. Not many people wear them, but they must mean something because the others barely glance our way as we pass. As if they're afraid to look at us.

A clanging fills the air of the camp, and everyone seems to freeze. The gray-bearded man appears in the center and looks up where our room was. The girl who told of my awakening stands outside, yelling something in their language. I wish now I could speak as they do. Whatever they're saying, it's about us because the robed people all pull out their weapons and ceremoniously remove their hoods. Then it's everyone, removing their hoods and yelling over each other. Weapons appear—chains, knives, one person with a clay pot—and they all move toward us.

The small boy from before is one of them, and he dodges legs. The knife in his hands glints under the sunlight.

"Faster!" I yell to Thorne.

We run, but there's only the edge of the rock and down. We race along the edge, but down is a long way. We'd never survive.

Thorne pulls me into a crevasse in one of the rock walls.

There's no way out of this.

I stand as still as I can on my shaky legs. Thorne's erratic breathing fills my ears. I exhale, and that's when someone reaches in for us. Hands come at us. Hands and then bullets. Neither of them get us because Thorne pulls us to the ground. A sound of something breaking echoes, and rocks tumble in around us. Hands grab for us from the other side, and someone finds my leg and I scream. Thorne reaches for me, but he's not fast enough. I cry out as my body slides across the rocky ground. I try to kick my free leg, to wriggle my other out of the men's grasp, but it doesn't work.

I'm brought before the gray-bearded man and tossed like a sack to the ground. Thorne's lip is bloody and swollen when they push him beside me.

"Nice try," the gray-bearded man says. "You almost pulled it off. To think we were going to give you a proper meal."

"What should we do with them?" one of the men asks him. The hoods have all been replaced to hide the Remnants' faces now that we've been caught again. They don't need to prove themselves anymore. That or they don't want us to see them. It was a test to see if they could find us.

The man raises a hand. "They are no longer our property. Their new owner is here."

There are least a hundred people watching us wordlessly from behind their leader. They circle us, and until the gray-bearded man speaks, no one even seems to breathe. The Remnants in the robes and long dresses all turn their heads toward the newcomer.

I hold my breath.

They've found me. This is how it ends after all this death and fighting: with the Elders dragging me back to the Compound. Will I become one of their experiments? Or will they kill me immediately?

But when I look up, it's not my father.

It's not him.

The man in front of us is tall, his pants marked with dirt and faded with age. He's got a dark goatee that covers his chin, and his hair is cropped short against his head. Arms bulge out of the rolls of his shirt sleeves, but his face isn't hard and evil as I expected. Instead, his eyes are a soft brown, warm like honey, and something familiar strikes me about them as he looks between Thorne and me, lingering longer on Thorne.

"I don't appreciate my cargo being handled like this," he says. His voice is deeper than I expected, coarse and relaxing, and his eyes seem friendly, even as his angles are sharp. He speaks with certainty and has a commanding presence. No one is able to look away from him. But, beyond that, I feel like I know him, even though I have never seen him before.

The gray-bearded man stumbles over his words. "They were trying to leave, sir, but we procured them again."

He bends down toward us, his eyes locking on Thorne's bleeding lip. He yanks my chin up, and his fingers are warm on my skin. "They're damaged. She looks sickly."

"Some things are damaged during shipping, as you know."

The man stands and faces the gray-bearded man. He towers over him by a foot at least. "No, I don't. If someone pays for a whole product, then they get a whole product." He digs in his pants pocket. Hands something to the gray-bearded man. "I believe that should be more than enough, considering the damages."

Then he looks to us. "On your feet."

Thorne sends me a warning through our connection, but I stand anyway. We can escape one man better than we can a whole camp. Our new owner gathers a set of chains from one of the hooded men. He cuffs us together and nods toward the gray-bearded man.

"Until next time," he says, and he leads us out of the camp, chains clinking against the hard ground.

He loads us into the back of a large black van, more gentle with us than I expected. The doors close and Thorne whispers, "We'll escape," as I sit next to him.

The man gets into the driver's seat, and when the door closes, he looks back at us. "You don't need to escape. I'm not going to hurt you. I promise."

His voice is heavy when he says it, and it sticks with me in a way that makes me believe him.

THE SKY IS SO CLEAR we can see the stars. There's a crisp breeze in the air that treads along my skin. The chains are digging into my wrist, leaving deep red cuts and bruises there. When the man hands us some food, I pause. Thorne doesn't eat either, and the man looks at us.

"It's not poisoned," he says, and to prove it, he takes a bite himself.

I shove the sweet, juicy bites of oranges into my mouth. Our new owner watches while we eat. His eyebrows crinkle together as he stands, unmoving, next the black van. Trees surround us to the left. Owls hoot somewhere in the distance. Crickets chirp. Without the chains, this would be a perfect night.

"We'll sleep in the van tonight. Head on in the morning. And I got your packs," he says. His voice still has a tinge of the coarseness in his words, but it's softer, lighter. Relieved. "They're in the front seat."

Thorne's stance hardens beside me. I wipe away some of the juice from my lips. "Thank you," I say.

He nods in response and takes a bite from an apple before turning away from us toward the trees. His hand runs over his short hair, and the whole motion sends me reeling. I know that movement. It is equal parts Thorne and Kai.

"Thorne," I say.

The man curses in the wind before he marches over to Thorne and yanks at the chain that connects us. They stare at each other, then the man twists on the chain until it falls away from Thorne's wrists. He does the same to mine, and it clanks against the floor of the van.

"I'm Neely," I say to him. The man looks at me, and there's something about him. He looks toward Thorne, waiting. Thorne says nothing. "What's your name?"

He doesn't respond at first. The silence is covered by the sound of life around us. The part of the world that has always been. "Asher," he says.

Thorne stiffens beside me, a heavy sadness passing through him. "I'm Thorne Bi—"

"I know who you are," he says.

My brain jumps into overdrive, and the sadness inside Thorne shifts to something confused. I wrap my hand in his because I know he's thinking that it can't be possible. Yet lots of things have turned out to be possible. I escaped. Thorne escaped. This world exists. Stranger things have happened. I force my eyes toward Asher. I can see it in the sweep of his dark hair, the chisel of his jaw, the smile that plays on his lips, and the warmth of his eyes—eyes I know so very well.

I look in Thorne's direction. He's staring at the ground, but I feel his surprise, his doubt, his excitement. "How?" Thorne asks.

The way Asher stuffs his hands into his pockets is so very Thorne. The look in his eyes, so Kai. Everything about him screams he's a Bishop. The brother they all believed to be dead is alive and in front of us.

"It's a long story," he says.

Thorne looks toward Asher. Watches him as he tries to avoid looking at us. We're all silent, afraid to break the moment.

"You look like her," Thorne says finally. And he does. Tanned skin and amber almond-shaped eyes, dark hair, and a softness to his face.

"I remember her less each day. And I didn't get to know you at all. Kai, though—I remember Kai."

"He's a good brother," Thorne says.

Asher's eyes flash from the trees and then to me. He looks down at our hands, which I forgot were even entwined. He looks back at Thorne.

"He's the best," Asher says.

Asher Bishop is right here. The boy who died seventeen years ago is alive. He's saved us. Thorne's just met his brother.

Thorne pulls his hand from mine, and a wall goes up again. He doesn't want me to know what he's feeling. I look toward him, but he doesn't meet my gaze. I wonder how they both got here.

The short answer, it strikes me, is because of me. My eyes dart back and forth between Thorne and the brother who's been gone for seventeen years.

Thorne has been gone for seventeen days, and the sky has been dark every day since he left. The fisherboats met a storm; no one has heard from them yet. No one knows if they are alive or dead. I know though. I can still feel Thorne—not that I can say anything.

I'm doing the shopping for Sara the day he comes back, and I feel him before I even see him as surely as one feels the sun on their skin. When I turn, he's running toward me. My heart is light, and my body anticipates his touch, fueled by the desire I feel through the connection.

By the time he reaches me, I can't control myself. My emotions and his tangle together—one big mess of love and longing. His hair is damp, clothes dirty, shirt sticking to his chest like glue. He smiles—the big, boyish grin that he's never outgrown—and my heart flops.

"I never thought I'd see your face again," he says in almost a whisper. I feel the truth of it, the relief of being here, coursing through his body. The love he has covers me like a wave, and the desire—the strong, strong desire—is the undertow. He's washed up in it, and I am, too.

His hands are running up and down my back. My branding is tingling, a mixture of emotions and his hot breath on my skin. Just as I remember the rules for residents about showing affection in public, he forgets. His mouth meets mine. The eggs I carry slip to the ground. I forget everything else right along with him. My hands wander, and my lips enjoy their moment as he fire devours me.

When he pulls away, it's not the embers that are still sparking within that worry me. It's not the fear that I want more of his touch. It's the people who are staring at us. It's the look on their faces—filled with warning and worry and shame that we kissed in public. It's the voice that shouts for us to run. It's the sound of everything falling apart, like the eggs I just bought now broken under the feet of the Troopers.

There's noise outside. Thorne leans against the door, panting with his hair sticking to his face. He touches my cheek and removes it quickly. "I'm so sorry," Thorne says. "I'm so sorry. I'm—"

I put my finger to his lips, and his eyes find mine. We broke a rule and everyone saw, and I should be sorry, be scared, but I'm not. There's a knock at the door, and we look away from each other as Kai comes in at the commotion. He's out of breath, staring at us, and he doesn't say anything, but the look in his eyes says he knows we did something wrong.

My father is standing on the other side of the door, Troopers lined up behind him. He looks between us.

"Take him away," Father says. The Troopers grab Thorne's arms and haul him away. I follow after them, Kai nearby, until my father pulls me by the arm. He studies my face like he doesn't know me at all.

"You were warned, Cornelia," he says. Then he drops my arm and follows the Troopers.

Kai steps up beside me and rests a hand on my shoulder as I try not to cry. Even without a branding, I can feel his pain as he watches the only brother he has left be dragged away. I don't speak, unsure of what to say.

THORNE AND ASHER SAT only feet apart all night, and neither of them knew what to say. We left the spot as soon as the sun broke through the sky. If ever there is a time to say things, this is it. Asher's been dead for seventeen years, a ghost, a reminder of some deep sadness that I never understood. Even when I tried.

Asher was only six when he died, the same time as their father. Sara never explained, even though it seems she has always been the center of loss. Her husband, her son, her real daughter, my mother, me, now Thorne. The vile taste creeps up my throat. I've made it worse for her now—first with me and then with Thorne. Kai is the only one she has left.

"What happened to you?"

Asher eyes me from a mirror in the front of the van. "That's a long story." Asher's only twenty-three, but the deep lines on his face make him look worn and tired. In the lighting, I can even make out gray flecks in his hair.

"We're not going anywhere," Thorne responds.

Asher locks his jaw, and the harsh line of it reflects back in the mirror. "I promised I wouldn't hurt you, and I meant it."

He's spunky. Like Sara. "Where are you taking us?"

"Depends. Where are you going?"

The silence resumes again. Thorne's hands are clenched at his side, and I hear the faint sound of his knuckles cracking. I still can't feel his tension, but with that movement, he confirms the nervousness is there.

"San Francisco."

There's another beat, long enough that life seems to pass us by. The sun breaks the sky through the branches. "I'm what the Remnants call a Chainer. It's my job to trade goods for people. Most Chainers do it for the profit. They make all the money and sell anyone to anyone else. They don't care. Me? I work with the Mavericks to give people a new life."

"A new life?"

"You'd be surprised how many people are sold every day. That camp you just left? They're the hub for human trade in all the camps. I get people from them all the time. Two weeks ago, I got a young girl—maybe seven or eight," he says. "Whole family died in a Trooper attack, and other Chainers found her in the desert when they scoped the area. Word got to me, and I took her to a settlement camp on the outskirts of the ocean. She'll be good there."

I touch the green bracelet on my wrist from Delilah. It's painful to imagine someone her age out there alone. "You saved her."

"I don't know about that. But I did give her a chance. That's more than most people get out here."

"How did you know who we were?" Thorne asks.

Asher clears his throat. "I didn't. I mean, I got word of two people from the Compound traipsing through the landscape and heard lots of ruckus at some of the camps about where they'd go next. They said one was the director's daughter, and that's who I came looking for. The Snatcher camp sent out a signal that they had prisoners for trade, and I'm the Chainer who does business with them. I didn't know I'd find you there until I was outside of the camp. I heard your name on the outskirts from some old guy in a beat-up truck."

Thorne nods in silence. I reach out my hand to him, and he takes it, squeezes it, and drops it.

"How long have you been one of these Chainers? How long have you been out here?" Thorne asks.

The soft hum of the engine fills the small space. We bump along over some rocky road, on toward wherever Asher is taking us.

"What do you know about me and Dad?" Asher asks.

Thorne shifts in his seat, clears his throat. "He was chosen by the Elders to go to the North. Mom was pregnant with me, and Kai was three. You wanted to go with him, and the director let you. You died there a couple months later when the Compound was infiltrated by rebels."

Asher smiles weakly. "That's not quite how it happened, but the Elders always spin things in ways that make them look good." He looks at me again through the mirror. "It's true that they wanted Dad for the trip, but it wasn't to the North. It was to the Middle, in the old region near the Great Lakes."

"There's a Compound there?" Thorne asks.

"Not anymore—it's fallen. But seventeen years ago, Father agreed to go. Lucian Ambrose asked for Dad's help, said the Elders wanted him to go, but he didn't want to leave his wife—and Lucian's father, the director, refused to let him go. Amelia Ambrose's pregnancy had been rough, and even at six months, she was having difficulties. The Healers feared an early and complicated delivery, and the director refused to have his son and daughter-in-law anywhere but the South."

He eyes me through the mirror. "I remember your mom. She always brought me lollipops, and I never understood where she got them. She would wink at me and tell me not to share my secret."

I swallow and try to nod, but it all gets stuck in my throat. My head doesn't respond to anything, only focuses on not crying. Thorne's hand finds mine. This is his brother, who he's found out is alive after seventeen years, and he's comforting me. I don't deserve him.

"The orders were only two months," Asher continues. "Dad would go to the Compound and help the director there restore order. Apparently, there was an uproar over some escapees in the North, and those in the Middle were attempting to overthrow the Elders. Our dad was one of those people who had influence among the Elders, so they agreed he could go. They assured Dad he'd be back before Mom had the babies."

"Mom's never mentioned that Dad was held in high regard," Thorne says.

"With him gone, she'd have no protection. I'm sure you've realized that Mom knows things that others don't. I was six the last time I saw her, but I knew that even then."

I know the truth of that statement as soon as he says it. Sara has always pushed the boundaries, challenged my father with a glance, told us things in her own secret way. She talked in code and lived in code and not much surprised her.

"So Dad was to go. I remember the day he told Kai and me. I wanted to go with him, that part is true, but they all told me it wasn't going to happen. It was no place for children. I was mad about it. I loved our parents, but Mom had Kai and the babies coming and Dad had no one." Asher pauses. In the silence around us, he takes a deep breath. "I snuck out that night, followed him, and put myself in the cargo unit of a trucker. I fell asleep there and woke up in MWC5. Let's just say Dad wasn't very happy to see me." Asher smiles to himself at the memory and then cringes. "I spent most of my time locked away in a bedroom. Sometimes I'd talk with other children. There was a lot of fighting, arguing, and discourse until they rebelled completely, and then it was chaos."

"My father sent yours into a rebellion?" I ask.

"I really don't think he knew what it was," Asher shrugs. "Maybe he did, but Dad and Lucian were friends. They grew up together more like brothers."

The van slows to a stop. Asher sighs and opens his door. Ours follow just after. It's good to stretch my feet, even if we don't walk anywhere. Asher watches me as I turn and bend to stretch, and then his eyes widen slightly. He looks away. He's just noticed my branding.

"It was almost three months later when Troopers stormed the Compound," he adds, "counteracted by the Mavericks."

"The Elders sent Troopers to take down their own Compound? Why?"

"The rebellion," Asher says. "The Elders' fear has always been losing control, so they eliminated the threat. The Troopers killed everyone who put up a fight and hauled the others away, while the Mavericks saved everyone they could. The last time I saw Dad, he pushed me in a hole under a building and told me not to leave until he returned."

"He's dead," Thorne says.

Asher nods, quietly looking around. The way he likes to avoid whatever he doesn't want to feel or see or explain is so much like me that I completely understand how hard this conversation is for him to relive. It's hard to let people in when all you want to do is forget and move on. "I tried to find him, but by the time I came out of hiding, everyone was gone or dead. I can still remember the sound of that Compound blowing up and disintegrating."

"What did you do?" I ask.

"I walked. I didn't get very far when I met a woman," he says. "She was with the Mavericks, helping the escapees find refuge and new life. She led me to a family who had a son near my age, and they let me travel with them. Most of the survivors came here, but others spread out along the way. Some even found freedom in San Francisco. Others never made it that far."

"Why stay here when it's dangerous?"

"I've been waiting."

"For what?"

He moves toward me, his fingers touching my neck quickly. "For you." He drops his hand and looks at Thorne. "The woman who helped me had that branding." He points to Thorne's neck, too. "She said to wait for the next pair to find me, so I have been waiting. She told me that they would be coming, and they would need me. I remember I asked her how she knew and she smiled, said she had dreams."

"Deanna," I say. Cecily's twin. They worked with the Mavericks after they escaped.

Asher nods. "Deanna said to go as far as we could and wait for the one who would follow in her steps. I didn't understand, but she showed me this branding. 'The mark will be like mine, that's how you will know.' So I did what she said. I had nowhere else to go anyway. I thought she was crazy over the last few years, that I was crazy for listening, but then I heard the news of the director's daughter and her journey. Here we are."

We're both quiet. My brain is on the verge of exploding. Seventeen years ago, Asher knew we would come. He waited, got a job as a Chainer, and happened to save us when we needed him. Just when I think there's no way out, there's a moment of hope. This world has more questions than I ever knew possible.

"Ready?" he asks, opening the door for us again.

"WHY DIDN'T YOU EVER come back to the Compound?" Thorne asks from the passenger seat. I sit in the back, but I lean into the open space between their seats. How different would his life have been with Asher in it?

"I would've upset society. If they saw me, if I'd tried to go home, they would've wiped my memory or sent me to another Compound. Or worse."

My mind flashes back to the safehouse and the torture room, but somehow, I know there are worse things in the Compound. Even if I have never seen them.

"What will you do with us?" I ask.

Asher smiles. "I have a man near San Francisco. His name is Eddie. We can be there in two days' drive."

"Then how long is it?" Thorne asks.

"Another two days. Maybe three."

I don't want to smile, but I can't help it. Five days until I'm there. I have eleven days left. I can still do this. The impossible suddenly seems a little more reachable.

I STARE OUT THE WINDOW while we pass through the Old World. This part of it is beautiful. Where the other pieces were dead and broken, this one feels newer. It's mostly desert sand and blue sky, but the clouds in the morning roll over each other with equal lightness, and as far as I can see, there are mountains and sand.

Thorne laughs, and I watch him with Asher. It's almost like they have never been apart. They've spent the whole car ride talking, and I felt it was better to not be included. I knew the stories Thorne told Asher in great detail because I had been there. Sometimes, he'd pause and ask me if I remembered a point and I'd answer, but then I'd retreat into myself again. I don't want to ruin this reunion for them.

"Kai's a Healer's aid. One of the best. He was always taking care of people, so it was a pretty easy fit for him." Thorne pauses. "Remember the shop Dad kept in the basement?"

"The wood shop?" Asher asks.

Thorne nods. He's relaxed around Asher; the tension in his body is gone. "Kai uses it now. He's really good at making things. He can spend hours down there shaping, sawing, building. Made a whole set of table and chairs in one week."

"Dad loved it down there," Asher says, and both boys get quiet. Then Asher turns his head to his brother and smiles. "I remember once when Mom made dinner and Dad wouldn't come up. We were halfway through whatever it was that she cooked when she stood up and started carrying it all downstairs. 'We eat as a family, Richard,' she'd said. I think we ate dinner down there every day that week."

"I've never heard that one. She doesn't talk about you and him much," Thorne says.

Aside from the mention of them on their birthdays and sometimes when Sara was feeling some kind of nostalgia, Richard and Asher Bishop had always been a mystery that we never investigated. At least not when I was around, and I was there a lot. They were a sadness for Sara, a weakness that she didn't want anyone to see. She was too strong for that.

"What about Mom? What does she do?"

Thorne pauses, and in the silence, I see Sara. A woman who is always smarter, braver, more determined than most. Never afraid to push the limits.

"When I was six, she delivered a baby for one of the neighbors," Thorne begins. "They came for Mom. She took us with her and sat Kai and me in the living room to wait. I don't know how long it was before we heard the baby crying. Ever since then, people want her to help. The Healers don't like it much since she's not one of them, but no one stops her. Not like they could anyway."

I remember hearing about that after it happened, years later, and Kai and Thorne talked about how the sound in the room went from silence to screaming to a baby crying. Kai would poke at Thorne and say he freaked out, but Thorne would insist that was Kai. And I would sit there, listening to a story I wasn't part of in this family that had been mine for two years and still felt like mine, but wasn't. Then I went home to my father. I know he tried his best considering his job and Mom and the lie we all lived for two years, but he has never been family in the same way they have. He loved me and I loved him, but he was only one part of me and they were the rest.

Asher stays silent after the story. What does he think? Does he miss his family? Sometimes having no family at all seems better than losing one. Especially that one.

"Mom always was feisty. I think she's still the most courageous person I've ever met," Asher says with a smile.

"You have her smile, you know," Thorne says.

Asher looks at Thorne and lets his smile really show. Thorne's right; it's exactly like hers. I can see it even from the backseat. And then the car is quiet, filled only with the sound of the wheels on the road. I long for more of their hushed voices.

THERE'S A HUSHED conversation coming from the kitchen when I open Sara's door. My arms are full of food from the grocer, and Sara's gentle voice floats toward me, her words lost in the shuffle of my feet.

"Don't tell me what Amelia wouldn't have wanted!"

I freeze. It's my father. What is he doing here? Why are they arguing about my mother?

Sara's voice is still calm. "Lucian, you're being irrational. You've been irrational like this for months. Rowan Perkins was a nice boy, an innocent boy, and the Elders were wrong in their reasons."

I gulp. Rowan was transferred earlier this week. They found some books from the Old World in his house—books that were forbidden, books that I'd been reading too—and sent him away.

"Their judgment isn't mine to question, and it's not yours either. In case you have forgotten, it's treason."

Treason? I try to see around the corner, but all I can make out is my father's head.

"Don't threaten me," Sara says. Her voice is fierce and has an edge to it. It's not a tone I've heard her use before, but then again, I've never heard my father, or anyone, talk to her that way. "I'm not afraid of you. I know who you are. I remember the scared little boy who cowered in corners from his own father. That's all you're doing now—cowering. Amelia would be disappointed."

"Do not push me," my father says through gritted teeth. I know the sound. Almost every conversation we've had lately has been forced like this one.

"This is my home. If you don't want to be pushed, you can leave it."

The sound of a chair scoots across the floor. My father's voice is sharp. "If it's true, then I hope you are wise enough to tell me. I can protect them. She is my daughter. Her safety is my concern. The Elders are wondering, all of a sudden, the same questions from years before, so whatever has happened—"

"There is nothing to know. Neely and Thorne are perfectly normal. They won't become what you say. Their branding is merely a marking like all the others. The Elders ran all those tests years ago, Lucian. Even if it weren't, I would not throw our children at their merciless feet."

"They believe those tests to be corrupt because of Liv Taylor. They want to know, Sara, and they will do whatever is necessary to find out."

"And you'll just let them do it? To your own daughter? To my son?"

The bottom of the bag I'm carrying collapses, and fruit scatters across the floor. I wince and try to catch them, but I'm caught as my father and Sara both look at me. For a brief reprieve, it's like it was a year ago when they were friends and we were some sort of weird family unit. Not whatever they are now. Whatever it is that he's becoming, I don't recognize it.

We all stare at each other while oranges roll across the floor.

"What are you doing here?" I ask my father. I try to look surprised, but I don't think he buys it. He knows I've heard too much.

"Just leaving," he says. He kicks an orange in my direction as he steps over an apple. Sara and I watch him as he goes, and when his hand is on the door, he looks back at us. "They warned Liv Taylor, too. Before."

Xenith's mom. I look between Sara and my father before he turns away. The door opens and slams shut. Sara exhales. She closes her eyes for a moment and then opens them with a smile.

"Let's get this mess cleaned up," she says, pulling the remaining bag from my hand and setting it on the counter.

"What was that about?" I ask, bending over to pick up an apple. I examine it for bruises, but it's fine.

Sara shakes her head and gathers up the oranges. "It wasn't anything."

I watch her and join her in silence until all the fruit is safely in a big bowl on the counter. She puts some water in the kettle.

"Why did he mention Thorne and me?"

"You heard that?" Wisps of hair fall away from her bun and line her face as she looks at me. Her mahogany eyes look darker. "What else did you hear?" she asks before she moves around the kitchen, putting the kettle over the fire in the hearth. At my silence, she looks back at me and sighs. "Lucian says the Elders are questioning the decision they made to keep you and Thorne together with the branding, but he won't tell me why. I don't think he knows. They don't really explain things to him."

I gulp back the truth. I know that no one has the twin branding anymore, that it had some results the Elders felt were deadly to others. What if they find out about the connection? Would they separate us? They must not know anything, or we wouldn't be here right now.

"What did the Elders warn Liv Taylor about?"

She sets some mugs on the counter. "When we were younger, I did things that challenged the Elders. We all did. We had secrets—Liv and your mother and me.

Secrets even your father doesn't know. It seems Xenith knows these secrets. Your father fears you and Thorne might know them as well."

"What secrets?"

We stand around in silence, and I wonder what secrets she's keeping. They have to be big ones if she can't talk about them. Finally, she looks at me. "The three of us protected each other until there was no one left to protect. But I will protect Kai, Thorne, and you. It's all I can do."

"Protect us from what?"

She hands me a mug. "It doesn't matter."

THIS MOMENT MATTERS. It will forever be the time when Thorne met his brother for the first time, maybe the only time, and because of that I don't want to intrude. I want him to have this. I rest in the back of van, eyes closed but not really sleeping as the road bounces me around as we drive.

"Do you still have the branding?" Thorne asks.

I peer toward the front of the van through my eyelashes. Asher stiffens next to him before turning his head. I can't see anything else, but Thorne says something. I re-close my eyes and try to focus on sleeping, but I hear Asher's voice instead.

"I saw you have the twin branding with Neely. How's that work?"

"My twin sister died at birth, and Amelia died giving birth to Neely. Do you remember Neely's grandpa?"

"The director then? He's a hard man to forget."

"Mom says he wanted Amelia and her child for something, and Lucian wasn't able to protect them. When Amelia died and my twin died, Liv Taylor saw an opportunity to protect Neely, so she switched them. Mom says she didn't even know at first. That she woke up and there were her two babies in her arms."

I listen and imagine that it's Sara telling us the story of waking up and holding us, how it was when she learned the truth. She'd always told in it in a whisper and only on the beach where it wasn't monitored, as if she was always scared someone would hear something different in her story.

"We were two when the director died and Lucian Ambrose took over. With him at the lead, I guess Liv came forward with the truth. It was a confusing year for everyone, but when I got older it seemed more obvious since Neely never looked anything like us."

Asher doesn't respond, at least not in a tone that I can hear. Thorne and Asher talk in low voices, and my mind runs back to what that must've been like for Sara. To hold me and think I was hers, only to find out it was a lie. To let me go. To watch me grow up and fall in love with her son. A part of her family, but not really.

Asher's voice is louder. "Deanna and her sister shared dreams, visions of sorts. It was the craziest thing how they could communicate. Do you and Neely have that?"

I watch Thorne through my half-closed eyes and see him nod his head. "I know how she's feeling all the time. When she's sad or happy or any strong emotion. We feel each other."

Asher whistles. "That can't be easy—not being your own."

Thorne shrugs. "I see it more like I'm part of something greater than just myself."

I've never seen us that way, not ever.

"Isn't it weird?"

I hold my breath, waiting for his answer. He's never been honest with me about it. Or if he has, it's not anything I've believed. I guess I expect him to feel the way I do.

"Sometimes," Thorne says. Relief fills my chest because all this time I never thought he felt anything about our connection except acceptance. "But it's always been part of me, and knowing her like that, knowing what she's really feeling? I wouldn't trade it. And trust me, sometimes it's intense."

Intense is an understatement. Sometimes I don't know which emotions are mine and which emotions are his.

"Neely can feel a hundred things at once, and she doesn't even realize it. She gets an idea in her head, and then she goes with it. It can be frustrating, but I always know why she does it. I can feel how positive she is that, whatever the outcome, the decision was a good one."

He's the same way. When he feels one thing, he feels ten other conflicting ones.

"Why would you follow her out here?" Asher asks.

I wait for that answer. I know he thought he'd lost me, but is that his whole motivation?

"She's been part of my life since I was born. It sounds odd, but when she's not around, it's like I'm half-missing too. I had to come." Thorne sighs. "And if I hadn't, I wouldn't be sitting right here."

"You felt like you were missing because of the branding?"

"I don't know. She thinks so, and maybe it is," Thorne says. His voice is just above a whisper. I have to strain myself to hear him. "For two years, she was raised as my sister, and while I don't remember a lot from that time, I remember her. When she didn't call Mom 'mom' and when she lived next door instead of down the hall, she was still Neely. This constant who always knew exactly what I needed and when. The first time I kissed her I knew everything was different. I was different."

Looking at where we are, at what we've been through, I feel like I'm the worst thing that's ever happened to him instead of the best. I've caused him confusion and trouble and pain. Yet he stays. Even when I run away, he's always there.

Thorne exhales. "It's all for a purpose. You, us, all of this."

"I can agree with that. Before I found my place, I didn't have a purpose aside from waiting for Deanna's words to come true. Then I found a place, and now the thing that makes me wake up in the morning is knowing that I'm helping others," Asher says. There's a noticeable joy in his voice, a conviction, and even though I can't see his face, I can bet it's embedded there in every pore. "What's your purpose—aside from following Neely?"

Before we left the Compound, I wanted to teach. To be with all those kids and watch them grow up, learn. Thorne never talked about what he wanted since he was passed up as a Trader.

"Aside from Neely," he says sharply, "I don't know. I used to want to study the Old World and understand how it worked. Catalog it, examine it."

"But now?"

"Now I'm in it and it seems depressing."

"Seriously." Asher chuckles.

Thorne turns so I can see the profile of his face. In the light and from the side, he looks more serious than I've seen him before. Driven and purposeful. "I want to fight them, to make the Old World new and to give people hope. Not for Neely or for history or for anyone, but for myself."

Tears flood my eyes. When had that happened?

"I've been aboveground and underground. I've seen people completely hide who they are and where they are just to survive, and that's not how it should be. Everyone deserves to live in the truth and live how they want," Thorne says.

"To be free," I add in a whisper. Maybe Thorne understands more than I believed.

THIS IS THE PART WHERE we say goodbye. As we get out of the van, I wonder if they'll ever get another chance together again. The ground feels odd under my feet after not walking for days. It takes a few seconds for the feeling to come back completely, and then I feel better than I have since I left home. Energized.

"I've known Eddie for years," Asher says. "Me and three other Chainers all use him."

"Where do you send people?" Thorne asks.

"San Francisco is the biggest remaining city, but there are three smaller ones that operate above- and below-ground. Some have been rebuilt, and there are a few established outskirts camps if people don't want a city."

We follow Asher to an old restaurant, and he pauses before we go in. "Don't put your pack down. And hold her hand," he says to Thorne.

Thorne slides his hand into mine without a question, and when we open the door, a bell jingles. We follow Asher to a seat. Thorne pulls me into a booth and sits next to me. People aren't staring at us directly, but their gazes drift toward us. It doesn't take a genius to know we are the topic of conversation.

The walls are yellow, the table is sticky, and mold grows in the cracks and crevices. There's a greasy smell in the air.

"This is where Eddie operates."

As Asher speaks, a grungy looking man approaches us. He's got a gut and a stained white T-shirt. His hair is mostly gone, and I can smell him, too—the same as everything else. He tosses a towel over his shoulder and pulls a notepad out of his back pocket. "What can I get you?"

We look at Asher.

"Three rounds of the special," he says.

The man grunts at Asher and writes it down. He hands Asher a paper with the number twenty-six. Then he's gone.

"That's not him, is it?" I ask.

Asher laughs, shakes his head.

"You could come with us," Thorne says to Asher. Asher stops laughing and his smile fades. "You could come with us and get back to Mom. She'd—I know she'd love to see you."

Asher looks as if he's considering it, but he shakes his head. "I can't go back there. I have a job to do here."

"We're going to help stop them, and then you won't need this job," Thorne says. "You can rejoin the family. Mom would be thrilled to know you're alive."

"If you do, then I'd love nothing more than to see Mom." He smiles softly and taps his fingers across the table. "But for now, I'm dead. And I'd prefer to stay the way I am." His words are soft, but his eyes hold a warning.

"Twenty-six," the guy from before calls.

"That's us," Asher says. He stands, and we all go to the back of the restaurant. Some of the others look at us when we pass them. Thorne has my hand again. The big, greasy guy opens a door, and we walk through it.

Eddie's room is in the back, and it's actually bigger than the whole restaurant. The lights are dimmed. Large plastic boxes with glass fronts line the shelves on the walls. Eddie sits in the middle at a card-table-turned-desk two metal folding chairs waiting for us. Eddie looks like a kid, with dark skin and soft boyish features. His black hair is pulled back in braids.

"Asher Bishop," he says. He extends a hand to Asher, and they shake. "These for me?"

"They're for you. Thorne and Neely."

He smiles toward us. "Hey, you haven't heard from Aarons, have you?" Asher shakes his head, and Eddie curses. "He went to camp El Paso this last week. Haven't heard from him. They got raided, you know? Cecily sent word a couple days ago."

"Raided? These two were there a week ago."

Eddie looks at us and back to Asher. "Then they were lucky."

"What happened?" I ask. Bile rises in my throat when I think about all the people we left there. More people are dead. What about Delilah? Joe and the baby? The Elders were chasing me. Me. This was me again.

"Not enough survivors to know for sure, but probably what they always do." Eddie's voice drops an octave. "They send the Cleaners, and when that doesn't work, they have other tools—like this bomb-like weapon that completely eats through anything in its path or a gas that can line the ground and set it on fire at their command or even good old force from the Troopers."

Everywhere we go, disaster follows close behind. The Elders will never let me go.

"Because of me," I whisper. My insides shake, weighted with sadness and hot anger. We just left them all to die. Thorne grabs me and pulls me close to his chest but he offers no words, and in his silence, I notice his feelings are the same as mine. We both feel guilty.

Asher comes over toward us, Eddie behind him. "Eddie will take care of you from here. You're in good hands." He looks at Thorne for another second. "I'm sorry it has to be like this. That I can't stay with you."

"I get it," he says back.

Asher looks me over with a smile. "Good luck."

Thorne holds out his hand for Asher. There's only a glimmer of hesitation before he takes it and then pulls his brother into a hug. It's brief, but I can feel Thorne's ease and sadness mingle together. There aren't any words or drawn-out pauses. There's not even a goodbye. We watch as Asher disappears back into the restaurant. Then we're alone with Eddie.

"Have a seat," Eddie says. We follow him to the chairs, and mine wobbles when I sit. Eddie scatters a few papers around his desk and looks up at us. "Did Asher tell you your options?"

Thorne shakes his head. Eddie looks between us.

"What I do is give people a chance. Where you came from or who you used to be doesn't matter anymore. All that matters is where you're going. Are you mountain people or ocean people? Farms or cities? I can put you anywhere. I can give you a new name, a history, a purpose. I help you find a new place to live. People from the old Compounds like to start over completely, and that's what we do. It's up to us rebuild this country." He picks up a paper from his desk. "Who do you want to be and where do you want to go?"

I inhale some air. We can go anywhere. I can be anyone. How easy would it be to just leave all this and run away? There'd be no questions of why I was being targeted, of Xenith or my father. Thorne and I could start over. Forget the deadline. Forget the Compound. We could be together and be whoever we want to be.

The thought is crippling. I wish I was that person who could just do it. I want to.

"Anywhere?" I ask.

Eddie nods. "Anywhere your heart desires."

Thorne looks at me, eyes sharp. He doesn't feel the same way, and I shake my head because I don't either. It's a dream, but there's blood on my hands. There will only be more until we end this.

"We need to go to San Francisco," he says to Eddie. "How soon can you get us there?"

"I have a trip going day after tomorrow."

Thorne nods. "What do you need?"

"Let's slow down," Eddie says with a smile. "You're the escapees going to find the Mavericks, right? The ones with the twin branding?" Word must have travelled through the Remnant camps about us. "Let me see it."

Eddie doesn't give us a chance to answer. He moves behind us, and his breath is close to my neck. He stares at them, as if they will disappear at any moment, before his fingers trail down my branding. His hand is gone just as quickly as it appeared, and then he's in front of us, leaning back against the table.

"I can get you there." Eddie reaches back and grabs a large camera. "Smile," he says. He takes a picture of me and then Thorne. "Come back in the morning."

WE WAIT IN THE RESTAURANT. Neither of us talks. I have too many questions and not enough answers. The questions are mine alone, and saying them aloud makes the uncertainty of everything too real. It makes the possibility of the things I dread all too real, inescapable. Even though I don't speak them, they still linger over me, keep me captive; a puppet on a string, that's all I am. I am bound to them, to Thorne, to the things that could exist but don't yet, and to Xenith. I am always bound to something, and that something is connected to the Elders.

"Eighteen," the same man from yesterday says.

Thorne and I walk the same path to Eddie. He's waiting for us when we get there, all smiles and a bright purple shirt. He claps his hands together when we sit and gives us both an envelope. It's nothing extraordinary, rectangular and tan with a metal clasp, and I pull out the contents slowly. A small blue card with my picture on it and a name: Amy Williams, seventeen. Mother: deceased. Father: a banker named Joe. We live at 52-B Claret Street. My birthday is listed as December. There's another larger paper that's folded, full of dates and places and names don't make sense to me.

"You're now Caleb Redding and Amy Williams, both seventeen, both residents of an outskirts city coming here for a check-in report with the Mavericks. They have people stationed at other camps, liaisons of some sort that report back and forth in person about camp functionality or needs."

"Why do we have to be other people? Are Amy and Caleb real liaisons?" Thorne asks.

"I put your name on a paper—Ambrose—and every Remnant in the Old World will be on alert. It's a precaution. The papers just show everyone that you've been saved and established somewhere. Otherwise there will be questions."

"Everyone has a paper like this?" Thorne asks.

Eddie nods. "Anyone saved from a Compound by the Mavericks. It will help make your story stronger."

"What happens now?" I ask.

"Now, you cover up that mark," Eddie says, tossing us a small box and bottle of concealer. Inside the box are small cloth strips lined with plastic. "Put that over your branding. Use the bottle—it will hide the look of the cloth. If people see that, then it's all over for you because they'll do anything for safety."

"Don't the Mavericks let people keep their brandings?"

Eddie shakes his head. "No." He pauses. "After this, you wait. We pull out from the dock at midnight tomorrow. Don't be late." That's all he says to us before he turns away and leaves us staring at our new identities.

I help Thorne cover up his branding with the sticky cloth strips. It takes a few minutes and most of the bottle, but the dark marks are almost unnoticeable. He does the same for me. The liquid is cold on my neck and has a weird iron scent. Thorne spreads it around with his fingers until all the traces of the branding are gone. He takes my hand before we go. The sensation is familiar, the magnets that pull us together, but we look normal. The branding is still there, just hidden, but to everyone else, it's gone.

Thorne and Neely are gone. Caleb and Amy remain.

At least for now.

"NOW, WE'RE GOING. Remember, be quiet," Xenith says. He puts a finger over his lips and races across the horizon in front of me, his blond hair the only thing noticeable in the darkness. The Compound teaches us to fear things that are different. I know he's no exception, yet I follow him blindly through the quiet night.

The air stings my face. I haven't felt it for so long that it feels foreign. The salty smell of the water rushes my nostrils, and I want to stand here, take it all in. But I can't. Not now. I will be back. I have to be back because the alternative leaves me dead.

"Keep up," Xenith snaps at me.

I pick up my pace, and we run across the sand. There's nothing to hide us. No trees, no buildings. We've already passed headquarters. It's good, in this moment, that the Compound is strict about sleeping hours and not crossing this side of the Compound. No one is out, and the Troopers don't come this far.

Xenith turns to the right and pulls me with him. We're standing behind the safehouse, and it's just big enough to hide us both. I'm careful not to touch the wall.

"We'll go that way. The barrier opening is about 100 yards away. Be careful that you don't step on anything."

Xenith points into the distance, through the shadows, and we move.

IN THE SHADOWS, we join a small huddled crowd. Not many people are there, maybe eight, but it's good that we aren't alone. Less obvious that we are running away from something. Eddie is quick in his orders, and no one else speaks. There's a small boy and his father crossing with us, an old couple, and three teenagers covered in piercings.

The boat is small. We squeeze inside together and sit shoulder-to-shoulder. Eddie tells us the trip is three hours, depending on if we run into stops or cautions or checks. We are to all remain still and quiet and never ask questions if we are stopped. Eddie does all the talking.

I sit with Thorne on one side and the little boy on the other. He has deep dark eyes that seem lost. His father's eyes are similar. He smiles at his son reassuringly, and we take off into the sea. I close my eyes when the boat sways and listen to the waves. The sound reminds me of home; I miss it.

Thorne's hand squeezes mine, and I wonder if he misses the sound, too. We sit that way for the rest of the ride, with his hand in mine and our bodies moving with the ocean. I keep my eyes shut and listen to the sound of the water on the side of the boat. I try not to hum along with it, even though it calls to me. I just listen. It's a good sound.

I TAKE IT ALL IN as we walk up the street. Everywhere I look is hills and ocean, an endless supply of rolling beauty. The sky is a light shade of gray, the color before the sun breaks loose on the day. I can smell the newness in the air, holding me captive to the illusion that everything will be easy and will work out.

We walk the empty streets, passing only a few people on their way to somewhere else. It's so quiet here, so safe. I'm not sure where I'm supposed to go.

"Let's go to the Mavericks," Thorne says. "We'll wait for them."

"Where are they?" I ask.

Thorne pauses. "They can't be that far away."

A HUNDRED YARDS IS FAR. *Farther than it seems. I equate it to the lack of light and the waves that sound farther away than ever before. We cross through a line of trees. It's odd that there are so many trees, so perfectly formed. But then, it's not odd; it's manufactured, here to hide something no one wanted any of us to see. Ever. The space between them is small, so we have to climb up a couple branches and go over them. The other side is truly another world.*

Small buildings rest everywhere. They're an ugly shade of gray, the color paper gets when it's waterlogged. Bodies of cars, tires, wire, metal slates, and piles of wood are strewn across the open area. There are more items—large metal pieces that we use for housing roofs, barrows, large cargo crates, tractors. I wonder why they are here or what's inside of them, but as curious as it makes me, I don't want to know. I imagine men in those little buildings and metal cargo crates. Men that sit at screens and watch us. That pull strings, directing people where to move. Men that build things to keep us under control and things to kill us when they lose it. A shiver runs down my spine as I glance at the gray shacks one more time.

Xenith puts a finger to his lips. Was I making noises? Maybe I was breathing too loudly. He points to his eyes and his fingers make a V shape toward the other side of the junk. I don't notice it at first, not until we take a few more steps. Then the large fence that trails toward the sky comes into view. The barrier. No one could ever go over it.

I step on something. It cracks underneath my foot, and Xenith looks up at me like a hunter who's found its prey. I'm frozen, staring at him. He puts his hands toward me, making sure I stay still, before placing one finger over his lips again. He sinks toward the ground, lays flat on it, and puts his ear against it. I don't know what he's listening for or why his ear is on the ground, but I don't move. I try not to even breathe.

He gets up and pulls me toward him and whispers in my ear, "Run now!"

WE RUN INSIDE the Mavericks' headquarters as soon as the doors open. The building is large, with floors made out of shiny tile that clinks when I walk. The entrance is blocked off by glass doors, and beyond that is a lady in a black dress suit sitting at a singular round desk. The image is jarring, not a real portrayal of the Old World. The Old World is out there where there's desert and abandoned buildings and people hiding underground, trying to live. Not here, at a desk with technology in a city where people are free to do more of what they want.

"You're here before I've even sat!" Her hair bounces around her. It's the color of the sunset in the summer, trapped on a head. "Good morning. How can we be of service?" Her eyes are on me, patient and waiting for me to speak. Can I just blurt all this out?

"I—we need to meet with someone."

"That's what we tend to do here. What's the purpose?" She smiles one of those fake smiles that I've only really seen in people like my father.

"I'm here to see Agent Handler," I say. I memorized the name a long time ago. "Salvation," Xenith had called him.

310

"He's unavailable unless it's an appointment or an emergency."

"I'm sure he'd have time for us," I say. I lower my voice to a whisper. "We're here about the Compound."

The woman's features shift into surprise, confusion, awe. I'm not sure why. She stares at us like we're aliens, and maybe we are. "Why would you need to meet with someone about that?" She's trying us, searching and waiting for a slip-up. Her gaze is threatening. I smile back, hoping it looks more innocent than it could ever be.

"I have some information and some questions. He'll want to talk with us."

She shuffles some papers around on her desk, and the keys clack under her fingernails. The noise echoes past us. She flashes her smile again, and her hair moves after her.

"Agent Handler isn't free until this afternoon."

"Is there anyone else we can talk with?"

"I'm sorry. He's the only one who takes meetings for that...issue."

"Fine," I say. "Put us down."

XENITH PULLS ME DOWN to the ground behind one of the cargo crates. He's lying on top of me, and I'm about to ask him what's going on when I hear a boom that makes the crate and the ground shake. I can't see, but I can imagine the image. Tearing apart, splintering, sticking pieces into the ground. Collisions happen all around me, items hitting the ground with booms and thuds, as if it was raining rocks.

A shout rings in my ears, along with the blast, until there's nothing but a high-pitch screeching in my head.

And then I hear the man again. "What the hell? See anything, Tom?"

"Nothing," another, probably Tom, replies. There are two of them. I hold my breath, willing them not to hear us. I'm so close I can taste it.

"Better look around. If the director wakes up because of the call, there will be hell to pay," the first guy says.

I hear them as they move. I think it's because my ear is implanted in the dirt. Their feet crunch the earth, and the flashlights graze us, near my head. I'm sure they've seen us. I'm holding my breath, trying not to move.

"Dave, look what I found."

Us. My heart races, pounds against my chest. This man has found us; he'll report us and my father will come and all this would be for nothing. I'm this close—this close—and now it's over. It's hard to breathe with the light shining near us. One inch closer and they'll see us, and then they'll take me to my father and he'll be relentless. He'll torture Xenith and me. He can't find us. Not when I'm this close to getting out.

The light moves away from us. "Must've been a bird," Tom says.

"It's always a bird. Stupid birds oughta know about the land mines by now," Dave says back.

My heart finally slows down, and the sound of their feet disappears. Xenith pulls me up and looks as relieved as I do. I whisper I'm sorry, and he nods back. It was a stick I stepped on. Just a stick. They really don't want people here.

Xenith leads me to the right along the fence. There's a piece of concrete about twenty feet wide, and it stretches underneath. It's attached to one of the little buildings and has a large door that rolls up and down that's open right now. Waiting.

"This is it?" I whisper.

"This is it."

"What is it?" I ask.

We stand a few feet away, ducked near the ground. I don't hear anyone or see anyone.

"This is the shipment zone. The freighter trucks bring all the supplies here, put them in the building, close it, and leave. Those men from earlier? They move it all from here to headquarters. When we need it, it's delivered to us," he says.

"How do you know that?"

He shrugs and avoids my gaze. "My family's been around for a long time."

I don't respond to his statement.

"See those boxes over there?" he asks. He points to a stack lined up by the side of the cement. "We need to get you in one of those."

I shoot him a look.

"Those are the empty ones. They take them away, refill them, bring them back. Guess where they go from here?" I shake my head. "The Old World."

My throat is dry. "What time does it come?"

"1:50. It takes three men exactly twenty-five minutes to unload and reload the truck. It leaves promptly at 2:18."

I look down at my watch. It's 1:45. Five minutes.

"Won't they notice if one of those empty wooden crates is heavy?"

His eyes light up. "I told you, Neely, my family's been around for a long time. No one will question anything. Come on."

It's not easy getting into a wooden crate. My knees are bent in an awkward shape against my chest, and for what feels like an eternity, I doubt I'm going to fit. But then I do. Xenith hands me my pack. There's hardly enough room for it to squeeze in, too. It's shoved between the box and my shins, half in my face as I hunch low.

"Are you okay?" Xenith asks as he stares at me.

I want to say no, of course I'm not okay. I'm running away in a box. I don't say that though. I say yes. He leans in, kisses my lips softly. I don't kiss him back—as much as one can not-kiss someone back, anyway. At least, I tell myself that I'm not going to, but then my body leans into him as I realize he's the last taste of something familiar. There's a slight smile on his face when he pulls away, and I know that I shouldn't have done that.

"It's a day or so in the truck, then you'll be at the Burrows. You'll be safe with them." Xenith's words rush out quickly, stumbling over each other. He pauses and looks at me. "Forty days from now, Neely, it happens."

His face is the last thing I see before he closes the lid and leaves me in the darkness. His scent fills up my box, the intoxicating smell of mint and earth and ocean. I can still feel his lips on me as I disappear.

THORNE AND I COULD DISAPPEAR in this park. We walk around like it's normal because that's all we can do. It's what Caleb and Amy would do. Thorne and Neely would be fighting, but they are gone. They were lost somewhere across the country in different spots on different days. Wherever I am—the real me—I hope she is fighting to find her way back.

Amy is too fake for me to be happy.

The park is beautiful, trailing the edges of the ocean, full of trees here and sand there. I like this part of the city better. We've spent the last few hours wandering through shops and stores filled with old books. We've been scrambling to fill our time with life. Neither of us is willing to say that we both feel it slipping away. I can sense it on him like cologne. He carries the fear with him. Sometimes he slips up and his worries flow into me through the connection.

I watch the people move past us. An elderly man watching the birds. A woman running with a baby stroller. A man with a dog. An old couple holding hands. Another man staring out into the ocean. They seem so carefree, so vibrant. I know it's this place, this freedom. I know it's changed them. And I'm on the cusp of it but as someone else. If I was here as me, longer, I know it could change me, too. This place takes away the darkness.

I bite my lip as Thorne stops walking and sits on a bench. It's got a good view of the ocean, and the trees shield us from the sun. Light drips onto my back and my head through the openings in the leaves. My eyes drift out to the ocean. In the distance, barely noticeable, I can make out the boats. Some have sails; some don't. All of them glisten and sparkle under the sun. It sends that soft memory of home rushing through me. I want to hate it back there. I want to hate it and hate them, but I can't.

They are all innocents, blinded and manipulated. They aren't at fault. They are fishermen and teachers and mothers and friends. They are pawns. The Elders are the problem, the game masters. I watch the boats moving on the water. They are moving toward something, and everyone at home deserves that.

Thorne holds my hand in his, and I hold him close. I can't see his branding, which is still covered on his neck, and it's weird, not seeing the mark on his skin. Even though it's gone, it still haunts me, and I wish I didn't hate it as much as I do.

"It's forever," Thorne says. "Like we're supposed to be."

I'm not sure how long we sit there, me looking out and him being silent, but then he's pulling me up from the bench. The wind is still. The sky is alive with color. The rhythm of the waves sounds like the song at home. I hum along with it in my head. Even if I had thirty more years, nothing would ever compare to this place and the freedom of it all. This place is good. Amy likes it here; maybe Neely could, too.

Shadows suddenly block the sunlight.

"This is a security check. Present your verification and security papers."

Two people dressed in black like the Troopers stare down at us, hands outstretched. They are in black, but they aren't Troopers. They don't look heartless.

"We got word of some unwarranted visitors. You understand," the second one says.

My racing heart slows down half a beat because they're not Troopers. They're not working for the Elders. It should calm me, but I can still feel my heart pounding within me. It's the first time I'm glad there's a cage there to hold it in. Without the cage, it would be roaming around the air and the world, ready to kill everything that endangers it. I imagine it, a roaring lion, hungry and ready to devour, its only purpose to escape and capture and protect the thing that keeps it alive. The world knows no fury like a heart on the prowl. I can feel the pounding in my head, reverberating there and shaking my memories into each other.

"Amy," Thorne says loudly.

All three of them are looking at me, a sea of eyes. Right, I'm Amy. I hold out my papers to the officers. Time stands still, and the lion trapped in the cage is ready to pounce. But nothing happens. They hand everything back to me and to Thorne.

"How are things in #11?" the second one asks.

I blink. Eleven. That's the camp where we live.

"Fine. It's all the usual really. Kids getting antsy, daytime restriction problems, lack of security measures," Thorne says.

The officer offers. "I get it. Grew up in #45."

Thorne nods like he completely understands the whole thing.

"Good luck with your visit, Ms. Williams, Mr. Redding," the first one adds. They move past us. I count to twenty, willing things to slow to a normal speed.

"What was that?" I ask.

"Sorry, you panicked. I didn't think you knew," he says.

"I didn't.

Thorne shrugs. "I talked a lot with Joe in El Paso. He said those were three of their biggest issues."

I had no idea that Thorne had asked about the camps or how they work. When he told Asher he wanted to help, he'd already been gathering information the whole time. He's a sponge when he wants to understand something. If he hadn't come, I wouldn't have been able to answer that question. I wouldn't have been able to do so many things that are possible because of him. He saved me again.

"We should go," I say.

AGENT NICHOLAS HANDLER'S crystal-blue eyes stare at me behind his dark-framed glasses. Even sitting, I can tell he's tall. Muscles bulge under his blazer, and he's younger than expected.

"What was your question?" I ask, completely sidetracked.

He leans back, and his chair makes this squeaking noise. He crosses his fingers in the shape of a triangle, tip to tip, and stares at me over his glasses.

"I asked, Miss Ambrose, what your plan was to save everyone?"

I swallow. "I don't have one."

He nods slowly. "And you, Mr. Bishop? Do you have a plan?"

Thorne shakes his head. Agent Handler nods slowly and rises to his feet. He moves in quick steps around his office, where every object is perfectly stacked and organized by size and color. "The thing is, it's only nine days before the Elders transfer your people. That's not a lot of time to make this happen."

He's right. It's not a lot of time. "Xenith said this is what you do, so I need you to do it. Whatever it takes," I say.

Agent Handler looks at me. His eyes meet mine for a second too long, and then: "What are you willing to lose to see this accomplished?"

I don't look away from him, even though I feel Thorne's eyes on me, too. I'd give up everything except him. But haven't I already done that just by saying yes to Xenith? Wasn't me coming here a risk of losing him? And me wanting something more than what we have? But he's still here.

"Everything," Thorne answers for me. I look at him. "She'd risk everything."

Handler's eyebrows raise, and he glances between us. I speak quickly. "Agent Handler, I don't want to be like my father. I don't want myself or anyone else to be changed by the Elders or used by them. Surely, you can understand what this transfer would mean for me."

He smiles—not in the funny way, but in some sort of way that puts me at ease. "Come with me," he says. He removes a pair of silver keys from his pants pocket and opens his office door.

Handler leads us down the hallway to a set of elevators. We ride them down to the basement. It's a long way down from the eighteenth floor, and the silence rests between us awkwardly.

WHEN THE ELEVATOR doors open, there are groups of people in line along the walls. Some are in lines at the computers, and some sit in circles and examine blueprints. Agent Handler leads us around the room toward the back. As we pass, people look up at us, some longer than others. There's a group of three people—one with green, pointed hair—encased in a glass room in the back, and they all look up at us when we enter.

The door hisses as Agent Handler closes the door. "Neely, Thorne, these are the commanders. Agents Carrigan, Mitchell, and Bane. They are my next in command."

I feel dirty next to Agent Carrigan's pristine white skin and blonde hair that falls across her ears. She smiles at me, her eyes sparkling, and greets us happily. Agent Mitchell, the one with the green hair, raises his eyebrows as he shakes my hand. Agent Bane, with his shirt really tight against his muscles, nods to us.

"What is all this?" Thorne asks, poking one of the buttons next to him. A screen changes, and Mitchell jumps in to change it back. Thorne stuffs his hands into his pockets.

Handler removes his jacket and leans against the wall. Even the white shirt is crisp underneath. A month ago I would've been like them, and now I'm more like a Remnant but not quite that either. I'm my own entity. A survivor.

"Those people out there," he says, pointing beyond the glass, "are helping us by providing possible extraction routes and strategy plans. Each group works on a different piece of the puzzle, and we will put the best elements together as an action plan for unification."

"Unification?" I ask. I've never heard of that.

Agent Carrigan is the one who answers, her voice high and light. "Everyone in the Compound is altered by the branding. It's something the Elders mastered before the Preservation so they could keep control." Carrigan points to my neck. "It changes the brain to subdue curiosity. The whole marking is a drug, constantly feeding into the brain. Without curiosity, there are no questions. Without questions, there is no search for truth and no need for free will, for decisions."

"It's quite effective when you think about it," Agent Bane adds, his messy brown hair sticking up all over the place like he'd been running his hands through it. He leans over the back of Carrigan's chair. "When people like you come to us or when we save them, we remove it and then place them in our new society. Unification."

"Why aren't we affected by the branding? I've never had a problem asking questions," I say.

I'm sure my life would have been easier if I had.

"The twin branding is different. In all cases that we've encountered, it created something new instead of taking away the curiosity. When the Lopez twins escaped, the Elders stopped the branding and separated all those who had received it before," Carrigan says.

"How does it work?" Thorne asks.

Agent Handler crosses his arms. "Twins were given a prenatal treatment to help the Elders find immortality, and when the branding links them together, it completes the process. From what you've told me, Thorne had the treatment, but Neely did not. Your body was not properly prepared for the branding, so when they branded you together, they created something else entirely."

I stare sideways at Thorne. One little lie from Liv Taylor changed all of our lives, made us something else. Every decision has led us here.

"And I have a feeling they didn't know what they'd created," Mitchell adds. We all look at him, and his green hair is odd to me. How does one get green hair? "I mean, if they had known, they would've made the two of you the biggest new experiment."

Liv Taylor saved us from that. It's why she lied to them. They'd suspected something after Cecily and Deanna escaped, after the branding effects were revealed. They wanted to make sure we hadn't been altered since we weren't properly branded, and her second lie kept us together.

Bane points to a screen, and a few images flash by. They look like pages from Old World storybooks. He stops on one of a man bent over a spring. "The Elders love to experiment." With a flick of Bane's wrist, the images change to small spheres forming, moving, turning into babies. "With twins, the Elders saw an opportunity to examine the effects of genetic splicing and connections from conception. Identical twins were viewed as the ideal study subject, the most like clones that the universe can create. Fraternal twins, on the other hand, added power to the idea that two separate beings could still be strongly connected.

Both of these things were of interest to the Elders, so they did whatever they could to find some answers. The tests have major side effects—morphing DNA into new abilities—but they didn't notice for centuries."

"Like the way Cecily and Deanna could share dreams?" I glance toward Agent Handler, and he adjusts his glasses on his nose.

"Exactly."

The images around us shift to pictures of children. Two in every shot: twins. Agent Carrigan smiles at me. Then she straightens up in her chair. "These are some of the identical twins from the last hundred years," Agent Carrigan says. She pauses on a picture of two girls, one with brown hair and one with blonde. "What's wrong with this picture?"

"They have different color hair," Thorne says.

She nods and flashes another. Identical twins with a different color of eyes or hair, a boy with freckles and one without. "The test made small superficial alterations after a few generations. Physically, there was no change, no indication that anything was amiss, but mentally, they were stronger, smarter, and in tune with each other. There's a study of twins placed in two different Compounds, and they could still communicate. The effects went to fraternal twins too—any children who shared the womb."

I wonder if that's how it works for Thorne and me. We can't communicate verbally or mentally, but emotion is a communication.

"But then, both kinds of twins started developing more significant traits, actual skills." Agent Carrigan flashes through some more pictures. All of these people could do something unique, and it's because of the Elders. Pictures of children zoom through my line of view, and one with blonde hair makes me think of Delilah. I hope she's okay.

The images pause on a picture. In it, the girls look identical, and it's easy to imagine the lines in Cecily's face now. Her eyes are the same shade of gray, but her hair is a dark shade of black.

"Cecily and Deanna Lopez were the first people who talked about what they could do, but I guess dreams of the future would cause that. There are others," she says, flashing through pictures. "Telecommunication, moving things with their minds, sensitivities to sound and light—more things than we can categorize. As a result of the testing, twins received enhanced mental connections manifested in different mental abilities. For every set of twins that were altered, hundreds more died."

Everyone is quiet until Agent Bane shouts from across the room. "What do you guys do?"

Shouldn't they know this? They seem to know everything.

"We share emotions," Thorne says.

"But they're not really twins, and the branding didn't work the same way," Mitchell adds. "Which explains that."

Everyone in the room grows quiet, and Mitchell doesn't even notice. I stare at him, waiting for something else. "What does it explain?" I ask.

"Sorry, he does that," Carrigan says quickly.

Mitchell nods and stuffs a hand into his pocket. "Every record we have are of mental abilities—things controlled by the mind—and none of the twins were inhibited by the branding. But yours is emotion-based. Do you feel each other's emotions in a physical manifestation?"

"Yes," we both say. The fire, the intensity, the swirling in the head, the weight in my stomach.

"That's because Neely wasn't prepared for the branding. It makes your connection different," he says. Agent Mitchell moves around the screens. His fingers move quickly, pulling up images. "You're the director's daughter, right?" I nod, and he rubs his hands together. I'm glad someone is excited. "Then your whole connection has adapted to each other because you have the gene. If you didn't, you would've been branded with no problem or effects at all since you didn't have the prenatal preparation treatment."

"What are you talking about?" I ask.

Mitchell looks at me like a rock has been dropped on my head, and I cross my arms. This is first I've heard of a gene, but my heart rate increases. I can't help but feel like everything is about to change. I'm about to change.

Mitchell sighs, pokes around on the screen, and changes some images. "About a century ago, the Elders tried to change the branding to be a control source, rather than a blockade. They tested in small groups, and your family was one of them. Three families were tested in that first trial. Two families were successful; one was not."

"Mine?"

"Yours. It took the Elders a few decades to figure out why, but then it was discovered that the Ambrose family carries a unique gene with this amazing plasticity to survive, to adapt. You bounce back quicker than most people. You survive," Agent Mitchell says. He barely has to pause for a breath, but I can't seem to catch mine.

"That's not true. This trip has been hard. The darkness, the sunlight, the heat—I've felt it all just like any normal person."

Thorne touches my arm. "Not since you were poisoned. Neely, I didn't tell you this, but you weren't breathing when they found you. You were dead. They only went to get you because I felt when it happened."

"What?" I died? How did I die? That's not possible. I would know if I had been dead.

Thorne's voice is low. "It was like before, when you drowned, only more intense. It felt like my body was dying with yours. I don't know how to explain it. They breathed life into you, shocked your heart, and then you slept for four days. You haven't really seemed tired since then, not like I have."

This whole thing is ridiculous. I didn't die. It's something else. I've been tired since then. Haven't I? I slept in the car ride with Asher. No, I didn't; I only listened and pretended.

"It's been activated then," Mitchell says. I pull my gaze in his direction, and he looks so excited. It'd be adorable if it wasn't all because of me dying. "The Elders discovered it while on their quest for immortality, and then they placed the Ambrose family in a position to be directors, starting with your great-grandfather, so they could track you. Obviously, everyone in your family has died, but it's because they were missing genes. They perfected and altered the Ambrose line, trying to create the perfect specimen that they could replicate, and we think they finally did. You. They need you."

I shake my head. This is too much to process. I'm some sort of creation that was manipulated into existence? "You're saying that they set up my mother and my father so that I would be born?" Even as I deny it, I remember what it said it my father's papers about pairing up marriages for reproduction.

Carrigan kneels down so she's closer to me. "They've been prepping your family for years, Neely. The Elders aren't immortal; they can die. Their study on twins has only postponed their death. They age, but at a way slower rate than us. If they could pair that with you, then they could survive anything—and live forever. As it is now, they can be killed or stopped, but with that gene of yours, they would be invincible."

They need me. That's why my father was fighting so hard to get me to take his place. That's why they were sending Thorne away. I finally sit down on that stool, head spinning. They'd planned for me since before I was born, a child with the perfect genetic makeup, so they could use me and live forever. My mother died only wanting to keep me away from them. Liv Taylor lied to keep it a secret and protect me.

I really have been a pawn. Since before I was born.

"Because you have plasticity, when you were born and rewired to Thorne, your genetic code adjusted. You became completely connected, which is how you feel each other. That makes you even more special."

"Why?"

"You're a threat. They can't control you, or they never could before. They could've found a way around that now, but you're safe right now," Mitchell adds.

"I don't understand. How?"

"That branding. If it was ever removed or anything happened to Thorne, then you're susceptible to the Elders. They could take whatever they want from you, and you couldn't stop them. The branding is a safety net for you; without it, they can manipulate your elasticity gene, you, for their purpose."

That's why the Elders wanted to transfer Thorne. Then they'd change his branding and ruin our connection. Have they known this whole time about our secret? Or was it just to get rid of him? If Thorne wasn't connected to me, I would only be a tool for the Elders' messed-up cause.

"Basically," Bane says, "without the branding, you're dead and the Elders win."

The one thing I've wanted to destroy is the only thing keeping me safe. I look at Thorne and he squeezes my hand, but it does nothing to calm the crashing in my stomach.

THE WAVES CRASH and squeeze into each other as I snuggle closer to Thorne. This is one of our last nights together before I die. I shouldn't be thinking about that, but the truth consumes my thoughts. I have one month, and Thorne will be gone for most of it. He leaves tomorrow for a weeklong fishing trip, and then he has another at the end of the month. Him being gone will be easier.

And not. Even sitting next to him, my body is on fire at his touch, and the branding does that. What we would feel like to me without our connection? If Liv Taylor hadn't lied to the Elders time and time again. If none of this had happened. What would being normal feel like?

"You okay?" Thorne asks me.

I nod, but I know he doesn't believe it because he inches my chin up toward his face. "You can tell me whatever you're thinking."

I sigh heavily. Can I really? "Do you ever wonder who'd we be without the branding?"

We've never had this conversation before. There was never a reason to, but now there are too many reasons. I know more than him, and it all feels false.

Thorne runs a hand through his hair and stares past me into the distance. "Of course I have."

"I guess sometimes I wonder how we would be if it wasn't that way, if we didn't have this." I touch the branding on his neck. "If we were our own person, completely without the other's emotions. If we had our own secrets and desires."

He smirks at me. "I have my own secrets, Neely."

"You do?" I ask.

He nods. "Sure. It's not like you're reading my mind. You're only feeling what I feel, and only when it's intense or something I want you to feel."

I scrunch up my nose. "It's almost the same thing, isn't it? Our pull is getting stronger. I can feel you more. When you're out with the boats and you get closer to shore, you get this moment of complete happiness, and I feel it like a shock to my chest."

"You make it sound like it's an annoyance," he says.

"I don't mind the happy things, but sometimes..." I pause. Sometimes I want to be my own person. This is a lost cause. "It doesn't matter."

"It does," he says.

I move so I'm facing him instead of curled up in his arms. "I guess I wonder sometimes what it'd be like if I carried all my own emotions and you carried yours, and we were normal."

"Harder," he says, as if it's the simplest answer in the world. "Right now we've got each other, and that's always made sense to me. Sure, it'd be nice sometimes to not have to worry so much about what you're feeling and why, but at the same time, if I didn't know that, I know you wouldn't tell me, and you'd be this mystery to me."

"You like the connection because it helps you understand me?"

"No," he says quickly, inching me closer so our bodies are touching. "I'm saying it wouldn't matter."

"But why?"

"With a connection or without one, we are still the same."

I nod, but I really wonder if we are. If we didn't have this huge emotional pull, would we be anything at all?

Thorne pulls me close, and I know he's done talking about it. I curl back into him, trying to clear my brain and stare over the ocean. How can he dismiss it so easily? The branding is everything we are, and without it, what are we? If I could ever get rid of it, what would happen to us?

"Look, a shooting star," Thorne says, pointing up. I see it too, a bright flashing light drifting through the star-filled sky and hurling down toward us. A dying star, the schoolhouse teacher taught us once. "Make a wish."

"What?" I explore his face, take in as much of it as possible. The soft angles and warm colors that are all him. I know I won't be seeing it much more.

"People in the Old World used to wish on stars. Shooting stars are the luckiest. Make a wish."

Thorne closes his eyes tightly. A smile spreads across his face like he knows I'm watching him. I close my eyes, too. The words are all jumbled in my head because there's so much I could wish for.

For all of this to be a dream. For me to not have to leave soon. For another way. For Thorne to come with me. For everything to go according to plan.

I don't wish for any of those things.

When I open my eyes, Thorne is smiling down at me. His warm caramel eyes are bright in the darkness, and a smile plays on his lips. There's this joy radiating from him that completely overtakes any of my own emotions, so overwhelming I'm tempted to let it consume me.

"What did you wish for?" he asks me.

I shake my head. "Isn't it tradition that you can't tell wishes?"

"That's only for birthdays. They have more power if you speak them."

I laugh. "I don't want to risk mine not coming true."

"You won't."

"What did you wish?" I ask, changing the subject from me. I don't know how to tell him my wish.

Thorne stretches his lean, tall body without his hand leaving mine. The movement is so swift and graceful. How did he end up being so good?

"I shouldn't tell you..."

"Because you don't want to risk it? I told you," I joke.

He shakes his head. "I won't be risking anything. I'm not worried because I already have you," he says, locking eyes with me.

My heart slows down and speeds up at once. He captivates me, and his emotions run through the branding, all lust and joy and passion. I feel my own guilt bubbling to the surface, but I hide it away as much as possible.

I'm not sure who moves first: him or me. It doesn't matter. Nothing matters except the feel of his lips on mine. Fire moves through me when we kiss, rushing over me like waves. His hand runs through my hair and over my skin, and I lean into the ground so he's closer to me. The branding is burning through my body while our mouths are entwined.

I steal a glance at the sky through half-closed eyes. I take back my wish, and I wish for him instead—forever.

But I don't mean it as much I as should.

I didn't wish for him the first time. I wished for the truth, for Liv Taylor to be wrong, for the branding not to be the reason we were connected. I wished for a life with no branding. A life that's completely my own. Even if it means that he's not connected to me.

THORNE'S HAND IS connected to mine as we follow the agents into another room. This one is deeper underground, and when Agent Carrigan flips on the light, it's a gray stone, small and cold, with a large machine in the middle of it that we can see through some plastic framing.

My head is spinning from all the information, from the idea that my whole life really was manipulated. That I died a few days ago and didn't even know it. That I'm really here. I don't want to admit I feel a little scared of what else I'm going to learn. Thorne lets go of my hand and sits next to Mitchell as he explains to him the way the computer works. Bane pulls up some more of those electronic files. A picture of an older man, balding and no smile, appears. Some more documents with the word "Unification."

Agent Bane clears his throat. He's all hard edges and angles and facts, even in the minutes I've known him. "There was a founding scientist, Leonard Taylor, who didn't agree with the Elders. After starting the Preservation, he learned he couldn't stop the branding, but he decided he could counter it. The Mavericks were started so we could establish Unification: the destruction of the Compounds, salvation of the people, and their reintegration into a new life."

A new life. It sounds so easy when he says it that way. An ache burrows in my chest. I want a new life, a new chance to live it. Freedom. That's why we're here, but we can never have it.

"Part of this allows us to remove the branding so that everyone can fully integrate into society," Carrigan adds. She points toward the machine. "It's a laser that removes the ink and the effect."

My ears are burning. "How do you do it?"

"It's something we've mastered. It's only ink, the branding, but they lace the ink with mercury," she says. I watch as a video plays showing the ink being mixed with a silver lava.

"They carve it into your skin, like a tattoo," Agent Handler says, "but the metals cause a chemical imbalance that allows them to have control. Everyone we've removed it from has behaved normally with questions and a desire for answers and no side effects."

It's amazing that they can do that, return us all to the way we were meant to be.

"Giving people back their free will to live a normal life is one of the only things we can do," Mitchell adds.

This is what I've wanted for a long time, and it's totally possible. Just not for me. That feeling is a sinking pit I could fall into. I can never be unbranded, never be my own. The only thing I've ever wanted can never happen.

"That's why this news of the new Experimental Ultimate Compliance is alarming," says Agent Mitchell. I notice for the first time that his eyes match his hair, both dark shades of brown. "This machine was created with the Preservation. If the Elders are changing the way the branding works, we may never get to save them."

What would the Elders do with the people they make serve them? What's the purpose? Why have they been taking down their own Compounds throughout history? Maybe they've changed their minds. Or they have found a way to make something better.

"Do you think they could've been experimenting with this on my father?" I ask.

The three agents look at each other. "It's likely, especially considering how much they want what your family has," Mitchell says.

"So it's true then," I whisper.

Thorne meets my gaze from across the small room. No wonder my father became someone else so quickly. He hasn't been the man who gave me the teddy bear when I was two years old, when he found out I was his. One day he came home and was horrible and blind, fueled by hatred and so unlike him. So unlike the man Sara said he used to be, the one I'd known.

They want me. They need me.

The Elders would burn down the Burrows and send Cleaners to peaceful camps. They would track us here and try to stop me. They would do anything.

The Elders will always look for me. I will always be branded.

If they succeed in the new Compound, everyone will be thoughtless, mindless, trapped in the darkness. No one will ever know the truth. They already stopped their curiosity, but it's as if the Elders want everyone to be machines.

I can never have peace. Never be free of them.

Thorne reaches out to me through our connection, and I look up at him. Tears burn at my eyelids, but I won't let them come. Not now. Even though the thought of it is terrifying me. They can't get Thorne, and they can't change the branding.

I have to stop them, to prevent everyone I know and love from being altered. That's what matters. And then we can get rid of the Elders forever. It's the only way to live.

"That's enough. We can all talk later," Handler says. He opens the door for us, and we step out. He pauses, looks back at Carrigan. "How's the layout team coming together?"

Carrigan shrugs, unsure. "Difficult. The insider information has been helpful, but this Compound's barriers are still presenting a problem. We could only figure out how to shut the barriers off long enough to break them if we had access from the inside. We need some kind of power redirection. That should disable the barrier alarms for enough time."

"We can't get inside until they're down," Handler says. He rests a hand on her shoulder. "You'll have to find a way."

I study all the faces as we exit the room. No one looks up at us this time, no one watches us go. It's almost as if, in less than an hour, we're already one of them.

"What was your plan before?" I ask Handler when we're in the elevator again.

"The same as usual," he says. "We've been planning to infiltrate your Compound for months. There are just a few kinks before we can go. We need to act faster now, before the transfer starts."

I exchange a look with a Thorne and then watch the numbers go up in the elevator, starting from two. *Five. Six. Seven.* We're so close to all of this that I don't know what to say. All they need is a redirection of power to disable the barrier.

Eight. Nine. Ten.

"Can you be ready before the Elders want to move us?" Thorne asks Handler.

A redirection. Something that causes all the power in the Compound to shift.

Eleven. Twelve.

"It's going to be tight, but we're almost there. We're only a missing a few pieces," Agent Handler says. "We find them and we're in."

Redirection.

Thirteen. Fourteen.

"I'll help you," Thorne says. He looks at me. Redirection. His eyes are warm, sparked with hopefulness.

Fifteen. Sixteen. Seventeen.

"Me too," I say.

Agent Handler smiles. "We're glad to have you."

There has to be something...

The light in the elevator flickers, and Thorne reaches out to me. His hand brushes mine, and a surge rushes through the branding.

I freeze and look up at Handler. "I think I know a way to take down the barriers," I say.

Eighteen.

The doors chime open.

THERE'S A CRACK, and my container is open, light pouring into the darkness.

For a minute, I let myself believe it's my father. But he's home asleep. It's not him. When my walls fall down, I hug my pack to my chest. Just knowing there's a knife there is reassuring, even though I never want to use it. There's a man staring back at me in a green uniform. He's got a flashlight and a smile.

"Thought you'd want to move around. It's a couple hours until the beach. That's where the Burrows are."

He has the strangest accent. He says around like "ahrand" and hours like "ahr." He's smiling, though, and he has a light.

"Water?" the guy asks me.

I shake my head. His face is round and chubby and red, but he's not a large man. His shirt has a white tag. His name is George. I open my bag for a second, just to make sure everything's there. Tucked deep inside is the map, some food and water, and then my eye catches something new. Xenith's copy of To Kill a Mockingbird. There's a page marked. I don't have to look at it to know what it is.

"That's a good book," George says.

I smile. "Where are you from, George?" I ask.

He doesn't get to answer. We both bounce as the truck jolts forward. There's a small bump, which I'm guessing to be the fence. I look down at my watch and push the button. Forty days left to save everyone.

EVERYONE PULLS US in separate directions when we step off the elevator. For the last few days, Thorne and I have been consulted in every aspect of the infiltration. I stayed up all night memorizing the entrance plan ever since I figured out how to redirect the power supply.

Sleep hasn't been my friend lately anyway; every time I close my eyes, I am plagued with images. Usually failed attempts at this plan, where I watch everyone die because of a miscalculation Thorne and I made. Where I watch everyone slowly lose their minds because of the Elders. Thorne says I'm too worried, but I'm concerned that he's not worried enough.

"Neely! You're here. Good." Carrigan moves around the glass room, which they call the Hub. Her heels are yellow today, just like her fingernails. She pulls up a screenshot on the computer. "What do you think of this?"

I scan the blueprint of the Compound, marked up with Xs to indicate where the Mavericks will break off to gather the people. Carrigan and Bane have covered all the basics: the center, the outskirts, and each area of homes separated into divisions. Fifty people are involved including us. Fifty people to save 743. They haven't accounted for the Troopers.

"Move people here and here," I say, pointing to locations on the screen. "And line more along the beach. Areas three and four can combine to get area five since it's small."

Carrigan squeals as she makes the changes. "That's so brilliant. You are made for this."

I laugh. "I don't know about that."

"Oh, I do. And you are. Not everyone can develop a strategy like this in two days. We've been at this for years."

"How long have you been here?"

"Six years. I've been with Handler since I was Mitchell's age. Fourteen." She clicks print on the screenshot. The sound of the printer whirrs around the Hub. "This is my family. Handler's been like a father to me. Mitchell is my annoying little brother, and Bane is—"

"This is good," Mitchell yells. He walks in with the printout in his hands. His hair is blue today, sticking out at the top of his head. "This is really good."

She points to me, and Mitchell looks in my direction. He nods his head, surprised, but doesn't say anything else.

"How's it going?" Carrigan asks.

Before Mitchell can answer, Bane pokes his head in the Hub door. At the sight of Bane, Carrigan shuffles and looks away. Mitchell smiles at her, and her face gets red.

"Handler needs you, Neely. He's in the office. Mitch, come on." I notice the look Bane gives to Carrigan before he leaves. Mitchell laughs and shakes his head before he follows.

She meets my gaze for a moment. "You should go," she says. She looks back at the paper. "Handler's waiting."

HANDLER, BANE, MITCHELL, and Thorne look at me when I open the door. They're huddled around a table, maps and blueprints scattered across it. Thorne smiles at me, tension disappearing from his face.

"Neely, great." Handler smiles. "Thorne says you'd be the expert on this area."

I close the door and join them around the table. I only have to glance down to see what they are staring at. The blueprint is too large, too pointed, too well-designed for me not to know.

"Headquarters," I say softly. "What is this for?"

All four men exchange glances. Much to my surprise, Thorne is the one who explains it. "You know your idea to redirect the power?"

I take a breath and nod. If we can get a large power source to operate when the barrier is already open, like at night when we're getting a shipment, then we stall it long enough to infiltrate. And the only thing with that much power is surrounded in windows and white walls, located under headquarters.

"We need to make him turn it on, Neely," Thorne says, taking my hand.

I know he's talking about the torture chamber immediately. Just the thought of what my father did to

Thorne, to us, I'm able to feel the pain of the shocks, of the screams, of the pricks across my skin and the heat that twists in my stomach at the memory. It was my idea to use the torture chamber, the most powerful thing in the Compound, so powerful each time he used it the lights in the buildings flickered. A redirection.

Mitchell's the one who explains it again. "The controls run off the same energy. Without your father's code to open the barriers, or a way to refocus the energy directed at the torture chamber so we can break through them, we can't access the control room."

"Why am I here?"

The men grow silent again.

"The director is the only one who can stop us," Handler says. "If he gets word of our arrival, he can stop us before we ever make it to the control room. Before we save one person. He can kill us all."

The "but" lingers in the air. I know what they're going to say. Thorne takes my hand, and I can't help but look at him.

"Only one person can get close enough to stop him."

Me—that's what they're not saying. Only I can stop him—but it's not fair because it's not even my father's fault. Thorne squeezes my hand, and I close my eyes for a second, try to remember the song I used to hum. It's not there. I've always known it would come to him or me. I've always known, but now it seems wrong.

"I have to kill him."

"You just have to distract him, to stop him," Thorne says quickly. I pull my hand away and stare down at the blueprints. The memories rush back to me of all the things he's done to me. Forbidding me from Thorne. Thorne screaming. His face when he made me watch. Him tearing my mother's picture. Locking me in the safehouse. Watching me, manipulating. But none of it was him. Not really...

"How do you plan to get in?" I ask, running my hand across the page. "It's better to use the third south entrance. It will take you to the floor directly and behind the Troopers, add an element of surprise."

"That's a good idea," Handler says. There's a softness to his voice that wasn't there before. I don't look up, but I can feel them all staring at me.

"I'm fine," I say. "I'll do whatever I have to do."

Thorne starts to speak, but I turn and walk away because, even after my father's evil, even though I want to hate him, the thought of killing him makes me sick. He's my father. The Elders made him this way, and if I do this, then I'm no different from them, despite my motives.

"WHAT'S IT LIKE?" MITCHELL ASKS.

I look up at him from the desk. "What's what like?"

His eyes explore the area of the Hub, jumping from computer to computer before they rest back on me. "The branding. Have you ever wanted it gone? It's got to be weird what you and Thorne can do."

I shrug and look away, just for a moment. There's no way to explain it; it just is. "I'm used to it now," I say.

But I still want it gone. Even knowing that without it I'm at the Elders' mercy, I still wish I could get rid of it. That I could know what it's like to be my own and that Thorne could know, and then we could decide what we wanted separately. That option is gone until the Elders are gone.

An alarm fills up all the space with a horn noise that grates my teeth together. I look up in time to see Bane burst into the Hub. He moves across the computers, typing in access codes.

"What's going on?" Thorne asks, coming in behind him.

"He's back," Bane says.

"Who's back?" I ask.

Bane doesn't answer, but Thorne, Mitchell, and I follow him out of the Hub. For the first time in a week, the groups stop working and all look at the door, waiting. We join Handler and the others in the center of the room.

"Who is it?" I ask Carrigan.

I don't get an answer, but when the door opens, I don't need one. My whole body freezes as everyone gathers around him, and my brain stops working at the shock of the familiar blond hair.

It's Xenith.

Xenith is here, staring at me. Here, shaking Handler's hand. Here, laughing with Mitchell, flirting with Carrigan. Here in front of me. And the way he's talking to them tells me he's been here before.

"Neely," he says. His voice is smooth and calm. The familiarity of it makes my heart skip a beat. It jars me. The last time I saw him—really saw him—he kissed me. I didn't have to think about it, but now? Now he's here.

"Neely," he says, pulling me into a hug. His voice is relieved, but my brain is spinning and I can't think of any words. Only images. Only him and our deal and Thorne's face when I told him. Only the numbers left on my wristwatch and...why would he be here right now? How is he here? I hate him. He's just as bad as the Elders because, whatever game he's playing, people died. People he sent me to see.

"You made it." He practically breathes it into my hair, and I know I shouldn't, but my mind drifts back to his bathroom. To his lips on mine. To the way he left me at the gate before my journey and held me when I cried out and tried to help me. He's always tried to help, and I realize I do feel something for him. I'm just not sure what.

Part of it is anger. He still sent me all this way and helped cause all those deaths. There's no excuse for that, right? I pull away from his embrace. No. There's not.

"Xenith, I assume you know Thorne Bishop as well?" Handler asks.

Thorne is beside me. He and Xenith stare at each other for a moment, a long and awkward moment, and then Thorne reacts. Xenith is on the floor before anyone can move. Thorne is shaking his hand, cursing from the blunt force of the punch, and Xenith is groaning. There's blood on Thorne's hand from Xenith's lip and I reach out for Thorne, but he pulls away and leaves us. I stand between them, halfway to Xenith and halfway to Thorne. Miles from both of them.

"I guess that was a yes," Bane mutters.

Everyone else rushes to help Xenith, bringing a cloth and some ice. And me, I just stand there and watch everything move around me. In all the chaos, it's only Xenith and me. Every word, every glance, every kiss comes down to this moment—and I realize it was all a lie.

Life speeds up to real-time. Xenith locks eyes with me, but I turn and race after Thorne.

SOMETIMES AFTER A long morning in the cramped schoolhouse, when the summer sun is hot on our skin and the humid air seeps into our pores, we race. The only relief from the heat is the ocean. Today is one of those days. The younger kids glare at us as they pour into the schoolhouse, their faces already blushed from heat. Rowen laughs at his younger brother, sticks out a tongue, and stands beside Kai on the starting line. I love running. Running is the only time I don't feel different.

Kai, Thorne, Rowen, Latavia, me, and six other second graders. Yesterday, Thorne won. Today, I'm determined it will be me. Xenith watches us from the distance; I wave at him.

"Come race," I yell. He looks surprised, and then he smiles.

Latavia pulls me aside. "Why are you inviting him? He's weird."

I watch him pick up his bag and tie his shoe. He's a little weird, but no more than Thorne and I are. I can't tell anyone that though. Not after Kai ordered us not to speak of it. "We're all allowed to race," I say.

Xenith joins me next to the line, a smile on his face. His blond hair falls in his eyes. I smile back.

"Why did you call me over?" he says.

"That's what friends do."

He laughs a little. "I don't really have friends, Neely."

"I'm your friend," I say.

There's a whistle to my left, and Rowen has his fingers in his mouth. Everyone on the line gets ready. I put one leg in front of the other and watch from the corner of my eye as Xenith does the same. Another whistle sounds, and then we're running.

I don't think while I run. I don't look for Thorne or Xenith or anyone else, even though I hear the other kids laughing. I zoom through the schoolyard, past the worker mill, around groups of working women and women with babies. I go past the grocery, through the courtyard. A group of Troopers sees us, and I'm pretty sure they run after us, but I keep going. The wind rushes through my hair. My feet pound, pound, pound against the ground. I feel myself breathing, racing against my heart.

Something crashes behind me. I look over my shoulder and see the bob of Thorne's head in my vision. He's smiling.

Ahead, the ocean crests along the horizon. I don't look back to see who else is still in this race with me; I'm almost there. That's what I focus on as I move forward, racing along the beach, fighting against the sand for support. Then I jump. The cool water catches me and wraps me up in its current. I dive under, let it wash over my head, and leap up with a gasp of air. When the water clears from my eyes, there are a few other splashes into the ocean, but I see Xenith first, smiling at me.

"Who won?" I ask, spitting out some salty water.

"You, but I was right behind you," he says.

We spend the next hour in the water. It's easy to forget that I'm different, that I have a secret, because in this one moment, I feel totally normal. Like another eight-year-old with friends. Not the director's daughter or Sara's not-quite daughter or the girl who can feel what Thorne feels. I am just me.

When the warning bell for dinner rings, we all slosh out of the water. My skin is wrinkled up, deformed, and rigid. Xenith is beside me, sand covering his wet feet.

"See you at dinner," I say to Xenith.

He reaches out to touch my arm, and I look back at him. "Did you mean what you said?" he asks. "About being my friend?"

I smile. "Of course. Everyone needs a friend."

Xenith smiles until Thorne and Kai approach us with my pack. His smile disappears, and he turns away from me.

"Why were you talking to him?" Kai asks.

I shrug. "He's nice."

"Mom says we shouldn't talk to him. She said he could get us in trouble," Thorne says.

"In trouble? He's just lonely."

"But Mom said, Neely," Thorne replies as if it's the most simple thing in the world. I watch Xenith walk off down the beach toward his quarters until he's a dark blob against the sun.

I FIND THORNE SITTING on the floor with his back against the crisp white walls. He doesn't look at me.

"Are you okay?" I ask. "Your hand is bleeding."

"Just go, Neely," he says.

"No." I crouch down on the ground and take his hand, which is red and cracked with blood spreading across his knuckles. "I didn't realize punching someone was so dangerous."

I expect his eyes to light up a bit at the humor of my statement, but they don't. There's no light on his face, no warmth, and he stiffens under my touch but doesn't pull his hand away.

"Tell me it's not true," he says, putting his other hand on top of mine.

I freeze and search his face, expecting an answer or an explanation to the question. There isn't one there. Somehow he's almost someone foreign to me. "What's not true?"

Thorne gulps back his nerves, and I see his Adam's apple dance in his throat. My own nerves spread through me, pulling at me. Thorne's not usually the nervous one.

"Tell me you don't have feelings for him," he says, then pauses for a second too long. "Lie to me, Neely."

I lean back on the floor, but he doesn't loosen his grip on my hand. "Come on! Lie to me!"

His voice echoes down the empty hallway, and when it fades, there's no sound but the two of us breathing. I feel everything at once—betrayal and sadness and hope and hatred. Part of it is mine and part of it is Thorne's, and it's all woven together in an indecipherable wave. My body doesn't feel like mine, like the spinning and tingling and fire are a storm of someone else. Tears rush at my eyes.

"Do you really want me to lie to you?" I whisper.

"You're pretty good at it. I asked you before—way before—what you felt."

Thorne's voice is laced with disgust. I know he's angry, upset, worried, and I can't say anything to make it better. Not with the connection, not with his hand on mine, not with the dead giveaway that would rush through both of us. "I'm sorry."

Thorne pulls his hand away. "I hate him," he says to me. "This was his plan all along. To take you away from me."

"I didn't know he would be here, Thorne, I swear. He played me, too," I say quickly. "I'm here with you."

He smiles, but it's weak and doesn't fully form. It's sad, doubtful. I've never seen him look so lost before. So much like how I've felt so many times. Then he looks at me, which is probably worse.

"I saw your face when Mitchell said they couldn't remove the branding."

"Thorne, I'm with you."

"For how long?" he asks.

Silence falls between us, filled only by the far-off noise of the infiltration team moving on without us. My head is on the verge of explosion—a kaleidoscope of love, hate, doubt, fear, uncertainty, hope. I can't separate one from the other long enough to figure out which ones I believe, yet all of them consume me.

"For always," I say in response.

He shakes his head at me. "I wish I could believe that."

And then he stands up and walks away, and he doesn't look back. Not once.

XENITH EYES ME FROM across the room through the entirety of the meeting. Try as I may, I can't avoid his gaze. I can't look away, even when my eyes wander. Even when I feel Thorne's insecurity through the connection. There's still something negative between us. Something that won't go away until Xenith does.

I'm not sure I want Xenith to go away.

I'm not sure I want him to stay either.

"We'll just have to keep looking," Agent Handler says looking at his watch. "Bane, Thorne, we have to go."

I steal a glance at Thorne when he gets up from the table. He looks back at me as he follows Bane and Handler, but he doesn't say anything.

When I look up, it's just Xenith and me. He's tapping his fingers along the edge of the table, and his eyes pour into me and through me. I shift in the chair. I should leave, but there's too much that keeps me sitting here. Too many things that connect me to him that I don't understand at all. For a second, it's as if they're all dangling in front of me and I could reach out and touch the answers. Questions form on my lips, but then he speaks and they all fall away.

"I was worried," Xenith says, leaning forward slightly. My cheeks flush a little too much for my own comfort, and I'm sure he notices. "I was worried."

"You were worried?" I say. "This was all you. You sent me out there!"

"You wanted to go."

"Do you know how many people I watched die?" I ask. My voice is rough, and the anger I feel toward him builds more and more inside of me as he just sits there. I didn't realize how angry I was until this moment, with his eyes on me and the room empty and all the questions burning toward the surface. "Do you know how many times we almost died?"

"But you didn't die." Xenith's voice is soft, almost like he's relieved. "I knew you wouldn't die, Neely, or I never would have risked you."

"The branding protects me from the Elders, and you sent me on a wild chase to get it removed."

Xenith shakes his head. "If you'd stayed in the Compound and done nothing, the Elders would have transferred Thorne, given him a different branding—one that isn't connected to yours—and then you would've been in their hands. In the Compound and at their will. I did what I had to do."

I shake my head and move from the chair. My hands are trembling. I can't help but believe him, and that's what I don't want to do. I move around the perimeter of the room, eyes on him. "Why would you send Thorne out here? How could you do that? We had a deal, and I trusted you, Xenith. You were supposed to keep him safe."

"I did. I sent him away. To you."

I stop and whip around to glare at him. "That is not what I meant and you know it!"

"You never said not to do it," he says with a smile. "Besides, he's safe from your father. *That* was your request—that I protect Thorne Bishop from your father in your absence. I believe those were the exact words used, and I did that. I even kept him out of reach of the Elders. No bonus required for that one."

I shake my head. "But you—"

He moves toward me and points to himself. "I upheld my end of the bargain, unlike you. You told him the truth the first chance you had." Xenith pauses. "I had to do it, Neely. Your father would have figured out that Thorne was involved somehow, and even if he hadn't, it wouldn't have mattered. Thorne was a target, too."

I know Xenith is right, but I want to be angry at him. It's easier than being something else.

"Trust me, it wasn't my ideal solution either. I thought I'd keep him there and keep an eye on him. It was only a month, and I could do that. But it didn't work out that way. He had questions, too many questions, and then he was really bugging me with all the whining about you, Neely. So I sent him to you," he says, his eyes examining me. "I thought you'd be happy to have lover boy with you."

"I was. I am," I say.

"I get why you told Thorne everything now. You're a horrible liar," he says.

I shake my head. "How did I let you get me into this position? You act like it's all a game to you, but it's not. It's my life. It's his life and hundreds of other people's lives." I step away from him, but he reaches out for me. I jerk back. "*Don't* touch me."

He holds his hands up in defense. "Allow me to explain, at least, before you write me off. This is not a game. I wouldn't gamble with your life, Neely. You have to know that."

"But you bargained for it," I say quickly.

"You don't even understand what that deal we made was about. It's not your real life, Neely; it's DNA. The Mavericks needed it, and I saw an opening. I haven't even taken it yet, so don't act like I did something horrible to you."

And I hate myself a little because I do know that. I can see it when I look him, when he talks to me, when he says my name. But that doesn't make it right. I'm not a prize or a pawn.

"You could've told me about the gene," I say.

"Probably, but we can't undo the past," he says with a sigh. "Look, I honestly didn't learn of the gene until your father changed, and then you were at my door and it all happened so quickly. There was enough going on."

I move to the opposite side of the room where the windows are. Outside, San Francisco is lively. I watch the Remnants from up here, and they look like ants. Like dust on a mantel.

Xenith moves closer to me as the energy in the room changes. I turn to him.

"Why doesn't the branding work on you? You ask more questions than anyone."

"I had it removed when I was six, and I came to the Old World with my dad."

That's a long time to carry the weight of such a heavy thing, to know that you're different than everyone else in your Compound. No wonder he's always been so standoffish. I reach out and touch his neck. It feels simple and plain, and he turns so I can see. The lines are still there, but the skin isn't raised.

"Ink. It's there, but it's faint underneath."

"So you knew all our lives. You knew what our branding was—what we could do. Way before you said it."

"Of course I did," he says, stepping toward me.

"I felt like a freak as a kid. You should've told me."

He shakes his head. "Told you what? That in all of history, twins had been separated or killed because they had special abilities? That the Elders were evil?

No way. Besides, you wouldn't have believed me with Thorne and Kai around to negate my every word."

"It was never like that."

"It was *always* like that. Not that it matters now. I assume you have something else you want to say—yell at me some more maybe?" he asks, crossing his arms.

I'm intentionally quiet. I want him to worry, to be uncertain about something, to waiver. But he doesn't. His eyes are soft and welcoming.

"Why do I even trust you?" I start to walk away from him, past him and toward the door, but he pulls me between him and the wall.

"Because I don't lie to you," he says. His grasp is tight on my arms, and my heart is racing faster than I knew possible. All my emotions are at war as he pulls me close like he did once in his quarters. I can feel his heartbeat too close to mine. My mouth is dry.

"Xenith..." I start.

"What?" he asks, his voice coarse and hollow.

My breathing is ragged as his lips moves closer. His breath mingles with mine, and I can almost taste the mint. His lips barely touch my own, a gentle flutter. I brace myself for more. His whole body tenses up, prepares, and I long for his lips in a way that scares me. He reaches out and touches a strand of my hair, sweeps it behind my ear, and then pours those blue eyes into mine.

"I missed you," he says in a whisper. I feel my body lean into him, torn between wanting and not wanting. He leans back into me, too, his lips close and his arms tight around me.

A shiver runs down my spine, and I pull away. Cool air seeps into the space between us. The gentle almost-press of his lips, the warmth of his body, the racing of my heart are all gone.

"You can't do that," I say, putting more space between us. "I'm with Thorne. You should go."

Xenith reaches for his notebook and moves back toward me. Not toward me—around me. He doesn't even look as he passes, but I hear him mutter "sorry." At least I think I do.

For once, I feel like I did the right thing with him. I trusted him, but now I really have to trust myself more.

"YOU TRUST ME, RIGHT?" Xenith asks. His voice is soft, and his eyes peek up to meet mine. We're both sitting on the couch, waiting for time to catch up to us. There are only two days now until I need to go. Until I leave the Compound.

"Of course."

"There's something I should say then," Xenith says. "I need to know you won't be miserable with me."

The room spins, a little out of focus at his words. I fight to breathe in some air, to calm down. "What?"

He shifts in the space next me. "I don't want you to be miserable. With me."

I shake my head, not sure what to say. I'd miss Xenith, but I love Thorne and he's not Thorne. Leaving him like this, without a clue and in pain, is something I try not to think about, but it's killing me.

"I want you to always trust me," Xenith adds. He reaches over and swipes a piece of auburn hair behind my ear. "I can't bear a world where you don't trust me."

"Xenith, I—"

"I can make you happy. I'm not Thorne, but I can make you happy. Keep you safe. I want that," he says. His blue eyes pour into mine, but I can't think of what to say. I don't even know if I'm breathing.

There's no precursor. No long, drawn-out explanation. There are just the words. Words that don't make any sense to me based on everything that's happened. I came to him for help and he gave it, but it cost me Thorne.

"The other night in the bathroom—that kiss is all I can think about. Pulling away from you was not easy."

I don't know what to say to him. Obviously my heart is with Thorne. It always has been and always will be. There's no question about that. Thorne is the one for me. He's the one. Always. Forever. Thorne.

"I don't want you to feel like you have to be with Thorne. The branding's the thing that makes you feel that way. If you didn't have it, Neely, I think you could love me."

I open my mouth to speak, but then I see the look on his face. He's so sincere, so unlike the version of Xenith he shows the rest of the world. This boy is the one who sat with me after my nightmares. His name is the one I call out now for comfort. That matters.

Xenith touches my cheek and pulls my face toward him. He has a way of doing that, a way which makes me weak and light-headed. He leans into me, quick and certain. His hand moves from my chin to my shoulder to my neck, and then his lips are on mine. It's instant, this attraction, and my mind is spinning with it as he pulls me against his chest and deepens the kiss. I don't think anymore. My arms wrap around him. My lips part, and his kiss devours me.

But then I remember why I am here. Because of the Elders, to save Thorne, to help my father, to learn the truth. I'm not with Thorne because of Xenith, and now he's kissing me and I can't do this. I push him away and move from the couch like it's on fire. I can't do this. I love Thorne.

And Xenith is the reason Thorne isn't there.

"But there is a branding," I say loudly. "And things aren't that simple. You can't just kiss me and try to make me trust you. There's too much at stake."

"You don't feel anything for me?"

"I love Thorne," I say.

"It's not real," Xenith says back. Every time he says that, it pierces me because what if it's not real? Or what if it is?

"Maybe it is real," I say. "Or not. I can't do that to him or to you until I know for sure."

Xenith's eyes darken, and I can see his disappointment. He really feels something for me.

"If all you say is true, then I deserve to find out the answers for myself. Isn't that why you aren't going with me?"

"When you find them, I'll still feel this way about you, and I'll still be here. I'm not going away."

"Then do what you promised me. Keep Thorne safe. Let me find the truth. Let me make my own decisions," I say.

He nods quickly, and then he leaves the room. For once since I've come here, my mind isn't racing. It's not filled with worry or guilt or questions. It's determined. I finally know this is the right thing to do.

FINALLY!

I stand up so quickly that the blueprints of the Compound scatter around me and fall to the floor. I pull one page off the floor and run out of the Hub, letting the door slam behind me. I haven't moved in so many hours that my legs could be jelly. I don't let it stop me. I've been working on this all day. I buried myself in it after I made Xenith walk out, and now I know the only way to distract my father.

I think I hear Carrigan yelling after me while I run. Xenith definitely calls my name. I move until I'm across the room, standing between Thorne and Bane and Handler.

"How soon can you get me out of here?" I ask. The three of them stare at me. Handler asks me to repeat the question. "I think I've figured a way to distract my father and get us all inside. But we need to act quickly—and now. By tonight, if possible."

Handler scratches his head and reaches out toward the paper in my hand. I hold it back so he can't see it and look at Thorne.

"It's me. I'm the distraction, and I don't have to kill him to get you in. The Elders want me, and my father has to listen to them. If I show up, uncooperative, they'll do whatever they have to do to get answers."

Thorne shakes his head, and I see spark in his eye pleading me not to say it. Because once I say it, I can't *unsay* it. I can't take it back. I've done enough not-saying things that I can't do it again.

"You were right: I'm the only one who can get close enough to him. We agreed I had to kill him, and this is the only way. He has to think he's winning if I'm getting anywhere near him."

And as much as I hate saying it, I know it's true. I'm the only one. This has always been about me, and I made it my mission to stop the Elders. This is the way.

Thorne stares at me in the silence, his eyes darker than usual, and I send as much through our connection as I can. The way I felt when my father used to look at me or leave me notes with my breakfast or smile. When I saw him changing. When he pulled Thorne from me after our kiss outside. The way I felt when he tore my mother's picture, when he tortured Thorne, when he locked me in the safehouse. When I found out that none of it was on his own. I have to go back.

And I have to do it alone.

Thorne inhales a large breath of air. "No way, Neely. No way."

I step closer to him. "You *know* it will work, Thorne. This is my job, remember?" His eyes are intense on mine, and in them, I can see that he does. He does.

"That's crazy, Neely," Xenith's voice calls out. I'm not exactly sure when he joined our circle. I try to ignore the tug that wants me to turn around, to respond. It may be crazy, but it's our best hope. Deep down, I think he knows it, too. Everyone does.

"It's a risky plan," Agent Handler says.

"You asked me what I'd be willing to lose to stop them," I say. "This is all I have. It's a risk, but this is our best shot."

I know it won't be pleasant, but I can hold up. I can adapt to it. I can survive a torture round with my father and do it so that everyone can get inside. "Can we be ready by tonight?" I ask.

Carrigan clears her throat from behind me. I turn and see her and Mitchell, whose hair is blue today. "Yes," she says.

I nod at her and look at the others. "Then, Agent Handler, please take me home."

THORNE INSISTED ON riding in the helicopter with me. I told him not to, but he refused to be anywhere else. It's just the two of us up here—and the pilot. I rest my head in the crook of his shoulder, and he laces his fingers with mine. We haven't said much, and in just a couple minutes, I'm going to be back in the Compound. Back home.

Home. What a funny word. This place was never my home, and now it is. Now, as I'm about to help destroy it—or, if that fails, be destroyed by it.

"I know you're still upset about Xenith," I say.

"It's fine. We'll deal with it later. Don't think about that going into this."

I reach up and touch his cheek. "I don't want my last moment with you to be one where you hate me."

"I don't hate you. I love you," Thorne says. "That's why it's so painful. To know that you're only with me now because you have to be."

I shake my head. "That's not true."

"It feels true," he says. "You don't owe anyone anything. We can find another way. You may not come out again."

I shake my head. "I owe so many people, but I'm not doing this for that. I'm doing this because it's right."

He presses his lips to my temple. "I love you."

"This isn't goodbye. I told you always," I say. I stand and strap the bag over my shoulders. Thorne watches as I tighten the straps of the parachute, and when I look up he pulls me into him. My hands trail up the back of his shirt, and my whole body burns up from our connection. I push myself into his kiss. Is this the last time I'll ever feel his desire for me? The last time our bodies will touch like this? It can't be. The thought is too devastating, and he feels it too because he's kissing me harder, more passionately, down my neck, with his hands in my hair and his lips back on mine. The fire burns through our connection, on my hand, in my chest—

"This is where you jump," the pilot yells back.

My skin is on edge, my brain trying to catch up. This is the end.

Thorne presses his forehead against mine. "I'm with you."

I nod as I move from him toward the door of the helicopter. After one last adjustment of the straps, I take a breath and jump. All I see is darkness.

Then I hear his voice.
"Welcome home, Cornelia."

END OF BOOK ONE

ACKNOWLEDGEMENTS

THIS BOOK HAS BEEN MY LIFE since 2010, so I'm beyond thrilled (and nervous!!) to share Neely's story with the world. I'm very grateful that I get to do it in a place like Spencer Hill Press that believes in so strongly in their authors and stories. Thanks to everyone at SHP from the editorial staff to the publicity team for their time, passion and creative ideas.

Thank you to Kate Kaynak, who connected with Neely and believed in this series. I have all the respect for you, and for the opportunities you've given me from intern to editor to author!

To my fabulous editor, who also has the pleasure of doubling as best friend, Patricia Riley, for always believing in this book and in me. This book is yours just as much as it is mine. (Maybe more.) Thank you a thousand times for being there when I wanted to give up. I can't express how thankful I am to have you as my editor. Thanks for talking through scenarios, for knowing my characters almost better than I do, for letting me live in your basement and for being adamantly against Neely eating trash. Thanks also to your husband and kids for letting me consume so much of your life—and your phone bill.

Hafsah Faiziel, thank you for the fantastic book cover!! You took exactly what I wanted and meshed it with what I didn't know I wanted, and I love you for giving my heart the perfect body.

Thank you my unwavering crit partner, Christina Ferko, who read every draft of this book (nine, to be exact), and never grew tired of it. Thank you for pushing me and teaching me and for always believing in Xenith. And to my other CP/best friend, Cindy Thomas, for this insane ability to talk me off of ledges and this insight to make me smile and keep me moving when I want to sleep. You are a joy.

To the entire writing community—there are more of you than I can list here. I may not have said you by name, but you're on my heart as I write this.

To Jenny Perinovic because Neely is your homegirl; Helen Boswell, who helped me figure out my science-y/genetic stuff. You are a lifesaver! To my agent, Nicole Resciniti, for seeing something here and telling me I can.

To Jenn Rush for the enthusiasm in my characters and this story. It has always meant the world, and for the fun distractions. I always thank the God that I have a friend like you. #hotboyswin

To the ladies of the HB&K Society—Amalie, Kristi, Angie, Kate, Cindy and Ariane—for being these amazing human beings and writers who inspire me to be more, try more and do more. I am so incredibly lucky to have all of you in my corner. Your support is endless, and I hope to repay the sentiment to each of you in some little way now and forever.

My best friend, Ashley Carmichael: I promised way back in high school that you'd get your own paragraph when this happened. Here we are. Thank you for pretending to care when I would IM you lines from all my writing or talk about my characters like people. Whether it was theater class or Harry Potter or singing duets on the phone or failing to meringue a pie correctly—you have been there. I would be utterly lost without your friendship; I'm not sure how that happened but it does mean you are stuck with me forever. (One day we can go be British and they will not know what hit them.) And I really hope this paragraph was worth the wait.

To my little sister Cierra, who, like Neely, is stubbornly passionate. It's a good thing to be because it means you won't give up. May all of my journey (and Neely's) show you that what you want in life is possible to achieve if give your all, even when it's hard. Probably especially when it's hard. If you live a life of passion you can achieve things you only dreamed of—and I know that you will.

And thanks to my mom for always knowing I had these grand worlds inside my head, even as a kid, and letting me live in them.

To end, thank you whomever you are reading these words. This book is a huge piece of my heart and I hope it can be part of yours as well.

ABOUT THE AUTHOR

DANIELLE ELLISON spent most of her childhood reading instead of learning math. It's probably the reason she can't divide without a calculator and has spent her life seeking the next adventure. It's also probably the reason she's had so many different zip codes and jobs.

When she's not writing, Danielle is probably drinking coffee, fighting her nomadic urges, watching too much TV, or dreaming of the day when she can be British. Danielle is also the author of SALT, a book about a snarky witch without magic. She has settled in Northern Virginia, for now, but you can always find her on twitter @DanielleEWrites.

Made in the USA
San Bernardino, CA
07 May 2014